QUEENS
of
WONDERLAND

QUEENS
of
WONDERLAND

A Defenders of Lore Novel

GAMA RAY MARTINEZ

HARPER Voyager
An Imprint of HarperCollinsPublishers

QUEENS OF WONDERLAND. Copyright © 2023 by Gamaliel Martinez. All rights reserved. Printed in the United States of America. No part of this book may be used or reproduced in any manner whatsoever without written permission except in the case of brief quotations embodied in critical articles and reviews. For information, address HarperCollins Publishers, 195 Broadway, New York, NY 10007.

HarperCollins books may be purchased for educational, business, or sales promotional use. For information, please email the Special Markets Department at SPsales@harpercollins.com.

Harper Voyager and design are trademarks of HarperCollins Publishers LLC.

FIRST EDITION

Designed by Angie Boutin

Title page background © marina draws/shutterstock; Card suits © luma_art/ shutterstock; Chess piece © Aleksandra_khv/shutterstock

Library of Congress Cataloging-in-Publication Data has been applied for.

ISBN 978-0-06-301468-8

23 24 25 26 27 LBC 5 4 3 2 1

In memory of Eric Flint.
I miss you, you old curmudgeon.

QUEENS
of
WONDERLAND

W hat about storks?"

Vanessa rolled her eyes at the question and wiped away the cobweb that brushed her face. The crypt's musty air made her cough. Her breath disturbed the thick carpet of dust on the stone ground. Aside from that, she hardly made a sound as she moved, unlike the man behind her, who still wasn't accustomed to things like walking through a forgotten crypt under the Tower of London.

"What?" she asked.

"Storks," Will said. The light of his lantern shifted as he spoke. "Do they really bring babies?"

She turned and gaped. "You don't know where babies come from?"

Will's face reddened. "I know where babies come from, but I found out a lot of things I thought were true actually weren't once I joined the Knights."

She allowed herself a half smirk. "It's not that they're not true. It's just that the truth is more complicated than you thought."

Will rolled his eyes. "Right. So what is the truth about storks?"

Vanessa suppressed a chuckle. Most people, when introduced to the supernatural world, didn't accept the more unusual parts as easily as Will. Of course, most people's introduction didn't involve being a prisoner in Neverland for six years before helping to save Peter Pan from his brother-in-law's evil twin. That sort of thing tended to open one's mind, and Will had progressed far in the year he'd been a member of the Knights.

"Well, that's actually more or less the same as it was in the old days. It didn't die away like some of the other myths. Storks draw their power from the belief of children, and that hasn't really changed. They usher souls into this world."

Someone grunted up ahead, and Vanessa turned and ran forward, not looking back to see if Will followed. She came to a stone door that had been forced open—recently, if the dust it had moved across the ground was any indication. The ghostly glow coming from within was even more indicative. She rushed inside, hoping they would finally find Michael and be able to get out of this crypt.

She came in just as the armored ghost stabbed its sword into Michael's shoulder, and the Knight dropped his own blade, grimacing in the pale blue light cast by the spirit. Ghostly weapons didn't cause physical wounds, but a ghost blade did rob all feeling from the limb it pierced. Michael wouldn't be able to use that arm for a few hours at least. He fell backward to avoid another strike. When he tried to roll to his feet, the ghost screamed. This spirit was no banshee, but those buried this deep in the crypt had died more than a thousand years ago, and that conferred a power of its own. The force of its cry slammed Michael into the ground.

Vanessa drew her bow, taking only a second to aim. She fired. The arrow passed right through the spirit. It staggered back a few steps before advancing again.

"Dammit!"

Vanessa drew another arrow. Her arrowheads were made of

gravestone, which could be used to ward off ghosts, but those older than a hundred years or so could often resist it. Against a spirit a millennium old, it would be little more than a bee sting.

Michael scooped up his sword in his left hand, then turned to her and scowled. "Vanessa, what are you doing here?"

The ghost was on him again before she could respond, so she loosed another arrow at it, distracting it for a second. Michael rushed forward. He wasn't as skilled with his left hand, but it was enough. The sword sliced into the ghost's belly, spilling out motes of blue light. The ghost screamed again, and the power in the cry drove Vanessa to the ground. The arrow she had been about to nock went skittering across the floor and came to rest next to the sarcophagus that the ghost had probably come from. The spirit lashed at Michael again, but he caught the attack on his own blade. For a moment, it looked shocked that any mere mortal weapon would stop its blade. Will rushed forward, having put the lantern down. His knife, like Vanessa's arrowheads, had been carved from a grave marker. The ghost flinched as the knife went into its back. Startled by the pain, the ghost's reflexes caused it to turn. Michael took advantage of the distraction. He stabbed his sword into the ghost's gut and drove it upward where the creature's heart would have been. Some spirits screamed when they were destroyed. This one, however, only gave Michael a hateful glare before collapsing into blue sparks and fading entirely.

Michael stared at the spot where the ghost had been, then fell to the ground. Vanessa ran to him and helped him sit up. His clothes were undamaged where he had been stabbed, but chips of ice had formed. His skin was cold as well. He looked up and narrowed his eyes.

"You didn't answer the question. What are you doing here?"

She rolled her eyes. "Normally, when someone saves you

from an ancient ghost, you say, 'Thank you.'" He gave her a level gaze, and she sighed. "The Court sent us."

Michael scoffed. "I don't have time to deal with them."

That took Vanessa aback. Michael's cavalier attitude toward the Court of Camelot, the leaders of the Knights of the Round, always surprised her. She had joined the organization when she was sixteen, after learning that the statues of the Cornhill devils weren't actually statues. The Lady had been impressed by her survival skills and had recruited her, and so Vanessa had learned obedience to the Court from the very beginning. It was the job of the Knights to protect the world from mystical threats, and Michael could eventually be one of their best—or at least he would be if his recent behavior didn't get him expelled. He tried to get up but fell to the ground again. She offered him a hand up, but he ignored her. It took him three more tries before he managed it.

"Michael . . ."

He dusted himself off with his good arm. "Thank you for your help with the guardian."

"A guardian?" she asked. "Not just a restless spirit?"

He turned away from her and put a hand in the open sarcophagus. He moved aside crumbled bones with a casual ease. Next to her, Will shivered in a way that had nothing to do with the unnatural cold of a haunted crypt. After a few seconds, Michael grinned. There was a clicking sound, and the tomb moved aside to reveal a stairway that descended into the darkness.

"You woke it on purpose?" Will's voice was something between a question and an accusation.

Michael nodded once. "I didn't want it to surprise me when I tried to get past it."

"Michael, this is exactly what the Court—"

Michael raised a hand. "If you want to come with me, I would welcome the help. If not, wait outside, and once I'm done, I'll be glad to hear everything the Court wants to tell me. Right now, I'd prefer not to have the distraction."

Vanessa's jaw tightened. She glanced at his limp arm, but he just huffed.

"Michael," she said in a soft voice. "You're obsessed with this."

He looked like he was going to argue, but he turned away after a second.

Will raised an eyebrow, and it took him a second to work up the nerve to speak. "You hurt that ghost. You have wisp dust, and you didn't get it from the Knights."

Michael glared before patting a leather pouch on his belt. Vanessa's and Will's eyes went wide. The Knights hadn't had any wisp dust since James Hook's crocodile had ruined their supply more than a year ago, and they were anxious to get more.

"Are you coming or not?"

For a second, she considered refusing to see what he would do. But Michael was just bold enough to go in alone, and as impaired as he was, he probably wouldn't survive. Finally, Vanessa gave a curt nod. "We may as well, but you have to come with us after you're done learning whatever you can down here."

Michael frowned but bowed his head in acknowledgment. "Fine. Let's go. I need to be done before sunset."

With that settled, he turned and walked down the stairs without taking so much as a light source. Vanessa glanced over her shoulder at Will, who picked up his lantern. Often, Vanessa wished other forms of illumination worked in places like this, but the cold power of the grave tended to short out more modern devices. She sighed and motioned for Will to follow.

Michael had gone only a few steps. He wore a necklace that

gave off a light so faint that she never noticed it before. It took her a second to recognize it.

"You have a phoenix feather?"

"An old one. I found it in an antique shop, if you can believe that. It doesn't have more than a few hours of light left in it, though."

Even with the feather and the lantern, the darkness was oppressive, and the air felt almost too thick to breathe. Vanessa held a gravestone arrow nocked. The arrowheads were heavy, and they threw off the arrows' balance. Consequently, they had a limited range and were a poor weapon in most circumstances. At least they were when one wasn't exploring a crypt inhabited by powerful undead. It wasn't wisp dust, but it was better than nothing.

"Why didn't you get the Lady or the Wizard to enchant you against spirits?" Michael asked.

"They sent us to come get you, but they didn't know where you were. If they had, you would have probably been expelled already."

Michael paused as he reached the bottom of the stairs. "How did you find me, then?"

"You may be good in the field, Michael, but you're not nearly as clever as you think you are. You've been seeking forbidden knowledge. I knew you would be searching for an oracle. There are only a few of those still active in London, and it wasn't hard to figure out which one had an entrance that had recently been disturbed."

"You didn't tell them?"

"I'm trying to keep you from being expelled. It was all we could do to get the gravestone weapons without arousing too much suspicion."

Michael shrugged as Vanessa and Will reached the base of

the stairs. He proceeded down a dark hall. There was no dust on the floor, and the sound of their footsteps was muted. If Vanessa concentrated, she thought she could hear whispering.

Michael paused at a fork. He pulled out a scroll and examined it.

Vanessa looked over his shoulder and hissed, "You took that from the catacombs."

Michael didn't look up. "Of course. Do you think I could figure out how to reach the White Lady on my own?"

"The White Lady is an oracle spirit?" Will asked.

Michael inclined his head. "A very powerful one, which is why she occasionally manifests on the Tower grounds, but she was buried down here."

Will shivered. "I don't suppose you have any more wisp dust."

Michael reached into the leather pouch on his belt. He withdrew a small handful of shimmering dust and sprinkled it on them. The cold power of the death fairies ran through Vanessa, and she resisted the urge to shiver.

"What answers are you seeking?" she asked after the sensation had passed.

Michael didn't turn around. "If you know well enough to find me, I'm sure you can guess."

"First, you didn't want anything to do with the Knights," Vanessa said. "Then, you dive so deeply into it that you risk losing yourself. You've become obsessed with finding Hook, Michael. You'll destroy yourself like this, and you'll probably take others with you."

"I know what I'm doing." He sighed. "How much does the Court know?"

"They know you've been ignoring orders. The vampire in Merton killed three people. If you had been there . . ."

"Do you have any idea how difficult it is to coax a nereid to the surface? It took me two weeks to find Dero, and that was due to pure luck. After that, it was a month before I got her to actually speak to me. If I had gone after the vampire, all that effort would have been lost."

Vanessa reached forward and gripped his shoulder. "Was it worth three deaths?"

He winced, though she didn't know if it was in response to her touch or the angry tone in her voice. After a few seconds, he pulled away from her and brushed at a cobweb that covered the passage. The temperature dropped several degrees as they moved forward.

It was a few minutes before Michael spoke. "Assuming I could have saved them."

She looked at the pouch on his belt. "If you were able to gather wisp dust, then you're possibly the Knight that would have been best able to deal with something like that."

Out of the corner of her eye, Vanessa saw Will rub his neck, though the puncture marks had faded. He, along with Vanessa, had been the ones to deal with the vampire. It had been a young one, only a few decades old, and Will had done well for his first major engagement since returning from Neverland. He had very nearly been turned before Vanessa had staked the creature and taken its head, but that sort of thing was not entirely unexpected.

"Here," Michael said.

They were in the middle of a passage. The stone walls ran before them on both sides before disappearing into the darkness. Michael pulled a tin of red paste from his pack and rubbed it on his palm, then he placed his hand on an unremarkable stretch of stone and whispered a few words under his breath. The red palm print glowed brightly, and the stone melted away, leaving what looked like a doorway, though Vanessa couldn't see past the threshold. Michael stepped through, and almost instantly the darkness swallowed him. A few seconds later, his voice drifted from within.

"Are you coming?"

Will paled and looked to her. If it were anyone else, she wouldn't have gone, but she and Michael had been through too much. She tightened her grip around her bow before nodding once and stepping into the passage.

2

The darkness resisted Vanessa, and she felt like she was moving through molasses. Sparks appeared all along her body, stinging and filling the air with the smell of burning skin. Strength flowed out of her, and every step was harder than the one before. A sharp pain came from her back, and she pulled out her arrows. The arrowheads glowed bright red. There was some sort of a ward here, something that guarded against both life and things that were proof against the undead. Either Michael had gotten extremely potent wisp dust or the age of the magic had degraded the barrier, because she was able to push her way through the shield.

After half a dozen steps, the darkness gave way, and she found herself in a dimly lit chamber. Unlike the rest of the catacombs, this room had been made of white marble as smooth as glass. The air held the musky smell of cheap perfume, and there was the perpetual chill she so often felt around ghosts. A closed sarcophagus made of pure white stone sat in the middle of the room. Carved letters written in some long forgotten language had been inlaid with gold. Vanessa had no idea where Michael had learned the oracle spirit residing here was actually the White Lady, one of the infamous spirits of the Tower of London. While some knew her as a powerful oracle spirit, her name was uncertain, even to the Knights.

Will bumped into her and Vanessa realized she hadn't moved since she'd come through the darkness. She stepped out of his way, and when she looked up, Michael was standing over the sarcophagus. He laid a hand on it. Apparently, he had cleaned the paste off his hand because he left no mark. He let out a long breath and waited for several seconds. Nothing happened.

"Do you know how to summon her?" Will asked, backing into a corner.

Michael shook his head. "All accounts I've read of her said that she appeared whenever someone came into this room." He tapped the sarcophagus. "Short of opening this up, I'm not sure. I don't particularly want to anger her."

Will looked around, never taking his hand off the hilt of his sword. "How long do we wait for her?"

Michael sat down near the sarcophagus. "As long as it takes."

Vanessa felt Will tap on her shoulder, and she turned around, but he was on the other side of the room. He noticed her looking at him and gave her a quizzical look.

"How . . . ?"

The scent of perfume became overwhelming. It was a sharp smell, like one sold by a street vendor, something far too cheaply made to belong to the woman buried in such an ostentatious place. Still, that smell was often described by those who had an encounter with this spirit.

Vanessa whispered, "I think she's here."

Will drew his sword halfway out of his belt sheath. Michael, who had apparently known what to expect, only smiled. White sparks swirled in the air above the stone coffin. They came together and formed a flame the color of new-fallen snow under the midday sun. It grew until it was the size of a human being.

The fire flared up, driving all of them back with its heat.

Vanessa had to look away. When she looked back, a woman in a flowing white dress stood on the sarcophagus. Her face was gaunt and her eyes sunken. Her dress shimmered and rippled in a nonexistent wind. She lifted a hand and pointed at Michael with a finger that was as much bone as anything else.

"Why have you intruded on my rest?" Her voice drowned everything else out, and it made Vanessa's head ache with its loudness.

"I have come to seek wisdom."

"I have no wisdom to give one such as you."

"One such as me?" He looked back at Vanessa and Will before turning his attention to the ghost. "A Knight?"

She sniffed. "A Noble."

"A Noble?"

"One who commands others, who spends their lives like they were coins in his purse, uncaring as long as he gets what he wants. My life was spent by one such as you."

"I never spent lives like that!"

"Did you not spend three such lives in your search for me?"

Michael shuffled back a few steps. "How did you know that?"

The oracle threw back her head and laughed. Vanessa felt like her blood had turned to ice water. It was all she could do not to turn and run back into the darkness. Her training allowed her to recognize it as magical fear, not that it made it any easier to endure. The rasping of Will's blade as he drew it from its sheath silenced the ghost. She glared at him, and he took a sharp breath and dropped his weapon. Ice that had formed on the blade shattered when it hit the ground, leaving the blade marred with rust. Then, the White Lady turned her attention back to Michael.

"You come to me for knowledge and are surprised when I know about your own past? Arrogance. How very like a Noble."

"I had to find you. It was more important than fighting the vampire."

She turned away from him. "What right do you have to determine the worth of others' lives?"

"He would not have left the vampire if he didn't know others would take up his task." Vanessa stepped forward. "We are the ones who destroyed the creature. We would not be here if he was the kind of man you say he is."

"You are here because your leaders demanded that you bring him to them. They are of the gentry, too, aren't they? This is all a game to their kind." She scowled, and Vanessa's bones felt like they were on fire. For a moment, she couldn't move, but when the ghost turned back to Michael, the pain vanished. "Still, it does say something that she would speak for you. What do you wish to know, Noble who is not a Noble?"

Michael gave Vanessa a smile of thanks, then turned back to the oracle. "I fought a powerful enemy some months ago, but he got away from me. I tried to stop him, but I was wounded. By the time I was well enough to search for him, he'd hidden from me. He has to be stopped, and so I come to you. Tell me where I can find the ghost of James Hook."

"James Hook." The White Lady drew out the name. "Yes, I felt his call when he first came to London."

"Right. He called up an army of ghosts, but he could only control weak ones. Do you know where he is now?"

The spirit raised a bony finger and drifted toward Michael. Vanessa drew back an arrow, but Michael waved her off. She lowered the bow but didn't put away the arrow. Will, too, looked on the verge of attacking. Wisp dust and gravestone together would make a powerful combination, but the White Lady didn't give them so much as a second glance. She touched Michael's forehead and he screamed. Within seconds, he fell to the ground and writhed, seeming unable to control his movements.

Vanessa drew back and fired, but the spirit broke apart into a shower of sparks, and the arrow passed right through the space where she had been. Vanessa drew her sword, a three-foot scimitar made of Damascus steel. Without needing to be told, Will stood back-to-back with her. She eyed the shadowed corners and scanned the room for any other sign of the ghost.

"Keep watch," Vanessa said. "I'll check on Michael."

"All right."

Vanessa knelt next to Michael and put two fingers on his neck. As soon as she touched his skin, Michael smiled, though he didn't open his eyes. His pulse was strong, and color was slowly returning to his face. Vanessa shook him gently. His grin widened until it took up half his face, far wider than his mouth should have been able to stretch. She gasped and pulled back. Michael opened his eyes, and his expression slowly returned to normal. He sat up and swayed for a few seconds before steadying himself.

"What happened?" he asked.

"Why don't you tell me?"

He blinked. When he saw Will with his weapon drawn, he shook his head. "You might as well put that away. She disappears once she answers the question."

"But did she? Answer the question, I mean."

Michael brought a hand to his forehead. "I think so. She showed me hearts."

"Hearts?"

"I don't know what it means, at least not yet." He got up. "We should go."

Wailing sounded through the chamber, and Michael drew his own weapon in his left hand. His right one was still limp. Vanessa tensed and Will got into a fighting stance. Michael motioned for them to follow and disappeared into the dark passage. Vanessa nodded once to Will before following.

A spirit dove out of the stone as soon as Vanessa emerged from the darkness. Her sword sliced through the air and reduced it to a shower of blue motes, leaving the smell of brimstone in its wake.

"Was that ghost wearing chain mail?" Michael asked.

A heartbeat later, Will cut another ghost out of the air with his dagger even as Michael took out two. Soon the room was flooded by the dead. The three fought through the chamber, advancing slowly. More than once, a ghostly weapon cut into Vanessa's flesh. It never hit her sword arm, fortunately, and she was able to keep fighting. Will wasn't so lucky, and he dropped his weapon before they had even reached the guardian's chamber.

Ghosts came at them from all directions. The tide waned as they neared the surface. One spirit stabbed a spear into her right calf, forcing her to drag her leg the rest of the way. Finally, after what felt like an eternity of fighting, they saw the glimmer of sunlight and made their way to it. Even Michael wasn't foolish enough to go into a ghost's stronghold at night once the spirits had been roused. Most of the ghosts stopped once the trio came into the sun, but a few pursued them into the Tower grounds. Vanessa took a second to glare at Michael before slashing at the largest one. That one caught her attack on its own blade. Fortunately, while it was strong enough to come out into the sun, daylight did weaken it. Its weapon snapped in half. The piece that broke off disintegrated before it hit the ground. She stabbed the ghost through the gut, and it screamed before falling to pieces.

Another spirit came from above, knocking her weapon aside. Will ran forward, gravestone knife in his left hand, and cut that one down before its blade cut more than an inch into her. She staggered. There were a half dozen others. Vanessa's reactions had been slowed by the myriad of attacks, and Will was all but incapacitated. Michael was still on his feet, but only barely. The three of them stood back-to-back.

"I don't suppose either of you have any ideas," Will said.

"Listen," Michael said.

Vanessa heard voices. They weren't the disembodied voices of the spirits. They were something far more mundane. Still, it was one of the most welcome sounds she had ever heard, and she let out a breath of release. There were dozens of different types of ghosts. In hoards, like when Hook had summoned an army of them, they could be brave, but in small numbers, they feared the attention of a crowd of living people. The ghosts fled into the opening of the crypt and the stones slid back into place, leaving a flat wall. Michael looked back at the wall as he sheathed his sword. Vanessa and Will did the same.

"We should get out of here before the Tower guards see us."

Before Vanessa could agree, a tour group came around the corner. The guide's eyes widened, but Michael got under her arm, angling his body so as to hide the fact that he was armed.

"We got separated from another group," Michael said, "then my friend sprained an ankle."

Given that her leg was still numb from the ghost's attack, it wasn't too difficult to be convincing. They were ushered out of the grounds. By then, Vanessa's leg had begun to tingle, though she still wouldn't be able to move it for a while.

"Thank you for your help," Michael said while they waited for a car. "I need to research what these hearts mean."

"Michael, you agreed to come with us."

"I don't have time for the Court right now."

"They're losing their patience with you," Vanessa said. "They're not just going to let this go."

"What are they going to do? Kick me out?"

"No, but they might deny you the use of their resources. You're not likely to find Hook if you can't get into the archives or the catacombs."

Michael stiffened. After a few seconds, he seemed to deflate. His thoughts were painted plainly on his face. If he had wanted to just lead a normal life, then there would be little the Court could do, but he wanted to further pursue a powerful ghost. That wasn't something he'd be able to easily do, at least not without access to the resources of the Knights. Finally, he nodded.

"Fine. Let's go."

4

The headquarters of the Knights of the Round were housed in an old building in one of the more unsavory parts of London. Spells had been laid on the house that prevented a casual observer from looking too closely. As Vanessa walked up the path to the front door, the hairs on the back of her neck stood on end. She felt like she was being watched and had to suppress an urge to walk away. She knew that was just a part of the defensive spells, but that didn't make her approach any easier. She lifted a hand to knock, and the door opened of its own accord. Will gasped, though he had been through this door a number of times, too. To his credit, he didn't show any other reaction. Michael stopped at the doorway.

"You're coming with me?"

Vanessa nodded once and grinned. "We brought you in. Technically, you are in our custody until we deliver you to the Court."

Michael raised an eyebrow. "Are you serious?"

Vanessa shrugged. "It's enough of a reason to get us into your hearing."

Michael laughed and went through the door.

"Isn't he worried?" Will asked.

Vanessa fell into step behind Michael. She had to have Will

help her keep up because of her numb leg. "He should be, but this isn't his first hearing. Actually, it's his third, though I don't know that I'd consider being the Knight with the most experience at this something to be proud of."

Michael chuckled. "It's my fourth, if you count the time you brought me here before going after Peter. I wasn't a Knight then, though. The Court is nothing to be afraid of, Will. They're just a bunch of people who were once relevant trying to impose their will on the rest of us. Ignore them as much as you can, and you won't do too bad."

"Each one of them was a Knight in the field for decades before being called to serve on the Court," Vanessa said. "You'd be wise to listen to anything they say, Will."

Michael just snorted. Will looked like a child torn between arguing parents. The hall they were in appeared to go on forever. There was a thick carpet of dust on the floor, and when Vanessa looked behind them, she saw their footsteps left no tracks. In her years with the Knights, Vanessa had been through this passage half a dozen times, and the Lady had spoken to her about the nature of the magic on the house. The distracter spells on it still made her dizzy, though, and it took everything she had to not throw up. Michael didn't follow any particular path. That would have been pointless here. The house itself determined where they would go, and it was only a few minutes before they came to a plain wooden door. Michael raised his hand and knocked once. The sound was much louder than it should have been, and it echoed through the hall. The door creaked as it swung inward.

The dark room had a single lantern which didn't illuminate enough to see the wall. On the far end sat the five members of the Court of Camelot. The King was in the center with the

Queen and the Wizard on either side. At opposite ends sat the Lady and the Knight Protector. Each of them wore a voluminous robe. Their hoods, which were decorated with gold inlays, hid their faces. They were surrounded by an air of overwhelming power.

Vanessa had never understood how Michael could stand before their judgment so confidently. She watched as he strode toward the center of the room without hesitation, and he stood before the table of the five people who might well have been the most powerful in the world.

The King looked beyond Michael to her, and Vanessa bowed to him. Will did the same, though Michael remained still.

"Sir Vanessa and Squire William, you were not summoned."

"We brought him here," Vanessa said, trying to keep her voice steady.

"I have no objection to their presence," the figure on the far right said.

The King stiffened at the Lady's words, but after a few seconds, he inclined his head. "Very well, you may remain." Then, he turned to the figure before them. "Sir Michael, you have been summoned because you have been ignoring our orders so you can pursue your own ends, and in doing so, you have been delving into matters best left in the dark."

Michael smirked. "You have a copy of the Necronomicon in the catacombs. If you really thought there were things best left in the dark, that would have been destroyed along with at least a dozen other items I can think of. The Knights wouldn't have kept records of how to use them. You know as well as I do that sometimes there are risks that need to be taken."

"But you are not the one to decide when that is," the Wizard said.

"Someone has to. Hook is out there, and none of you are doing anything."

"There are many powerful spirits in the world. We don't actively go after them unless there is a need," the Wizard said. "You disturbed one such spirit this very day, if my sources are correct."

That made Michael wince, and Vanessa understood why. It was one thing for the Court to know in general what Michael was doing. If they knew enough details to know exactly what he had been up to, then they could probably stop him if they decided it was really necessary.

"A lot of Knights consult oracle spirits," Michael said.

"Is that your only excuse?" the King asked. "They are not to be trifled with unless there is need."

"Hook unleashed an army of ghosts on London."

"And after you stopped him, he retreated into the darkness like such spirits always do. That is the only reason we have granted you the leniency that we have, but our patience is at an end."

"So that's it, then?" Michael asked. "I do what you don't like, and you throw me out? At least you do until you need me again."

Vanessa held her breath, worried that the Court would do exactly that. Michael had walked away before, but being expelled was a different matter entirely. They might even order all existing Knights to cut off contact, and she didn't know what would happen if they did that, especially with Will. Finally, the King spoke.

"No. Despite all your brashness, you are indeed a valuable asset to the Knights. You lack only discipline. We are revoking your status as a full Knight of the Round. You are hereby reduced to the rank of Squire. You are denied access to the catacombs, the archives, and every other resource of the Knights unless you are accompanied by the Knight to whom you have been assigned."

Michael stepped forward. "You can't!"

"We already have," the Wizard said. "You are also put on probation and are not eligible to be raised to full Knighthood unless a member of this Court agrees to remove that probation."

Michael clenched his fists, and Vanessa worried he would do something foolish. A heartbeat later, however, his shoulders slumped and he bowed his head.

"To whom will I be assigned?"

"We will see if any volunteer to take you on," the Lady said. She then turned and looked right at Vanessa. The King cleared his throat, but Vanessa was already stepping forward.

"I volunteer to take on Squire Michael."

"You already have a squire in your care," the King said.

"He acquitted himself well against the vampire and the ghosts we faced this very day. He has the discipline of a member of His Majesty's Royal Navy. He is close enough to full Knighthood that I would not be overly burdened by taking another squire."

"It is not without precedent," the Lady said. "Knights have had two squires before."

"When we have had more squires than Knights."

"Regardless, I have no objection to this," said the Lady.

"Nor do I," said the Knight Protector.

The King, the Queen, and the Wizard all exchanged glances. Vanessa needed one more to agree or else Michael would be given to someone else. That probably wouldn't be a terrible thing, assuming they found someone who would take him. Unfortunately, Vanessa wasn't entirely sure that Michael wouldn't quit on the spot if he had to submit to the authority of someone he didn't know.

Finally, the Wizard nodded. "I will consent."

The King was probably glaring at Vanessa, though she couldn't see into his hood. Finally, he inclined his head. "Very well. Squire Michael will join Squire William as the ward of Sir Vanessa Finch." He looked at the three of them. "You may go."

I guess you're going to expect me to do what you say now," Michael said once they had left the house.

Thunder rumbled overhead, and Vanessa glanced upward. The air lacked the smell of an imminent storm, but it wouldn't be long in coming, either. She gazed blackly at Michael.

Will surprised them both by speaking up first. "Michael, they stripped you of your rank. If you keep pushing them, who knows what they'll do. They could kick you out entirely."

"They wouldn't dare," Michael said. "How many others do they have who are friends with a god?"

Vanessa put a hand on Michael's shoulder. "That won't stop them and you know it. If you try to turn Peter against them, you'll go from being a disgraced member to a target." She let out a breath, leaving it unsaid that since she was the Knight who knew him best, she would probably be the one sent to take him down. "Let's just work together on this. What is this about hearts?"

He sighed. "I don't know. I saw hearts. At least a dozen of them. One of them was pulsing, and the others swirled around it." He brought his hand to his forehead. "It's all still a jumble."

"Real hearts or drawings?" Will asked.

"What?"

Will drew a heart in the air in front of him. "A real heart

doesn't look anything like this. What kind of hearts were you seeing?"

Michael thought for a second. "Drawings. They didn't look like organs."

"It's probably not some kind of blood sacrifice then, but that's still not much to go on," Vanessa said. "We can go into the catacombs tomorrow to see what we can find."

"Why not tonight?"

She gave him a level look. "I'm only just now regaining the ability to use my leg. Your arm is still hanging limply at your side. There are things down there that could kill us all if we're not careful. We all need some rest right now."

"I don't need any—"

"Wendy and Jane would be glad to see you," Will said. "You've hardly been by since we returned from Neverland."

"I don't really have time."

"Visit with your sister, Michael," Vanessa said. "The catacombs will still be there in the morning."

"But—"

"I would listen to her, Michael Darling," a feminine voice said from behind. "You were very nearly kicked out of the Knights not an hour ago. This is not a good time to disobey your commander."

Vanessa spun. A robed figure stood behind her. The gold inlays in the inside of her robe identified her as the Lady, though the silvery gray hair revealed her identity just as clearly. Will sputtered something and bowed deeply, though that wasn't required when speaking with one of the Court. Michael scowled and took Will by the wrist. The two of them walked down the street, leaving Vanessa with the Lady. The Noble waved a hand and the air around them shimmered. Vanessa's skin tingled. Not many Knights were skilled in magic. Vanessa herself had undergone enough training to know that she lacked all but the most basic abilities in that area. Like the Wizard, though, the Lady was an exception.

"It's been a long time, Vanessa."

"Thank you for your support, Lady." She looked at the air around them. "A proof against eavesdropping?"

The Lady inclined her head. "I'm glad you still remember some of what I taught you."

Vanessa offered a small smile. "I was worried the Court wouldn't approve of putting Michael under my command."

"It was a near thing. The Wizard owed me a favor or he would have voted against it. I hope your friend is worth it."

"He's obsessed with finding Hook."

"Perhaps with good reason. That spirit almost destroyed us."

"Then why haven't the Court made finding him a priority?"

"What makes you think we haven't? After all, we haven't stopped your friend from pursuing his goals, and we had you and William ready to go after that vampire."

"If you had assigned Michael to this, we wouldn't have needed this hearing."

"Every Knight has to learn to obey orders."

"Is that you talking? Or the King?"

The Lady laughed, and it might have been Vanessa's imagination, but the nearby house seemed to brighten a little. "He's not nearly as bad as you think. He cares about our mission deeply. That, more than anything else, is what set him against Michael."

Vanessa nodded. "Is there anything else you can do to help?"

"What was it I heard about hearts?"

Vanessa related what Michael had told her, but the Lady shook her head. "Visions like that are all about the details. How many hearts were there? Were they all the same? Were they drawn hearts or actual ones? To just say there were hearts tells us nothing. Even all the secrets of the catacombs won't help you if you have only that."

"They were drawn. Will thought to ask that."

"Did he? Impressive." Thunder rumbled again. The Lady looked up, and it stopped instantly. Even the air around them warmed up a little. Vanessa let out a small gasp, and the Lady grinned. "What of the rest?"

"I'll get more details from him."

"Let me know when you do. I will give you what aid I can."

Vanessa bowed her head. Even more than the Wizard, the Lady was a master of the more abstract branches of magic, such as divination and prophecy. It was entirely possible that there was no one in the world more qualified to interpret Michael's vision.

"I assume you'll take him to the catacombs in the morning."

"No, Lady. Tonight." Vanessa laughed as the Lady cocked her head. "You don't know him like I do."

IT WAS NEARLY THREE O'CLOCK IN THE MORNING BEFORE Wendy Darling came out of Number Fourteen. She practically glided across the sidewalk, moving so quietly the sound of the crickets hid her footsteps. She came to rest beside Vanessa. She carried an umbrella against the rain, though it was still light enough that Vanessa enjoyed the feel of the drops against her skin. Wendy didn't say anything until Vanessa did.

"You don't seem surprised to see me."

Wendy sighed. "Why should I be? You are almost as predictable as Michael."

Vanessa gave a small smile. "Will he be out soon?"

"In a little while. He hasn't quite convinced himself to sneak out yet."

"Will he bring Will?"

Wendy shook her head. "He thinks I'm still asleep. He would never risk waking me just to get Will. Even if that wasn't the case, though, I doubt he would try. He respects our family too much. I'm sure Will will join you after sunrise, though. I assume he knows where you'll be."

Vanessa nodded. A light flickered in the house. Wendy let out a small chuckle and shook her head.

"What is it?" Vanessa asked.

"The nursery. It's Jane."

"Why would your daughter be up at this hour?"

"To say goodbye to Michael, of course."

"She knew?"

"It's funny that even you, a woman who deals with things out of people's nightmares, have trouble understanding those of us you call the Unveiled. Will is like that, too, you know. He might have been in Neverland for years, but he was never one of Peter's like we were. We recognize what the beginning of a journey looks like."

It took a few minutes for the front door to open. Michael stepped out. He scanned the darkness. When he saw Wendy and Vanessa, he seemed to deflate. He walked over to them.

"I should be surprised to find the two of you here, but somehow, I'm not."

The nursery light went out and Wendy raised an eyebrow. "What did Jane say?"

"She just wanted to wish me good luck."

"I guess you want to go to the catacombs?"

Michael nodded. "For a start."

6

"Do you remember how many there were?" Vanessa asked as they approached the dark house.

Michael thought for a second and wiped water from his brow. The rain had stopped, though the chill in the air told Vanessa it would probably start up again before too long.

"Thirteen," Michael said eventually. "There were thirteen hearts. Each was slightly bigger than the one before. The biggest one . . . no, the second biggest one was pulsing."

Vanessa made a mental note of that. "Anything else?"

Michael thought for a while. "It's silly."

"What is?"

"Will mentioned I was grinning when I woke up. I think that's related."

Vanessa shrugged. The grin had been odd, but she didn't see how it could be relevant. All in all, it wasn't much. Perhaps the Lady would find something in it, but Vanessa doubted it.

The hooded form of the Knight Protector was waiting for them as they entered. She looked over to Michael before returning her gaze to Vanessa.

"The Lady said you'd be coming soon, but I, at least, thought you'd have the decency to wait until morning."

"But you're here now anyway?" Vanessa asked.

"You don't just prepare for what you think will happen." The

Knight Protector handed Vanessa a sheet of paper and a pen. "You have a message for the Lady?"

Vanessa took the items and swiftly jotted down everything Michael had told her. Oddly, focusing on writing helped her ignore the disorienting effects of the magic. Once she was done, she folded the letter and handed it to the Knight Protector. "We need access to the catacombs."

Vanessa could imagine the Knight Protector's gaze searing Michael from within the hood. "It's rare that a Knight takes a squire into the catacombs, especially one so recently in disgrace."

"Michael has been in the catacombs several times already. It's not like he doesn't already know what's down there."

The Knight Protector snorted. "As I recall, however, the last couple of times you entered, you had a battle. That is not the sort of thing we want to encourage in the storehouse of the most powerful items in the world."

"Well, it's not likely we'll find Hook down there," Michael said, "and I don't imagine you've captured another wraith."

"If we had, we certainly wouldn't let you down there." She gave a mirthful laugh. "Very well. I grant you leave to go into the catacombs, though you may not remove anything without my explicit permission. The Wizard placed wards on the potions, so don't think you'll be able to sneak another one out of here."

Michael huffed derisively. "I promise you I'm not going to try the same thing twice. Let's go."

"Remember your place, Michael Darling," the Knight Protector said in a firm voice. "You are no longer a Knight. You may not give commands to those who are, and you certainly may not give one to me."

"You already granted permission for us to go down there. Does it really matter who gives the order?"

"Yes, it does."

Michael stared into the hood for several seconds. Vanessa began to worry that they would be sent away. The Knight Protector shifted her weight into a fighting stance. Even Michael blanched at that, which was understandable given that the Knight Protector might well be the most skilled sword master in the world. After a few seconds of uneasy silence Michael turned away.

"I'm sorry." The look on Michael's face told Vanessa that those words had cost him a great deal. He looked up at her. "By your leave, Sir Vanessa."

The Knight Protector's posture shifted slightly, and Vanessa had the impression she was smiling. The Noble of the Court inclined her head. She motioned toward the interior of the house. Vanessa started walking right away. Michael hesitated, but he, too, followed before Vanessa turned a corner. As before, she didn't try to go anywhere in particular, trusting the magic of the house to lead them where they needed to go. The longest Vanessa had ever wandered the headquarters of the Knights was two hours, so she was glad that after a mere fifteen minutes, she came to a door that tingled under her touch.

It looked old and rotted, as if it would fall off its hinges at any second. She pulled it open, and it creaked loudly. It felt far heavier than its appearance suggested. The wooden stairs beyond looked to be even older than the rest of the house. They descended into darkness, and she thought she heard wind howling below. Though she had been down them several times, she couldn't help but feel apprehensive as the first step shifted under her weight. It was all an illusion, of course. The stairs were actually worked stone that were almost as old as London. The illusion was meant to confuse any intruder who ever made it this far. Even the sound of the wind was something created by magic.

Michael snorted and pushed past her. One of the more physically inclined Knights, he had developed a certain contempt for the more subtle branches of magic, such as illusion. Every step he took gave the sound of wood cracking, but that didn't deter him, and after a few seconds he had moved beyond her sight. She sighed and picked up the pace. After a few minutes, the illusion vanished, revealing natural-looking stone. Humidity hung thick in the air.

She reached the bottom and took a deep breath. There was enough magic in this place to sink the British Isles, and she could never enter this place without feeling a little frightened. Nearby, an underground river spilled onto the shore. Michael was examining several nooks in the wall, each holding a magical container. She saw the magic lamp that Michael had used to destroy his evil twin, as well as the cornucopia, the original one that had been used to feed the infant Zeus. There, next to Baba Yaga's cauldron, was the Cup of Jamshid, which the rulers of the Persian Empire had used to maintain power for centuries. He took it and headed toward the river, but Vanessa stepped in front of him.

"Michael, the river is dangerous. You know that."

He hesitated. "Is the water elemental still there?"

She nodded. "The Lady had a hell of a time binding it again after you set it free. She won't be happy if she has to do it again."

"Well, that means that water is full of magic. That would probably make the cup work better anyway."

"We don't have any nixie dust. If it breaks free . . ."

"It won't, not if the wards are any good, and knowing the Wizard and the Lady, they are."

In spite of his confidence, he approached the river slowly. He held the cup down and allowed the gentle current to fill it. Then he came back to Vanessa and showed it to her. The substance in the cup didn't look like water. Rather, what appeared to be liquid smoke swirled within. Vanessa stared into it and dozens of images half formed in front of her eyes, far more than should have been able to fit in such a small object. She felt herself getting lost in it until a strong hand gripped her and pulled her back. She nodded in thanks to Michael.

"Scrying tools are tricky," Vanessa said. "Do you have any idea how to use that thing?"

"I think so." He dipped his finger in, and when he pulled it out, a wisp of smoke swirled around his hand before vanishing. "It's supposed to respond to the need of the one using it. It would be easier if I had some right to the Persian crown, but I think I can make it work."

He touched a finger to the surface of the liquid again, and it crawled up his hand until it covered his wrist. This time, instead of removing his hand, Michael breathed out slowly, and the smoke drained back into the cup. The skin of his arm took on an ashy color, but he pulled his hand out of the smoke and shook it a few times. Color flowed into it. Images rose from the cup and danced above it, but they were vague and indistinct, and Vanessa couldn't see any form to them.

Once again, Michael placed his finger on the liquid's surface. The images above the cup faded as new ones formed from the smoke. This time, they were smaller, and Vanessa could make out even fewer details than before.

"I think the smoke is blue."

"What does it matter?" Michael asked as he poured out the liquid, which evaporated before it hit the ground. "It's not working. Vanessa, don't the Knights have a crystal ball or two around here? I was there when we found Circe's lair. She had to have something."

Vanessa felt her face heat up. "You're never going to stop bringing up Circe's lair, are you? She was known for human transformation. She was not an oracle."

"Fine then. How about one we got from somewhere else? There has to be something."

She thought for a second. "I think we might have a crystal ball in one of the upper levels, but even the Lady has never been able to get it to work reliably. That's never been my skill or yours."

Michael scowled and walked to the river again. This time, the water stirred, but he didn't seem to notice. He dipped the cup in and brought it back. He repeated the exercise, but the smoke was even wispier than before.

"Let me try," Vanessa said.

She hesitated, shuddering at the potential for disaster. The last time she had used an item from these catacombs, it had left her writhing on the ground with the right half of her body burned. Fortunately, the Knights had access to more potent healing than the rest of the world, and she had recovered quickly, but it still wasn't an experience she wanted to repeat. Of course, the silver bow of Artemis had never been meant to be used by human hands. This object should be safe. In theory.

She took the cup and dipped her finger in. Warmth suffused her body, and she smelled the scent of roses mixed with that of fresh paint. Smoke rose from the cup in a constant stream. It swirled, and for a moment, it solidified. The image looked like a turtle more than anything else, only it had hooves. The head and tail looked like it had come from a calf. She stared at it for a second. It seemed to see her and looked surprised before it dissolved a heartbeat later.

"What was that?" Michael asked.

"I have no idea."

"That's about as helpful as the hearts," Michael said. "We may as well try that crystal ball. It can't be any worse than this."

She replaced the cup and headed up the stairs. This time, Michael had the grace to follow. It took them a while to find it. The crystal globe was small enough to fit in the palm of her hand, and its smooth surface felt warmer than the rest of the room. Vanessa had seen the Lady use it. When it worked, it would fill with a color-changing fog, and the images would appear inside, though their meaning was often obscured. They each tried to use it, but it just remained a transparent sphere. By the end, Michael was so frustrated that he lifted the crystal ball over his head. Vanessa realized what he was doing just in time and grabbed his wrist.

"What are you doing? You can't break an item from the catacombs. You're in enough trouble as it is."

Michael struggled against her for a second before relaxing. She took the crystal ball from him and replaced it on the chest they had found it in. Then, she moved to stand in front of Michael.

"What's wrong with you? It's never been like you to be quick-tempered."

For a moment, it looked like he wouldn't answer. Then, his shoulders slumped. He was about to speak when his eyes went wide. Vanessa followed his gaze and gasped. Smoke had filled the crystal ball. A pale blue light shot from one side of the small sphere to the other. Three shadowy figures followed it. Then, as quickly as the smoke appeared, it vanished. Michael stared at it for several long seconds before sighing.

"Why are you so obsessed with Hook? Michael, this is destroying you."

He shook his head. "I have other sources. I was trying to avoid using them, but it doesn't look like I'll be able to."

"Sources worse than the White Lady?"

Michael waved that off. "Knights have used the White Lady before."

"The Knights have used everything." She raised an eyebrow. "Almost anything. Michael, there are things that are forbidden to us. This isn't like going against the orders of the Court. If you cross those lines, you won't only be expelled. They'll send someone to kill you."

"Calm down, Vanessa. I'm not going to summon a demon or call up the dead. I wouldn't go that far, not even for Hook."

"Then what are you talking about?"

He let out a breath. "I guess if I don't tell you, you'll follow me."

She nodded. "Of course, and you know I'm better at trailing people than you are at spotting them. Even Will's gotten pretty good at it."

"You may as well come with me, then."

T he Knight Protector searched them, first physically.
Then her eyes glowed green from within her hood as
she examined them magically, but when she found
none of the items from the catacombs, she let them pass. She
did give Vanessa a letter from the Lady, though. Apparently,
the Noble had an idea about what Michael's vision had meant,
but she didn't want to give more details until she was sure. She
had gone to one of the Knights' hidden libraries to research it.
Michael wasn't happy about that, but he was too focused on his
new goal. They left the house just as Will was approaching. He
took one look at their faces and fell into step behind them.

"Where exactly are we going?" Will asked.

"Beremondsay."

Vanessa raised an eyebrow. "Okay, can you be more specific
than the district?"

"You two don't have to come."

She frowned. "There's a lot I don't have to do, Michael. I don't
have to take responsibility for you, and the Court could assign
you to someone else."

Michael paused. "We all have choices in life, Vanessa."

He kept walking. Vanessa and Will exchanged glances before following. It was a long walk, but Michael refused to hire
a taxi or to take some other transportation. It was well into

the afternoon before Vanessa realized they were heading for a graveyard. By then, the rain that had been sputtering all day was now coming down in full force. It took the edge off the summer heat, not that that made being soaked any more pleasant. She put a hand on Michael's shoulder. He looked back at her but kept walking. She shouted over the loud thunder and heavy rainstorm, trying to keep up with Michael as he came to the gate.

"You said you weren't going to call up the dead."

"I'm not."

"Is there another oracle spirit here?"

"Not as far as I know."

"You know, you're infuriating when you're like this." She rolled her eyes and sighed. Completely drenched, she chose to give up.

He laughed and walked in. The cemetery was empty, and the air had taken on a chill. Will kept a hand on his gravestone dagger as they moved. Michael came to one particular gravestone and rested his hand on the earth. Vanessa's blood went cold. She didn't know what she would do if he tried to call it up, but instead he withdrew his hand, and a shimmering ball of golden light emerged from the grave.

"Is that a fairy cage?" Will asked.

Vanessa realized he was right. Golden bands of energy fenced in a pale blue figure. With the cage around it, she couldn't tell what kind of fairy it was. Of course, the fact that it had been kept in a cemetery told her everything she needed to know.

"You captured a will-o'-the-wisp. Michael, that's . . . When did you even . . . ?"

She couldn't think of the words to finish her sentences as Michael nodded once. Still, she had a hard time believing it. Wisps were one of the most dangerous creatures under the sun.

They could suck out one's soul if you weren't careful. They had angered a tribe of wisps once and had been lucky enough to get away, but that was nothing next to holding one prisoner for who knew how long.

"Michael, this may not be forbidden, but it's not wise."

"Who knows more about the dead than wisps?" he asked. "Besides, you saw what the crystal ball showed us."

Now that she thought about it, the shadow-like figure had looked like a wisp, and the three figures following it could well have been the three of them. That didn't answer everything, though.

"Michael, if you captured this wisp, then you must have already tried to have it lead you to Hook," Will said. "In fact, I'd be surprised if it wasn't the first thing you tried. If it didn't work then, what makes you think it's going to work now?"

"Before, it hadn't been a prisoner for three weeks."

"Three weeks?" Will asked. "Are you insane?"

"Where did you think I got the wisp dust?" He lifted the fairy cage. "Well, you know what I want. Can you lead me to James Hook?"

The fairy said something in haunting song. Vanessa had learned some of the fairy language, though she couldn't make out the words. From Michael's expression, though, what it was saying didn't please him. He began pushing the cage back down into the earth. It hissed and Vanessa wrinkled her nose against the burning smell it released. The fairy shone brighter, and its song grew louder. Vanessa found herself staring at it. She reached forward to grab it, but Michael turned away from her, blocking her sight of it with his body. She blinked and came back to herself. There was a flash of light out of the corner of her eye. Will was looking toward the other end of the cemetery, but she guessed he had seen the same thing she did. Balls of pale blue light drifted close, and the temperature dropped so rapidly that some of the wet grass froze. Their haunting song filled the air, and Vanessa found it hard to focus.

"Michael, there are other wisps."

"I know. They always come when I bring this one out."

That brought her out of her daze. "Always? Michael, how many times have you questioned it?"

"Half a dozen or so." He stopped pushing the cage down. Instead, he picked it up and shook it over them, showering them with dust. The song of the wisps around them grew harsh, though it had lost much of the alluring quality. One of them zipped toward the trio, but Michael absently batted it out of the air.

"Michael, we need to go. Now. You're taking this too far."

As if on cue, a ghost rose out of a nearby grave. Off in the distance, she saw several more. Wisps didn't command ghosts, but spirits were attracted to the death fairies. With so many wisps, they would soon be overrun.

"I'm not done yet."

"I hate to do this to you, *Squire*, but you will come with us, or I will see that you're cast out of the Knights of the Round. They won't go after you for this, but they will turn you away."

"Vanessa . . ." Michael scowled at her.

One of the ghosts drifted too close, and her sword darted forward, slicing a line along its arm. It drew back, and Vanessa began moving toward the gate. "Now, Michael." Her voice was stern, and her patience incredibly thin.

He glared but gripped the fairy cage and shoved it into his pocket. The wisps came closer as did the ghosts. Michael moved toward the gate and motioned for them to follow. A ghost darted at him from above. He cut at it, but he didn't notice the one coming at his back. It stabbed into him. He arched his back and opened his mouth, but his cry was frozen in his throat.

"Will, get him. I'll hold them off."

Will rushed to his brother-in-law and picked him up in a fireman's carry. Three ghosts flew at them, but Vanessa's blade sang through the air, spilling ethereal entrails. Another one stood in their path. Vanessa didn't think. She just struck, losing herself in the battle. The Lady had been her mentor in mystical matters, but Vanessa was one of the few Knights to have been trained by more than one member of the Court. She had learned the sword from the Knight Protector herself, and there were few people on earth or any other world who were her equal with the blade.

Ghosts screamed as they fell before her. The wisps never came close enough for her to hit, but they, too, fell back once the trio had passed through the gate and left the graveyard. It made a sort of sense. The walls of a graveyard had a certain power of their own, and spirits did not easily pass through them. She didn't lower her weapon, though. The rain was coming down harder now. With the threat gone, her wet clothes began weighing her down. Ice crystals had formed in a few places, indicating the ghostly attacks had gotten closer than she'd thought. They needed shelter, but fortunately the Knights had a safe house nearby, so they went there. Though she kept a wary eye out, neither the ghosts nor the wisps prevented them from reaching their destination.

Three Knights were in the common room of the safe house, and all of them studied the bedraggled trio. Vanessa didn't say anything, and after a few seconds the Knights resumed their conversation. The organization, after all, had protocols about interfering with one another.

This particular safe house looked like a hotel. The man at the counter would report that there were no vacancies to anyone who wandered in by chance, but he just handed Vanessa a key with the number three on it. They went down the hall, opened door number three, and stepped inside.

There was no bed in the room, but a wooden couch and two chairs with scarlet cushions set around a low table. They were decorated in an Asian style with plants and birds delicately painted in white. Bookshelves were stuffed with tomes; part of the Knights of the Round's archives. These were mostly about dragons and were written in many languages. Under other circumstances, Vanessa might have taken a few minutes to peruse the contents, but she didn't have time for that now. She turned to glare at Michael as he sat down.

"You brought that thing in here, didn't you?" Vanessa asked.

"Of course. Do you have any idea how hard it is to capture a wisp in a fairy cage? I wasn't about to just let it go."

"Michael, you're going too far."

"What about Peter?" Will asked.

Both Vanessa and Michael turned to him. "What?"

"Have you tried asking Peter?" Will asked. "He's a god, and Hook was his enemy for centuries. If anyone would know where he is, it would be Peter."

Michael's shoulders slumped. "I tried. Getting any information out of Peter is like trying to get the wind to talk. I finally got him to tell me that he's not in Neverland, but more than that?" He shrugged.

Will stared at the floor for several seconds. When he looked up, his eyes were wide, and he spoke in a voice barely above a whisper. Vanessa felt the hairs on the back of her neck stand on end before he had said anything. "What about Mora?"

The witch had lived in Neverland for centuries and was

probably the most individually powerful mortal in either this world or Neverland. She had formed deals with many of its inhabitants before being expelled by Peter. Most worrisome, they had each given her a drop of their blood in exchange for her aid in helping Peter, and there was a lot she'd be able to do with it. If Michael went to her, she might well be able to find Hook, but who knew what price she would demand in return?

"I tried." Michael's voice was hardly a whisper. "I couldn't find her."

"You tried to find Mora?" Vanessa shook her head. "With all your other attempts, I guess I shouldn't be surprised with this one."

"In the catacombs, after I couldn't find Hook, I looked for her. That was why I tried the cup twice. But you can't find a witch as powerful as she is unless she wants to be found. I even thought about going to the rest of the Knights. Maybe some of our magic users would be able to do something."

"They would never help without permission from the Court." Vanessa gave him a level look. "Which they might have granted if you had actually bothered to ask."

Michael snorted. "I have other ways to look now. Thanks for your help in that, by the way."

"Help? You mean when I forced you to leave that cemetery before the ghosts froze your blood?"

Michael laughed. "Oh, come on. You don't really think you forced me, do you? You gave a very convincing show, though. I'm sure the wisps hate me now."

"And you think that's a good thing," Vanessa said in a flat voice.

"Of course it is. Wisps are attracted to ghosts. This one knows where Hook is even if she won't admit it."

"And you expect her to help you after all that you did?"

"Of course not. I expect her to do everything she can to destroy me as soon as she gets free."

"And once again, you think that's a good thing." She was trying not to let the anger come through in her voice, but she wasn't doing a very good job.

"Where do you think it's going to go?" Michael asked. "It'll head straight for the most powerful enemy of mine it can find, and that will mean Captain Hook."

Vanessa sat down and tried to process everything she was hearing. The cushion was thinner than she would have liked, and after a few seconds she stood up again and paced through the room. Michael actually seemed patient for once. Will obviously didn't know what to say and occupied himself with a book that had been left on the table.

Finally, Vanessa spoke. "So you're going to track it. Do you have any idea how dangerous that is? If it finds out and calls the rest of its tribe—"

"—it could lead me into a trap. Without backup, it could suck out my soul or worse."

She glared. "Without backup? You did this whole thing on purpose, didn't you? It was just to force us into this position."

He raised an eyebrow. "You can walk away from me at any time. Even now, there's nothing stopping you."

"Did it ever occur to you to just ask for our help?"

"Would you have given it?"

"Yes!" Will replied, putting down the book with a heavy thump. "Are you really so dense that you haven't realized it yet, Michael? Me, Wendy, Vanessa, we all love you in our own way. We're not going to leave you alone in this."

This surprised Michael more than anything he had heard so far, and he was struck speechless for several seconds.

"Really?"

"Well, I wouldn't have put it quite that way," said Vanessa, "but yes, Michael. If not, I wouldn't have put myself on the line by making you my squire. The Court will be watching me closely now, and they'll hold me accountable for anything you do. The Lady may be on my side, but that will take me only so far. She won't violate her oaths any more than any of the others will. I trust you, but you also have to trust me. Now, come on. Let's see where this wisp leads you, and hope our souls are in one piece by the end of it."

8

On the way out, they grabbed a loaf of bread and some cheese from the safe house's supplies. Vanessa hadn't eaten since the day before, and the meal, sparse as it was, took the edge off her hunger. They went several blocks from the Knights' safe house before Michael pulled out the fairy cage. The golden light shone brightly as the fairy within struggled against its bonds. Being away from a graveyard had muted its power, though it was still quite dangerous. They ducked into an alley, and Michael held it in front of his face.

"It's past time you cooperated. Do you know where James Hook is? Tell me."

The wisp glared and spoke several harsh words in the fairy tongue.

"I'm offering you the same deal I always have. Lead me to James Hook, and I'll let you go."

Again, the fairy spoke.

"You expect me to believe you? If I let you go, you'll run away."

It spoke so rapidly that Vanessa doubted she'd be able to understand even if she had been close enough to hear.

"Fine," Michael said. "You give me your sworn word that you'll go straight to where Hook is right now, and I'll follow you. If you agree to this, I will release you."

"Agreed," the fairy said, using one of the few words Vanessa knew.

Michael tapped the fairy cage. Each touch released a note that blended with the one before. The golden bands lashed out, releasing the wisp even as they wrapped around Michael's finger. The fairy cried out in joy before flying up and disappearing over the building. Michael grinned.

"As long as you let fairies think they're tricking you, they're so easy to manipulate."

"You didn't make it agree to take a route you could actually follow."

"And it assumed I had no way to do so." He chuckled. "I've been searching for this ghost for months. I've learned a thing or two about following spirits, and I do have other resources."

A raven landed on the edge of the building above them. It sang for a few seconds before taking off. Michael nodded. That was one of the few things about Michael that Vanessa was actually jealous about. When they had gone after Peter Pan, Michael had drunk a dragon's-blood potion. That had allowed him to learn the languages of certain animals, including birds. The Court had been angry that he had drunk it without their approval, but once done, there was nothing they could do about it.

"Come on. It's not far."

Michael led them a few blocks away. Vanessa expected it to be an abandoned building or a dark alley. Instead, they came to a small park. The sun shone brightly above, and the wind carried the fresh smell that always happened after the rain. It looked nothing like a place where they would find one of the most powerful ghosts to ever walk the earth. Michael looked surprised as well. Children played all around them, and a young couple strolled through, avoiding the puddles the recent storm had left.

"This can't be right," Will said.

"Ravens aren't exactly the most reliable creatures," Michael admitted, "but still I didn't expect this, especially when going after a wisp."

"Let's look around," Vanessa said. "Maybe the raven was right, and there's something we're missing."

They searched the park for nearly two hours. There was nothing that they wouldn't expect to find in a city park. Once, Will thought he had found a crystal and wondered if it possessed some mystical properties, but it turned out to be made of plastic and had probably fallen off some child's toy. Michael even tried talking to some of the other birds, but none of them had seen anything.

"I can't believe it. Hook got away from me again! Dammit!"

People stared at him, and Vanessa shushed him.

"He's still out there, Michael." Vanessa spoke quietly. "There are other ways to find him."

"What ways? I've *literally* tried everything."

Vanessa motioned for the two to go with her, and she led them to a bench in a shadowed corner of the park. They all sat down. The bench was still wet, but then, their clothes were soaked, so it didn't make much of a difference.

"Maybe he's been destroyed," Will said. "He doesn't strike me as someone who would have trouble making enemies, and from what you told us, he was hurt pretty bad. Maybe he never recovered."

"If only it were that simple," Michael said. "I've seen signs that he's out there. The wisp couldn't have sworn an oath if it didn't know where Hook was. That sort of oath is one of the few things that can bind them."

"How far could the wisp have sensed him?" Will asked as he brushed at a bee buzzing near his face. "Could it have felt Hook across the country?"

"No, I don't think so. As far as I can tell, their senses don't extend more than a few dozen miles or so."

"So regardless of where the wisp is," Vanessa said, "Hook is either in the city or close to it."

"Where Hook is *now*," Will said.

"What?"

"That's what you made the wisp promise, that it would lead you to where Hook is now. What if Hook was here a little while ago? Could you track him, somehow?"

"Maybe," Michael said. "Birds won't go near him, but if he was here, he might have left some sign." He reached into his pouch and pulled out a handful of wisp dust. "I'd hate to use so much of it since I don't have a source for more, but it's the only idea we have."

Vanessa raised an eyebrow. "What are you going to do?"

"There are a lot more uses for wisp dust than the Knights know about. It can be used to find traces of ghosts. It takes a lot of dust, and I don't like wasting it, but Will does have a point."

Vanessa glared at Will, and the squire had the grace to look embarrassed. Vanessa turned back to Michael. "We're in the middle of a park, Michael. The Court won't be happy about this."

"How are they going to find out?"

Vanessa gave him a level look. "Because we're in the middle of a very public place."

"No one who sees this will have any idea what it is, and it's not flashy enough to stick in people's memories," Michael said as he threw a handful of dust into the air.

A thin band of the dust shimmered and began drifting northward, though there was no wind. Michael and Vanessa exchanged glances before running after it. It drifted toward the edge of the park and disappeared into a bush. Michael dove into it. Vanessa and Will exchanged glances and Michael rummaged through the bramble. When he came out, he had cuts down his arms, and his clothes were covered in mud. In his hands was a dead rabbit. Its fur was completely white, though patches of it had fallen out. Its face was frozen in a look of terror, and it was so stiff that for a moment, Vanessa thought it was made of stone. There were no visible wounds. She had heard of rabbits dying of fright, but she hadn't actually seen it. It smelled like it had been dead for some time, though if that were the case it was amazingly preserved.

"What do you make of this?" Michael asked.

"I have no idea," Vanessa said. "You're the one that has a way with animals, and with dead things for that matter."

"This isn't natural."

"Obviously. Do you think Hook did it?"

"It seems likely, but I don't understand why. I mean Hook is evil, but I don't see him going around killing small animals just for the fun of it, especially if he's trying to hide."

"So what?" Vanessa asked. "You think this particular rabbit is special?" Even as she spoke the words, a chill ran through her. Some rabbits *were* special. She reached forward. Michael raised an eyebrow but let her touch the dead creature. There was a slight tingle against her skin. The feel of its magic so nearby caused fear to well up inside of her. She was pretty sure she knew what this was, but she had to be sure.

"Vanessa, what is it?"

"I'm not sure," she said, scooping up a handful of dirt, "but if it's what I think it is, it could be very bad."

She sprinkled the dirt on the dead rabbit. A few specks of it shimmered when it touched the creature's fur, and Vanessa caught the smell of roses. She told herself she was imagining it and repeated the process. It happened in exactly the same way.

"What's that?" Michael asked. "Why is it sparking?"

"So much for that," she said under her breath. "It was just dirt, but there's only one reason dirt would respond like this."

"It's part elemental?" Michael asked, though the tone of his voice said that he hoped it was true but didn't believe it.

"No, this creature is a burrower. It has the ability to cross between certain worlds by digging. Hold on, I have to check something."

She drew her dagger and held the blade so as to see the rabbit's reflection in it. She studied it for several minutes and started to feel relieved until she noticed that some of the patches of fur that had fallen out in the physical creature were still present in the reflection. She moved the knife around the dead animal and found that the patches that were missing on one side were present on the other.

"Dammit! It looks like it's been to the other side of the mirror. Michael, this is bad. This creature couldn't just cross between worlds. It leaves a wake, and if you follow it, you can end up in whatever world it's going to."

"So it's not very skilled if it's leaking magic like that," Michael said.

"It's by design."

"A fairy creature?" Michael asked.

Fairy creatures had been known to lure the unwary into their worlds. Something like that would be worrisome, but that would at least make sense. This was far worse.

"This is a *white* rabbit, in the service of the Queen of Hearts."

"And Hook was here a little while ago," Michael said, looking over the rabbit's body. "A ghost could kill like that." His nose wrinkled at the foul smell. "In fact, I don't know anything else that can."

"We don't know for sure it was Hook," Vanessa said.

Michael nodded and they spread out. This time, they knew

what they were searching for, and it didn't take them long to find it. Near the bush was a small hole. They had missed it when they were first looking because there was nothing at all remarkable about it, but now Vanessa stuck a finger down it and felt the faintest hint of magic. It was definitely a hole to another world. She ran her finger along the edge, and it came away glittering. They were ice crystals. She let out a breath and nodded.

"Hook has gone into Wonderland."

9

Vanessa placed her palm on the hole and pressed, but the barrier between worlds resisted her. Just the fact that she could feel it was a good sign, however. She wasn't skilled at this, and if there hadn't been a recent crossing, she wouldn't have been able to feel anything at all. She stood up, but Michael stuck his hand in the hole and pressed into the ground, expanding it. He grunted with effort before he withdrew, his hand covered in mud.

"Michael, that won't work. The hole is just a representation. Without the magic giving it form, it's just a hole in the ground."

"How do we give it form, then?"

Vanessa shrugged and patted the rabbit corpse. "I'm not sure. Maybe we can do something with this, but the Lady only taught me a little before deciding I don't have the temperament for this sort of thing. She would help, though, if we asked."

"No, I don't want to involve the Court."

"Why not? The Lady is on our side."

He stiffened and clenched his teeth. After a few seconds, he relaxed, though only slightly. He stared off to the west, and Vanessa had the impression he was looking toward Neverland. He met her gaze. "If we let the Court know where Hook has gone, they might send someone else."

"Would that be so bad?" Will asked. "I mean Hook almost

killed the two of you. I'm certain he would have killed me if I had ever come to his attention. We still have no idea how many people died that night because of the ghosts. Maybe others are more qualified." He snorted. "Maybe they should send the entire Court, with what Hook almost did."

"We're not there yet," Vanessa said. "If Hook was a big enough threat, they might go after him, but taking that many powerful Knights would be seen as an invasion of another realm. That's not something the Knights would ever do lightly. As for sending someone else, who do you think they would send, Michael?" She turned to Michael, her eyes staring directly into his. "You know Hook better than anybody. No one has spent nearly as much time in another world as Will has, and nobody has been to Wonderland at all since the . . . since Alice herself."

Michael raised an eyebrow at her hesitation. "No, I still don't trust them. We'll find a way without involving the Court."

"You know the Lady already knows about your vision, right? Thirteen hearts, like a suit of cards. A grin like the Cheshire Cat. I promise you, she'll have realized it means Wonderland a lot quicker than we did."

Michael looked away. "No Court."

"Michael, you know you're not actually in charge, right?" Will asked.

"No," Vanessa interjected, "but I understand Michael's hesitance. We'll do it your way, for now, Michael, but if we hit a dead end, I'm contacting the Lady."

He frowned, but he had no choice.

"Sir Charles Flamel lives nearby. He's a skilled alchemist, not a field agent. He might be able to help, though I take it you don't want to ask any of the other Knights for direct aid?"

Michael shook his head. "Telling one of them is as good as telling the Court directly."

"You know, for someone who willingly rejoined us, you're very reluctant to trust us." He glared at her but didn't say anything, and she sighed. "I helped him deal with a rogue werewolf once. He owes me a favor. He'll let us use his laboratory. I know enough that I might be able to get what we need to follow Hook."

"Fine," Michael said. "Are you sure you want to carry the rabbit like that?"

Vanessa put it in her coat. "It's not the sort of thing we should carry out in the open, even if it wasn't a magical creature."

"I just meant that I have a pack we can put it in."

She considered for a second before shaking her head. "Keeping it close to the skin of a living human can help to preserve any residual energies."

"Really?"

"Maybe you should spend more time learning about things like this and less time chasing after ghosts. There are a lot of things that can disrupt magical energies. We found this out in nature—" She looked at the landscaped grounds of the park. "Of a sort, anyway. That would have preserved most of it, but moving it will cost a great deal. I'm not happy about the smell, but I can get over that."

Sir Charles's house was less than a mile away, though "manor" might have been a more accurate description. Marble pillars held up the porch, and expertly carved statues perched on the lawn. With four stories, it was at least four times the size of Vanessa's own house.

The Knight's servingman answered the door. As soon as it was open, there was a loud whistle from inside, like a teapot but a hundred times louder. The smell of sulfur billowed from inside. The servingman flinched but didn't otherwise respond. Apparently, this sort of thing was common in the house.

"We are here to see Sir Charles."

"Of course, and what may I tell him this is about?"

"Perhaps you didn't hear me. We are here to see *Sir* Charles."

The servingman winced again, and Vanessa could practically tell the moment he realized that only another Knight would refer to his master by that title. "Ah yes. Forgive me. I will retrieve him presently."

He disappeared into the house, and after a few minutes, they were greeted by the Knight himself. He was short and wiry for someone who had been sent out to fight a werewolf. His hair stuck out in every direction, and the pungent smell of garlic wafted about him. Still, he held himself with a certainty that Vanessa had rarely seen.

"Vanessa, Michael." He eyed Will. "I heard you had taken a new squire—the one you rescued from Neverland, right?"

Will nodded and extended his hand. "William."

The man shook his hand. "A pleasure. Now what can I do for you?"

"I need a favor," Vanessa said.

His smile faded a little, and his eyes darted to Michael. "Vanessa, I've heard of some of the things he has been up to, and I want no part of it. No matter what, I am loyal to the Court." Charles looked directly at Michael, now with a mix of disgust and apprehension.

Michael rolled his eyes and looked to Vanessa, his expression showing his contempt for Charles. Vanessa ignored him.

"I'm not asking you to go against your oaths, but we do need access to your lab." Vanessa sighed when Michael cleared his throat. "And a little privacy. I give you my word that nothing we do will go against the rules of the Knights."

Charles cocked his head. "You were never an alchemist, and you're, at best, an absolute beginner at any of the magical arts. What could you want with my lab?"

Vanessa shook her head. "I can't tell you that."

"There are some dangerous potions that could be brewed. The Court could hold me accountable for any potion that comes out of my lab."

"Like you said, I'm not an alchemist. I don't have the skill to brew anything truly dangerous."

"You may not have the skill, but I know your reputation. More important, I know his. The two of you have a way of man aging things that should be impossible. You might have found some new formula, for all I know."

"That I was good enough to brew? We only need your lab for an hour or so. That's not enough time to make even the simplest concoction."

"I don't know." He spoke slowly, and Vanessa knew she almost had him.

"You know me, Charles. I've given you my word that nothing we do here could in any way be seen as violating the rules of the Knights." She hesitated, glancing at Michael. "We just need to examine something, nothing more."

Charles pursed his lips for a few seconds. "Very well. With you giving your word, I'll trust you. Do you need any special materials? I managed to get my hands on some Korrigan eyes recently. Those can be helpful in divining information."

Vanessa thought for a second before shaking her head. "I doubt I would know what to do with them. I just need basic materials. A little copper, some basic herbs, and a way to heat them."

"I have all those in abundance. It's this way."

The house was sparsely furnished, which was an odd contrast to the ostentatious outside. There was hardly any furniture, and the blue carpet was splattered with unidentifiable stains. Charles led them downstairs, and Vanessa noticed runes etched on the stone. She rubbed her hand on one as she passed and thought it felt a little warm.

"Reinforcing the structure?"

"Ah yes. Some compounds can be rather explosive, and it would look a little suspicious to my neighbors if my house were to suddenly collapse in on itself."

Vanessa shivered at that but kept walking. Unlike the house above, the lab was extravagantly furnished. Bottles were arranged in neat lines on half a dozen heavy oaken tables. Each bottle was labeled in a neat hand, and the herbs were grouped by place of origin. Charles even had some creatures that, as far as Vanessa knew, were extinct.

She examined a jar of dark green powder. "Blue rose thorn? I thought those only grew in Atlantis."

Charles laughed as he led them to the table on the far end of the room. "You don't want to know what I went through to get those. Here is the main workstation. You should have everything you need right here."

"Thank you."

Charles hesitated, but Vanessa gave the stairs a pointed look. The Knight sighed and started up them.

"Do you trust him not to spy on us?" Michael asked her in a low voice.

"Oh, I'm sure he has the means to watch everything that goes on in this room, but Charles is an honest sort of person. If he was going to monitor us, he would be up front about it."

As soon as she heard the door shut, she pulled the rabbit out of her coat and placed it on the table. Locating a container of fine salt, she took a handful and drizzled it around the corpse to preserve the magical energy. She took a pinch of mustard seed and ground it in a mortar and pestle.

Will looked over her shoulder. "What is that?"

"Eye of newt."

Michael took a seed out of the container and raised an eyebrow. "Really?"

She chuckled. "In a way. Long ago, witches didn't want the names of their herbs known to the general public, so they made up code names. It does add a little dramatic flare, don't you think? 'Eye of newt' certainly sounds better than mustard seed." She picked up a few petals of dried chamomile and put them in. "Blood of Hestia." A few sprigs of wormwood. "Hawk's heart." She ground them until they had formed a fine powder. Then she took a silver knife off the table and sliced it across her palm. Blood dripped into the mortar, and she mixed it until it had formed a paste. With a half smile, she added, "Sometimes what they called 'blood' was actually tree sap, but in some mixtures, there's no substituting the real thing."

She put the mixture in a beaker and lit a fire under it. While it heated, she scraped some copper dust into it. The paste gave off a dim glow that could have been mistaken for a reflection of the candlelight. It released a clean smell, and her nose felt cold. It reminded Vanessa of being on a mountain. At the same time, she tasted wild berries. A single curl of smoke rose from the mixture. She dipped her finger in. In spite of the fire, the substance was so cold it burned. It felt soft, like fur. She withdrew her finger and dragged it across the rabbit's fur. The body twitched, and Michael gasped. It opened its eyes but didn't move after that. Vanessa looked into those eyes and a wave of cold washed over her. She realized she was breathing heavily and forced herself to calm down. Will looked worried, but Michael just stared at the rabbit.

"So?" he asked.

"I'm not sure," Vanessa said. "It should have given me some kind of insight into how to use its powers."

"Maybe it did," Will said. "The rabbit had to dig, right? Maybe you do, too."

Vanessa shrugged. "Transference doesn't normally happen with a formula this basic, but it's possible. When Michael first drank the dragon's-blood potion, he had to hear animals before he could learn their languages. If something similar happened here, then we should hurry. Effects like this tend to wear off quickly."

She reached for the rabbit, but before she could touch it, it went up in a flare of purple fire. A heartbeat later, there was nothing left of it, not even ash. Both Michael and Will had backed up, but Vanessa examined the area where the rabbit had been. She thought she sensed something, a tingling across her skin, but it was gone a second later.

"Well, that was unexpected." She looked at her companions. "Let's go."

10

Are you sure I can't do anything else?" Charles asked as they stepped through the door of the manor.

"Dispose of the paste I made," Vanessa said.

"Dangerous?"

"Inert. I didn't intend it for long-term use, so I didn't add anything to preserve it. It'll probably start to smell before too long. I would have cleaned up after myself, but—"

He waved her off. "I've made a couple of divination potions in my time. I know that sometimes, you need to act right away. I'll take care of it."

"Thank you." She hesitated. "We might have to dig up your garden a little."

He looked at his neatly planted rows of plants and opened his mouth to speak. After a second, he huffed. "I probably don't want to know."

"No, you really don't."

"Fine. Try not to damage anything, and stay toward the north side of the garden. I don't have anything too rare planted there. It was good to see you again."

"You too."

He closed the door. Vanessa looked up and down the street. There were a few people out, but she didn't want any magic to

dissipate. She knelt down in the dirt at the far end of the garden and used her dagger to dig a small hole. She looked over
her shoulder to the window of Charles's house, but if he was
watching, he wasn't doing it in an obvious way. Vanessa took
a deep breath and searched within herself for the same feeling
she had gotten from the rabbit. She felt a quiver within her and
seized it.

She was in a dark forest. A wide grin appeared before her,
but that was it. Just the grin. She felt something small crawling
on her skin, and somehow she knew it was exactly three inches
tall. An ax shone as it came down on someone's neck. Vanessa's
head swam with images that made no sense. Flamingos swung
at balls that were actually rolled-up porcupines, and birds swam
in a sea of tears. It was too much. The magic felt like it was torn
from her grasp. She found herself on the ground, gasping. Michael and Will were next to her.

"What was that?" Michael asked.

"You saw it?"

"I think we both did," Will said.

"It was even stronger than the vision the White Lady gave
me," Michael said.

"I'm not sure," Vanessa said. "I don't think that was a vision, exactly. It was like we were everywhere at once. I think
we passed partway into Wonderland. There wasn't anything to
concentrate our location, though."

"What do we do about it, then?"

"Back to the park," Vanessa said. "If I try again at the original hole, that might give me the focus we need to get all the
way through."

"You said the effect wouldn't last long," Michael cautioned.
"Is there still enough for you to make it through?"

Vanessa closed her eyes and concentrated. Now that she had used the ability, she could sense it within herself. It was slowly fading. "I think so. There's enough for one attempt, at any rate, as long as we do it quickly."

"Lead the way."

11

T he hole had almost completely fallen in on itself. As Vanessa ran her fingers around its edge, she felt no magic, but when she reached into the hole, she felt a vibration. Something in the hole resonated with her. She plucked at it until she held it between her fingers. It was frail, and she knew it would rip if she wasn't careful. She interwove it with the fading magic she had gotten from the rabbit.

A sudden whirlwind of energy whipped all around them. The color of her surroundings bled away, and she felt herself being pulled away from the park, from London, from the world itself. She was being drawn someplace else. Her companions were next to her, but everything else was a blur. Then they were falling down a great hole. She couldn't see where they had fallen from or where they were falling to. There were shelves all around them, cluttered with all sorts of items. She even thought she saw the empty jar of orange marmalade that Alice had found so long ago. A room with a myriad of doors came rushing up to meet them. This was exactly how Alice had done it. It was going to work.

Then they hit a wall.

There was no other way to describe it. The room was below them, but they had hit an invisible barrier. It still felt like they were falling, and her hands could move freely through the air below them, but they didn't fall.

"So what do we do now?" Will asked. "We're not going to be stuck here forever, are we?"

"I don't think so," Vanessa said. "Maybe if we were actually in Wonderland, that would be something we would have to worry about."

"If we're not in Wonderland, then where are we?" Michael asked.

"Where were we when we were sailing from Neverland? We are in the space between worlds."

Michael managed to turn enough so that she could see his face. He narrowed his eyes. "We didn't all study under the Lady, Vanessa. What does that mean?"

"If we don't find a way to make it through quickly, we'll be pulled back."

"How quickly?"

Suddenly, there was a rush of wind. They flew up the hole more quickly than they had fallen, so quick that she couldn't see any of the items. The next thing she knew, they were ten feet in the air. She barely had time to cry out before crashing down onto the park's muddy ground. She bit her lip before her mouth opened, and she tasted blood and mud. She groaned as she got up and felt her face redden when she saw at least a dozen people staring at them. Beside her, Michael struggled to his feet. He brought his hand to his head. For a moment, he looked like he would fall over, but Will helped him to stay up. In spite of being the newest of their number, he had handled the ordeal better than they did.

"What happened?" Michael asked.

Vanessa looked around and gave him a level look. He seemed to notice the people for the first time. He closed his eyes and shook his head. The Court wouldn't be happy about this. Fortu-

QUEENS OF WONDERLAND 67

nately, nothing too extravagant had happened, as long as you didn't consider three people shooting up into the air extravagant. Hopefully, it wouldn't be too big of a mess for the Knights to clean up.

"The safe house?" he asked in a low voice.

"No, Michael, it's time."

"Time for what?"

"Time that we admit that we can't do what we need to do to finish this. We need to see the Lady."

He paled and shook his head. "Vanessa, no."

"This isn't up for discussion, Michael." She was having a hard time keeping her voice low enough that the crowd wouldn't hear. "We've been on enough wild goose chases."

"I don't want to involve the Court."

"Let me put it this way, Michael." She shook mud off her hands. "I am going to see the Lady. You are welcome to come with me, but if you don't, the Lady will know that you have disobeyed orders. She won't stand by you then, and you'll be expelled. Not that being in the Knights will do you any good anymore. We have no other paths open to us."

Michael frowned. Will nodded behind him, which was a relief. She hadn't been quite sure who he would end up following, though given that Will had been a navy man, it made sense that he respected the chain of command. Though Michael didn't turn to look, he seemed to understand. He motioned for her to lead the way. She resisted the urge to smile, worried that if she gloated, he would change his mind. The crowd parted for them. They couldn't walk very quickly, and the fall had hurt them all in one way or another. Vanessa's right leg hurt if she put too much weight on it. She sighed. Just when she had recovered from the ghost attack, too.

They hired a taxi. After seeing how muddy they were, the driver didn't want to take them at first, but once Vanessa offered him triple his normal rate, he became much more agreeable.

"Jane was happy to see you," Will said once they were in the car.

Michael smiled, something that had become far too rare in the past year. "I've missed her."

"You should come visit more often," Will said.

"I haven't had time," Michael said.

"We make time for what is important, Michael. I lost a lot because I went away to fight in the war. I'm still not sure it was worth it. Don't throw away what you have in us."

Michael looked out the window but didn't say anything the rest of the way. They were dropped off a few blocks from the headquarters and limped to the old building. As tired as they were, the magic defending the place almost sent them running. Vanessa had to stop three times just walking the path before she finally made it to the door.

As before, it opened before she touched it. This time, rather than creaking, the door spoke in a high-pitched voice: "Hello."

Vanessa drew back. She looked back at Will and Michael, but both men looked as surprised as she felt. She examined the entrance, but it was the same old thing that had always hung here. When she peered inside, she resisted the urge to gasp. Instead of the old building that the illusions had so often projected, the hall was filled with fog. It was so thick that she couldn't see more than a few feet ahead of them.

"What do we do?" Will asked.

"We go in," Vanessa said. "Whatever the illusions are showing us, this is still the headquarters of the Knights, and we are welcome here."

She took a step and the fog swirled around her. She had the momentary sensation of being strangled. Michael followed and gasped, his hands going to his throat before realizing the sensation was artificial. "Are you sure?"

"Okay, I know that wasn't particularly pleasant. But after all you've been through, you hesitate before a little fog?"

"I don't surround myself with hostile magic if I don't have to."

"What about when you surrounded yourself by ghosts and wisps in the middle of a graveyard?" Vanessa asked.

"That was necessary."

"Well, so is this. Now, come on."

The fog grew thicker as they walked until they couldn't even see the walls on either side. Behind her, Michael cursed. She turned around. He was standing on one leg and gripping his shin. He knelt and picked up a metallic outline of a rooster.

"Is that a weather vane?" Will asked.

The fog swirled around them. Tendrils of it reached into Vanessa's mouth and nose. She gagged and heard the others doing the same.

"Oh, you should not have said that," a dull voice said. "It doesn't like to be called that."

Vanessa looked around, but she didn't know who had spoken. Michael was staring at the rooster in his hand.

"Who said that?" she asked.

Michael indicated the rooster. Vanessa cocked her head.

"That wasn't very polite," the rooster said. For a second, she could only stare. It turned to look at her, squeaking as it did. "You should probably apologize."

"Apologize for what?"

The tendrils of fog wrapped around her neck. She had the sense it was angry, though she couldn't feel the fog. Will looked like he was completely tied up, though the mist didn't seem to actually inhibit his movements.

"You called the fog vain," the rooster said.

"No, I didn't."

"Yes, you did, unless you were calling some other kind of weather vain. I don't see anything else, so I'm pretty sure you were talking to the fog."

"No, I meant you."

"Me? How could you possibly mean me? I'm neither weather nor vain."

"No, I mean—"

The fog grew even thicker until she couldn't see the others. Water droplets formed on her forehead. When she reached up to wipe them away, the fog thinned again, and the weather vane was gone.

"Well, that was odd," Will said.

"I've never seen the spells like this." Michael moved one of his hands back and forth, causing the fog to swirl around his fingers.

"Me neither, but it does seem familiar somehow."

Will looked around. "If you say so."

She kept walking. The ground beneath her became softer, like soil. She touched it and found that it was grass. The fog obscured the walls of the passage, and when she groped for them, she couldn't find them, which was more than a little disturbing. She thought she heard running water and headed in that direction. After a few seconds, they came to the flowing water. The fog didn't allow them to see very far, so she couldn't tell if it was a stream or a river. She walked along the shore until she found a squat stone building. She exchanged glances with the others. Will walked up to it and touched it before looking to her and shrugging. There was a single wooden door. She pushed it open and went in. The fog was just as thick inside as out, and they couldn't see any detail of the interior.

"Vanessa, where are we?" Michael asked.

"If I'm right, we're in a river bank."

Michael blinked. "You mean we're in a building on a river bank."

"Not here," Vanessa said. "We're *in* a river bank."

"Indeed," someone said from just beyond their sight. The voice was distorted, almost like it was heard from underwater. "How may I help you? Would you like to make a deposit or a withdrawal?"

Vanessa could just make out a large desk, though the fog was too thick to determine what it was made of. She sat down next to it and motioned for her friends to do the same.

"That depends," Vanessa said. "Are you just a river bank or can I deposit other things?"

"There are a number of things we can store," the voice said. "What did you have in mind?"

"Fog," Vanessa said.

"Ah yes. We are a fog bank as well. How much would you like to deposit?"

"All of it."

Vanessa thought she could see the outline of a humanoid figure. It bounced. "Oh, miss, that is wonderful. Yes, we can accommodate you."

"Thank you. Can you do so immediately?"

"Yes, of course. We will start right away."

Instantly, the fog vanished, and they found themselves in an empty building. Marble pillars lined the walls, and there was a row of desks with a printing calculator on each one. There were no people, though. Even the person they had been talking to was gone. The desk in front of them had a single slip of paper, which Vanessa took. She read it aloud, her voice echoing in the cavernous chamber.

"Five million cubic feet of fog."

"Vanessa, none of this makes any sense," Michael said. "It's like the world has gone insane."

"Right," Vanessa said. "That's a good sign."

"How is it a good sign?"

"If you can't handle this, then you have no business in Wonderland," Vanessa said.

Michael paused. "Have you been there?"

Vanessa pursed her lips. "No, I told you. No one has been to Wonderland since Alice herself."

"Then, how is it you know so much about it?"

"This really isn't the best time," she said. "Come, without the fog, we might be able to see the way we should go."

"Would it really be that easy?" Will asked. "Just deposit the fog in a fog bank and then go outside?"

She got to her feet and headed toward the door. "You'd be surprised how often problems like this have a simple solution." Michael scoffed, and she gave him a level look. "We tried your way, and it didn't work. Besides, you know as well as I do, that once we get into this house, it determines where we will go. You won't be able to get out of this place until the house lets you."

"Why didn't we just wander through the fog until we found what we were looking for, then? It would have been exactly the same as wandering through hallways."

"Call it a hunch."

They stepped out of the bank and found themselves in a sparse forest that smelled heavily of pine. Birds chirped in the branches overhead; the river gently lapped on the shore. In the distance a hill rose up, and they saw a figure standing atop it. Vanessa gave Michael a pointed look and headed in that direction. It only took her a few minutes to recognize the robed figure of the Lady. She approached her mentor and inclined her head.

"Vanessa, it is good to see you."

"Lady. Did you do this?"

"Of course."

"Why?"

"Because you are going to Wonderland, and you need to be prepared."

"How do you know what we need?" Michael asked.

"Your vision, Squire Michael."

"You understand what it means?"

"Of course. It was only a matter of time. Thirteen hearts." She reached into her robe and pulled out a deck of cards. She spread the hearts out before them and tapped the queen. "The second from the biggest was pulsing. The pirate has allied with the Queen of Hearts. Everything centers on that. Then, there was the grin you wore when you woke. That comes from the Cheshire Cat. It has a habit of appearing where it was least expected."

"I suppose you're an expert on Wonderland, too, but you haven't been there either, right?"

The Lady threw back her head and laughed. Tendrils of blue light slithered out of her and wound around their legs. Will tried to shake them off, but it didn't work. The whole thing struck Vanessa as funny, and she started laughing. Soon the others were laughing as well. It took a few seconds to realize she couldn't stop. Before she had a chance to do anything about it, the laughter faded. The Lady's hood had fallen off, though Vanessa knew her well enough to know that wouldn't happen unless she wanted it to. She had alabaster skin. Her hair had been golden in her youth, though time had transformed it into silver. Her face had wrinkled, though there was still strength to it. Her eyes, as blue as the summer sky, met Vanessa's before turning to Michael, who was still catching his breath. To his credit, he inclined his head.

"Lady, does this mean you're going to help us?"

"Yes, of course. You were correct in assuming I am an expert on Wonderland, but you were wrong in one respect. I have been to Wonderland as well as the Looking Glass Land."

"I thought no one had been there since Alice."

"That is true, as far as I know. I was six when I saw the white rabbit and chased it down its hole and seven when I visited the other side of the mirror."

"You are Alice. *The* Alice?"

"And I was only slightly older than you were, Michael Darling, when I first crossed into another world."

12

Vanessa had known the Lady's secret, but the others were dumbstruck by the revelation. The true identities of the members of the Court were known by only a few. The story of Alice was known to every Knight, but that was entirely different from meeting the legend herself.

"Lady," Vanessa said. The Lady smirked, and Vanessa cleared her throat. "Alice, we tried to cross into Wonderland, but we were blocked."

The Lady waved her hands. A vortex of blue light surrounded them. Once again they found themselves falling, though this time they fell even faster than before. The rush of wind was deafening. They reached the room with the doors but couldn't touch the ground. The Lady's face hardened. Lightning shot down from the hole above, filling the air with the smell of ozone. The bolt dissipated before it hit the ground. She threw her hands down. The barrier bent away from them but it held. Vanessa braced herself to be thrown into the air again, but they found themselves standing on a hill instead.

"Well, that was interesting. The way into Wonderland has been blocked."

"By whom?" Vanessa asked.

"It's hard to say," the Lady said. "Wonderland isn't like Neverland. It doesn't have a single all-powerful ruler. If Squire

Michael's vision was any indication, it was the Queen of Hearts, though she lacked the power to do so the last time I saw her."

"So then what do we do?" Michael asked. "Hook is in Wonderland. Whatever he's doing there, you can be sure it won't be good."

"Calm yourself. Sealing off a world entirely is not an easy thing to do. There are always secret ways, small ways. I know magics that have originated in places other than Wonderland, and I doubt the queen would even know to block those. Before I help you, do you understand what you're asking?"

"I've been to other worlds before," Michael said.

"Don't exaggerate your experience, Michael Darling. You have been to one other world, where you were directly involved in the business of its creator. That offered you a certain degree of protection. You won't have that in Wonderland. More than that, Wonderland is a land of madness. The laughter I infected you with earlier is nothing compared to what you will face. It's not like anything you've ever experienced."

Michael raised an eyebrow. "You did read my report, right? The one where I talk about almost being drowned by mermaids, the weird duplicates of my siblings who built a magical boat for us to cross between worlds, and the tribe of gremlins who conscripted us into fighting a ghost army?"

"Yes, I read your report. The things you are talking about made sense. They followed a certain logic. Wonderland has no such constraints. If you think depositing fog in a fog bank is nonsensical, then you have no idea what you will face in Wonderland. How is a raven like a writing desk?"

"What?"

"How is a raven like a writing desk? It is a simple question. Ponder it, and it may give you the barest idea of what you will face."

Michael clenched his teeth but nodded. "Whatever it is, I can handle it."

"Yes, I'm sure you can. At least you are better able than most, but you should be prepared."

"So how will you get us there?"

"Song, I think."

"Song?"

"There is powerful magic in music. Like all things, one must simply know how to employ it. It is a trick I learned from a siren I met long ago. For all that he is, I doubt very much Hook knows to guard against this kind of magic, and the Queen of Hearts certainly doesn't."

Michael looked at Vanessa, who shrugged. She didn't know anything about this, but like Charles had said, she was, at best, an amateur at magic.

"What do you need to make it work?" he asked the Lady.

"Simply for you to tell me that you are ready. Before I do that, however, I must make you my vassals."

"Your vassals?" Vanessa asked. "Aren't we already? We're Knights of the Round, and you are a member of the Court."

"No," she said, "not vassals of the Court or of the Lady. Vassals of Queen Alice."

"I wasn't aware you were a queen," Vanessa said.

"Then you should reread the chronicles of my adventures. When I crossed into the mirror, I moved across the land. Once I reached the end, I was crowned. I was only seven when that happened, but that title was never revoked, and I am still a Looking Glass queen."

"We're not going into the looking glass," Michael said.

"The two lands are more closely aligned than you might think, and it may well help you to be the vassals of a queen."

"Won't you be coming with us?" Vanessa asked.

"I'm afraid not. My entering Wonderland with the explicit purpose of opposing the Queen of Hearts would be the same as me declaring war on Wonderland, both as the Lady of the Knights of the Round and a Looking Glass queen. I am not prepared to do that just yet. This is all I can do for you."

She went to each of them in turn and placed a hand on their shoulder. Vanessa felt a surge of warmth flow through her, and for a moment the image of a huge chessboard appeared in front of her eyes. She blinked, and the Lady was moving on to Will. As soon as she was done, the trees around them seemed to bow. It was more than a little eerie, even considering the fact that they were all actually illusions created by the Lady.

Michael's eyes darted from one to another before he spoke. "If there is nothing else, then we're ready to go."

"Are you certain?"

"Yes," Michael said.

The Lady raised an eyebrow. Michael clenched his teeth and turned to Vanessa. "What do you think?"

Vanessa suppressed a smile. "Oh, are you looking for my opinion now?"

His face reddened, and she could tell that he was struggling not to snap back at her. She let out a small chuckle and turned to the Lady. "At your leisure, Lady." The Lady scoffed, and this time, it was Vanessa's turn to feel embarrassed. "Alice, I mean, provided there is nothing else you think we need."

The Lady—for Vanessa could only ever think of her as "the Lady"—smiled. "That is everything. *Will you walk a little faster? said a whiting to a snail.*"

Vanessa blinked. "What?"

"There's a porpoise close behind us, and he's treading on my tail."

"What is she talking about?" Michael asked.

"I think it's the spell," Vanessa said.

"See how eagerly the lobsters and the turtles all advance!
They are waiting on the shingle—will you come and join the
  dance?
Will you, won't you, will you, won't you, will you join the
  dance?
Will you, won't you, will you, won't you, won't you join the
  dance?"

Vanessa felt faint. The colors in the world around her bled together. The illusions on the house became transparent and melded with the reality they had been hiding. Vanessa's feet started moving in a dance. She knew she could stop them if she wanted to. She saw Michael and Will standing still, though they obviously struggled to do so.

"Don't resist it," Vanessa said. "You have to let it happen."

"Why?"

"No time. Let it happen or be left behind."

Michael started moving with the same sinuous movements she was doing. Will swayed at first. Then he started to dance. The three of them moved around the Lady. When she spoke again, her voice had a musical quality to it.

"'You can really have no notion how delightful it will be
When they take us up and throw us, with the lobsters, out to
  sea!'
But the snail replied, 'Too far, too far!' and gave a look
  askance—
Said he thanked the whiting kindly, but he would not join
  the dance.

Would not, could not, would not, could not, would not join
   the dance.
Would not, could not, would not, could not, could not join the
   dance."

The world faded, leaving only a few splashes of color swirl-ing around them. Other colors joined in. Garish oranges and bright yellows. Putrid greens mingled with whites that were purer than snow. Every new color was an extreme of one form or another. Only Will and Michael were visible to her, dancing in the void. The Lady's voice rang clear, though it had no source that Vanessa could see.

"'What matters it how far we go?' his scaly friend replied.
'There is another shore, you know, upon the other side.
The further off from England the nearer is to France—
Then turn not pale, beloved snail, but come and join the
   dance.'"

The colors of the world faded, leaving only the bright ones of a vivid new world. Those expanded and started coming to-gether. Blues split apart and formed the sky and the sea. The greens became seaweed, though a small portion of them formed into a blob. Yellows and oranges became the clouds at sunset. Browns formed the ground and mingled with the green in front of them. The Lady's voice was fading, but Vanessa could still hear her song clearly.

"Will you, won't you, will you, won't you, will you join the
   dance?
Will you, won't you, will you, won't you, won't you join the
   dance?"

The colors snapped together. They now stood on a rocky shore. There was a forest to the west and a mountain range far in the north. The blob of color resolved itself into the figure of a turtle with the head and hooves of a cow. The Lady's voice faded to be replaced by the sound of waves crashing on the shore. The smell of salt filled the air, and the turtle creature let out a long breath.

"That was rather rude of you."

13

The crashing waves were so loud that Vanessa wondered if she had really heard the creature speak. Her companions' expressions, however, told her that they had heard it as well. All three of them stared at the turtle creature. It moaned as it stared down at them.

"I'm sorry," Vanessa said. The salt was so thick in the air that she could taste it. "What exactly did we do that offended you?"

"It's rude not to know when you are being rude."

"We're sorry, Mister, uh, Turtle," Will said in a marveling tone. Vanessa could hardly blame him. Even among their order, a turtle with fur was hardly a common sight.

The creature stood up straight. "Turtle? You think I'm a turtle? Do I look like any turtle you've ever seen?"

"Well, no," Will said.

"Turtle indeed. I am a mock turtle."

"What is a mock turtle?" Michael asked.

"Oh, I'm not surprised you haven't heard of my kind, as rude as you are. Most of us have been made into soup."

"Mock turtle soup?" Vanessa asked. "But that's not—"

She hesitated. In the real world, mock turtle soup was made from the hooves and head of a cow but prepared in such a way as to be an imitation of turtle soup, one that was far less expensive than the real thing. However, they *were* in Wonderland, so it made sense that here the soup would come from a creature such as this.

"I'm sorry, perhaps we should start again. I'm Vanessa."

"That is interesting."

"It is?"

It used its hooves to brush away some sand that had gotten in its fur. "Well, I don't want to be rude, unlike some people. You told me something that was obviously important to you. I didn't want you to think I didn't care, so I pretended it was interesting."

"Well, what is your name?" Vanessa asked.

"My name?"

"Yes." She hesitated for a second. "It's rude not to share your name when someone has given you theirs."

"Is it? Well, I suppose it is. I am Tort." The mock turtle saw their shocked reactions and scowled. "Yes, as in 'tortoise.' My parents chose the name so that I would always remember that I could be whatever I wanted to be."

"But a tortoise?" Michael asked.

"There you go. Back to being rude."

"Look, I'm sorry," Michael said. "I just didn't expect . . . well any of this."

"That's no excuse to be rude."

"We're looking for someone."

"Changing the subject is—"

"Yes, rude, I know. Let's just agree on the fact that I'm rude and move on from there."

"Michael," Vanessa said.

"We don't have time for this."

"Barreling through a situation won't work here. You'll end up going in circles until you go mad, if you're lucky." She let out a breath. "Remember, this is Wonderland."

He looked like he was going to argue, but he seemed to deflate. "Fine, we'll do this your way."

"As we should," Vanessa said wittingly. "Tort, please forgive my friend. The person we are looking for was very rude to his mother. He is anxious to have an accounting for that."

"Well, I suppose I can understand that. Being rude to a person is one thing. Being rude to their mother is quite another. Of course I will help. Tell me of this person you are looking for."

"He's a ghost," Vanessa said.

"A dead man? Well, I suppose that is a proper punishment for being rude to a person's mother."

"Actually, he was dead when he was rude."

"Ah yes. A person who was rude in life is often that way in death."

Michael rolled his eyes and sat on a rock. He stared out to sea, obviously trying to distract himself.

"Can you help us, Tort?" Vanessa asked. "Have you heard of a ghost coming into Wonderland recently? It would have only been in the past day or so."

"Many ghosts have entered Wonderland in recent days. I don't associate with such creatures, so I don't think I know the specific one you seek."

"'Many'?" Vanessa asked.

"Yes. Death washes over this land like the waves on the shore. People of all sorts die, but they remain. Just the other day, I saw the spirits of a walrus and a carpenter walking along the shore. Oyster ghosts surrounded them, eager for revenge." He pointed to a stretch of wet sand. "They devoured the pair right there."

"What would oysters want revenge for?" Will asked.

"Why, for being eaten, of course. It was awfully rude of

them." The mock turtle's head perked up. "Is it the walrus or the carpenter that you seek? Or maybe one of the oysters?"

"No, not any of them," Vanessa said. "The one we're looking for is a pirate. One with only one hand."

"One hand? Perhaps the ghost of a clock to tell you the hour."

"A clock isn't alive," Will said, walking up to stand next to Vanessa. "Even if it were, clocks have two hands."

"You did say you were searching for someone that isn't alive, so a clock fits." Tort turned away from them. "If you weren't so rude, you might know that a clock that can tell you both the hour and the minute has two hands, but one that can only tell the hour has but a single hand. I'm sure they would find it quite rude to be reminded of the fact that they lack what so many of their peers possess."

"I'm sorry," Will said.

Vanessa moved in close to him. "Why don't you let me do the talking?"

Will looked almost grateful to hear that. "That's probably a good idea."

"No, Tort. We're not looking for the ghost of a clock. We're looking for the ghost of a human. He has a hook for a hand and is probably one of the rudest people in the world."

"If you seek one of the rudest people in the world, then you need only look beside you."

Michael groaned but didn't say anything.

"But he is not dead."

"Are you certain? There is a foul odor coming from him."

She resisted the urge to laugh as she heard Michael get to his feet. After a second, she composed herself. "That was rather rude, Tort."

The mock turtle suddenly looked horrified. "Oh my, it was

rude, wasn't it? You have my sincerest apologies for that. I can't believe what I did. How can I make it up to you?"

"You could tell us if you've heard of someone like I've described to you."

"Hmm, let me think. I do not know if any pirate ghosts have come into this land, but I spend most of my time on this rock, so unless they pass by here . ." It shrugged, which looked truly odd for a turtle with a cow's head. "I have many acquaintances who are better informed than I am. I could ask one of them if they have heard anything."

"That would be much appreciated. May we go with you while you do?"

"I suppose so. It is the least I could do after being so rude."

Slowly, Tort stood up and walked off the rock. The hooves should have made it clumsier, but instead, they had the opposite effect. The mock turtle looked more like a satyr than an awkward half cow half turtle, dancing from step to step before thudding on the ground. It motioned for them to follow. In spite of its grace, it moved exactly as fast as one would expect a turtle to go.

"Over here," someone whispered.

Vanessa looked around. A man was peering at them from behind a rock. He had sandy brown hair that looked like it had never been combed, and she caught a faint whiff of tea. She couldn't see the rest of the man's body, but on top of his head sat a tall hat made of some purple fabric. It had a wide brim and a card reading, "In this style 10/6." He waved at her, and she stopped. Tort didn't notice Vanessa stop, but the other Knights did. They stopped and stared. Michael saw the hatter almost immediately and pointed him out to Will.

"Come here," the hatter whispered.

She looked to Tort who had progressed only a few feet,

though the mock turtle hadn't noticed the hatter. She thought of the lessons she had learned from the Lady, not just the magical ones but the ones on the nature of reality as well. In Wonderland more than most worlds, it was dangerous to avoid such things. She crept toward the man, motioning for the others to do the same. As soon as she got close enough, he grabbed Vanessa and pulled her behind the rock. Will and Michael rushed forward, each with a sword drawn. They held their weapons to the man. The hatter, however, seemed not to notice them. Instead, he stared at Vanessa, his long face twisted with fear.

"You must be careful. You are in grave danger."

"Danger?" Vanessa asked. She motioned and the two men put away their weapons, though Michael kept his hand on the hilt. She rolled her eyes and returned her attention to the hatter. "Tort doesn't strike me as a particularly dangerous being."

"That's *why* it's so dangerous. You can't trust it."

"Why?"

"Because it is a creature of the Queen of Hearts. It is completely loyal to her. It's one of her lieutenants."

"What could it possibly do for the Queen of Hearts?" Vanessa asked. "It doesn't seem terribly useful."

"It's a watchman." Will glanced back toward the mock turtle, who was still walking. "The queen must know someone could come into the world here."

"Exactly so," the hatter said. "She lacked the power to close off this entry, so she sent someone to watch it."

"A mock turtle as a guard?"

"Would you ever suspect something like it?"

Vanessa and her friends exchanged glances. "No, I suppose not."

"No one would. He no doubt intends to lead you to the queen."

"Would that really be so bad?" Michael asked. "I mean if she's in charge around here, she might be able to tell us what we need to know. That's what my vision indicated anyway."

The hatter plopped down on the ground and rubbed his chin. "You know, she might, provided she's in a good mood, and all her roses are red, and she's had her tea, and you give her a good unbirthday present."

"Unbirthday?" Michael asked.

"Yes, of course, provided, that today is her unbirthday. I'm not really sure."

"No," Michael said, "I mean what is an unbirthday?"

The hatter was so shocked that his hat fell off. As if it had somehow been restraining his hair, it bounced up. The hatter scooped up his hat and put it on. Sand had gotten into it and spilled over him. He sneezed, and some of the sand blew into Vanessa's face. She brushed the grainy substance away.

"You don't know what an unbirthday is?" the hatter asked.

Michael rolled his eyes. "Obviously."

"Why any day that's not your birthday is your unbirthday."

"So today is her unbirthday unless, by chance, it happens to be her birthday."

"Yes, of course. It's quite a risk to take."

Michael laughed. "I don't think so. I mean it's my unbirthday today, too. For that matter, it's all of my companions' unbirthdays."

"Really? Mine too!" Suddenly, he looked worried. "What are the chances that it would be four people's unbirthday? Surely, we won't find another. Why the odds of that would be astronomical!"

"Astronomical?" Michael asked. "Are you serious?"

"Oh no," the hatter said. "Never. You never want to be serious here. There are grave consequences if you are."

"He does have a point," Vanessa said. "This isn't a place for rational people."

"How are we supposed to find Hook, then?" Michael asked.

"What's the difference?" Will asked. "I mean it's just like Neverland, isn't it? They both seem to be playgrounds for children."

"A playground with pirates and monsters," Michael said.

"A dangerous playground, certainly," Vanessa said, "but a playground nonetheless. Wonderland is different. It is a land of madness."

"Would you say the Lady is mad?" Michael asked with a smirk.

"I think she understands it. I'm not sure you can make it through Wonderland without doing that much, any more than you can make it through Neverland without understanding what it means to be a child."

"What about me?" Michael asked.

"You have to learn."

"I don't think that'll be an easy thing to learn."

"You have to bend sometime," Vanessa said. "I'm afraid this land will break you if you don't."

"Oh yes," said the hatter. "I was like him when I came to this land. I refused to understand it, and so I became what I am now." He took off his hat and bowed. His hair was still full of sand, and a hermit crab was crawling around on his head. "Now, where were we? Ah yes. The queen. She will chop off your head, you know, and that's almost always fatal."

"Almost always?" Michael asked.

"Yes, of course. Do you have any idea how serious cutting off a head is? Very few people can survive that."

"Who do you think could survive that?"

"A household," the hatter said. "It would be hurt, certainly, but it could survive. I don't think you're a household, though."

Michael stared at the hatter for several seconds before throwing up his hands in frustration.

"Hello?" Tort's voice sounded from the other side of the rock.

The hatter's face twisted in terror. The hermit crab, which was still on his head, clung to his hair for a second before falling to the beach. The hatter started to run, but Vanessa grabbed him before he had taken a single step. He tried to pull free, but he was remarkably weak.

"Please," he whispered. His face had gone pale. "Please, we have to go. If it sees us, it'll capture us, and then we're done for."

"Then we shouldn't attract its attention. Be quiet." Vanessa turned to Will. "Can you lead it away?"

"The mock turtle?" Michael asked. "Are you serious? We could fight him off without breaking a sweat."

"I'm not being serious," Vanessa said. "I've tried to explain this to you. This isn't the place for being serious. I think we'll get more from listening to the hatter, which is why Will is going to lead the mock turtle away."

Michael rolled his eyes at her, but Will nodded. He stood and listened for a few seconds before disappearing around the rock. She thought she heard the mock turtle's footsteps stop.

"Is that you? Oh come now, you're being awfully rude. Wait for me."

There was the shuffling of footsteps as Tort moved away from them.

"He won't be long," Vanessa said. "I gather Tort isn't especially fast."

"Do you know any mock turtle that is fast?" the hatter asked.

"No, I don't suppose I do," said Vanessa, "but if we don't trust what the mock turtle said, we need to find help elsewhere. I don't suppose you know where to find a dead pirate."

"In the sea, obviously," the hatter said. "That's where dead pirates normally end up." He put a hand over his right eye and began walking stiffly. "Arrr, walk the plank."

He took a few steps and vanished, falling into the sand. Only his hat remained on the surface. Before Vanessa had a chance to do anything, his head popped up again, and she resisted the urge to laugh. "Yes, I imagine you could find quite a few pirates there, but the one we're looking for is somewhat more mobile than those. He's a ghost."

"The seas also hold a number of ghost ships. Why I heard of one piloted by a Dutchman—"

Michael clenched his teeth and looked on the verge of screaming, but Vanessa gave him a stern look. He let out a breath and nodded once. Vanessa returned her attention to the hatter, who was pulling himself out of the ground.

"Yes, I met him once. That's not the kind of ghost we're talking about. This one moves around on land and has a hook for a hand."

Once again, the hatter plopped down on the ground and rubbed his chin. "I can't say that I have heard of such a being, but I know of someone who has."

"That's exactly what the mock turtle said," Michael said. "Why should we trust you more than we trust him?"

"Why, because I am telling the truth, of course."

"That's an easy thing to say."

"It is not. Do you have any idea of what must go on in the brain to control the tongue, the mouth, and the lungs? Why, it staggers the mind to know even a fraction of it. It's a wonder anyone can say anything at all."

"You know of such things?" Vanessa asked.

"Why, of course. I am a hatter. I am familiar with all things that happen in the head."

"Never mind about that," Vanessa said. "Who do you know that might help us?"

"The dormouse."

"A mouse?"

"Not just a mouse," the hatter said. "A *dormouse*. I assume this ghost of yours came into this world at some point."

"Well, yes."

"The dormouse knows many things. It's always the one who told us stories, every one of them true. More than that, it is familiar with doors and with those who pass through them."

"It knows everyone who comes into this world?"

"No, of course not. Only the ones who pass through the doors. It wouldn't know of you, for instance."

"The room we saw," Vanessa said. "At the bottom of the hole."

"It was blocked," Michael said.

"But something has to have blocked it," Vanessa said. "It makes sense that Hook would have gone through it if he had known to block the access."

Just then, Will stepped around the rock. He wore a wide smile.

"Tort?" Vanessa asked.

"I convinced it we were walking into the sea. It followed."

"How did you manage that?" Michael asked.

Will laughed. "Let's just say its mind is just as fast as its feet. It wasn't hard to trick."

"We have a lead," Vanessa told him. She turned to the hatter and asked, "What is your name?"

He cocked his head. "Why, I don't believe I have one. I have always simply been the hatter."

"'Hatter' it is, then," Vanessa said. "Lead us to your dormouse."

14

The moment they stepped off the beach, they found themselves in a forest. Vanessa turned around, but she didn't see so much as a grain of sand. She walked back a few steps, but the beach was gone. The others were looking at her, and she motioned for the hatter to continue. The forest grew dark, and cobwebs stretched across the path. They passed a number of forks in the road, but the hatter pranced down one and then another. Vanessa thought she heard him singing something about an unbirthday, but she doubted she heard every third word. Eventually, they came to a signpost. The signs—"Here," "There," "Away," "Far," and "Dormouse"— each had an arrow pointing in a different direction. The hatter examined them for what felt like forever before picking a path not indicated by a sign.

"Wait a second," Vanessa said.

The hatter paused for an instant before continuing. Vanessa sighed. "Shouldn't we follow the sign that says 'Dormouse'?"

The hatter laughed. "Why would we do that? The dormouse is an enemy of the Queen of Hearts. It wouldn't stay where a sign was pointing in its direction."

"Finally, something that makes sense," Michael said.

They continued down the dark path until it opened on a clearing. There was a table long enough to seat at least two dozen people. Each one had a place set, as if for tea. Three tea-pots steamed in the middle of the table, and the smell of the biscuits made Vanessa's mouth water. They hadn't had the time for a proper meal since this whole journey started, and the hunger was catching up with her. The hatter sat down and began cutting bread. He moved with the speed of one who had done this often. In a few seconds, each plate had a slice. He then began pouring tea until steam rose from each cup.

"Sit, please sit."

Vanessa sat next to him, but Michael groaned. "We don't really have time for tea."

"I doubt you have ever even met Time," the hatter said. "No wonder you don't have it."

"Time isn't a person," Will said, then looked at Vanessa and Michael. "Is it?"

"To the Greeks and a few others," Vanessa said. "It wouldn't really surprise me to learn it exists in Wonderland in one form or another."

"That's not the point," Michael said. Then he sighed and sat across from the hatter.

Vanessa took a sip of tea. It tasted of mint but was too hot. The hatter brought the teacup to his mouth and drank it all in one gulp. He took a nibble of cake.

Then he exclaimed, "Change time!"

He got up and moved to Vanessa. Though he was a small man, and Vanessa was well used to combat, the hatter effortlessly pushed her out of her chair. Somewhat amused, Will and Michael got up and moved over one chair. Vanessa picked herself up and moved to sit in what was apparently her new seat, but there was a small mouse curled up in the center, sleeping soundly. Its tail was wrapped around its body, and it was snoring softly.

"What's this?" Vanessa asked.

The hatter huffed. "The dormouse forgot to switch places."

"What?" The word drifted up from the animal, though as far as Vanessa could tell, it hadn't actually woken.

Michael got up and ran around the table. He stared at the dormouse for a second as if he didn't know what to do about it. Then he prodded it with one finger. It stirred but didn't wake up. He looked up to Vanessa, who shrugged. She poured a little tea on a plate and blew on it for a few seconds. Then, she overturned it on the mouse. It coughed a little as the tea soaked into its fur. It opened its sleepy eyes. It saw the hatter.

"Oh no. Did I forget to move seats again?" it asked.

"Yes, I'm rather cross with you."

"I'm sorry, dear friend." It spoke slowly, its eyes closing a little with every word. "Perhaps I can make it up to you in some way."

"Well, I suppose you could tell us a story. You tell such delightful stories."

"No, we don't want a story." Michael banged his fist on the table, rattling the dishes.

"Of course we do," Vanessa said. "Can you tell us the story of the pirate who became a ghost?"

The mouse slumped. "I don't think I know that story. You will have to ask the queen."

"The mock turtle tried to lead us to the queen. The hatter said she would kill us."

The mouse closed its eyes and laid its head down. "No, not that queen."

"What do you mean 'not that queen'?" Vanessa asked. "This is Wonderland. Isn't it ruled by the Queen of Hearts?"

The dormouse perked up. "There are many queens in this

world. The Queen of Hearts is certainly the most vile, but there are other queens in this land."

"Really?"

"Of course. In fact, there are four queens that are of Wonderland." The mouse's tail moved, forming each shape as he spoke them. "The Queens of Hearts, Spades, Diamonds, and Clubs. Each rule a different area."

"I suppose that makes sense," Vanessa said. "In fact, we probably should have guessed it would be the case."

The hatter buttered a slice of bread. He cut it into the shape of a heart and handed it to her. He gave her such a sad look that she felt obligated to take a bite. The butter tasted faintly of honey, which she enjoyed.

"We are currently in the lands of Hearts," the hatter said, "but the other queens are near as well."

"So it's one of the other three queens that we need to see?"

"Three? What makes you think there are *only* three others in Wonderland?" the mouse asked.

"Didn't you just say there were three?"

"I said there were many queens, not three."

"But you said there were three others in Wonderland."

"No, I didn't."

Vanessa scowled. "Yes, you did."

"No, I said there were three others *of* Wonderland. That's not the same thing at all. There are six queens in Wonderland at this time."

"Six? Who are the other two?"

"What do you mean other two? There are five besides the Queen of Hearts."

Vanessa clenched her teeth. Michael grinned but didn't say anything. Will seemed to be having the easiest time of it, so he stepped forward.

"Which queen should we see to hear the story of the pirate?"

"The White Queen, of course."

A chill ran through Vanessa as she thought of the chronicles of the Lady's adventures. "The White Queen? From the Looking Glass Land?"

"Yes, of course. Both she and the Red Queen have come here regarding the war the Queen of Hearts has waged to conquer all of Wonderland."

15

Vanessa stared at the dormouse until the creature fell asleep again. Then she looked around at her companions. The hatter had sat down and was drinking tea. She prodded the mouse with her finger until it roused a little and blinked sleepy eyes at her.

"The Queen of Hearts is at war with the other queens?"

"Yes, to claim all of Wonderland."

"Where can we find the White Queen?"

"Why, she is sitting at the end of this table."

"No, she's not," Vanessa said, though as soon as the words passed her lips, she realized she was wrong. At the far end of the table sat a woman dressed all in white. She wore a crown made of ivory. She had pale skin, though Vanessa couldn't decide if it was alabaster or maggot white. The White Queen met her eyes, and Vanessa resisted the urge to shiver. Her eyes were silver.

"Welcome to Wonderland, vassals of my peer."

"Where did you come from?" Vanessa asked. "You weren't there a second ago."

"Regrettably, I don't know. I know little of what came before. I only know what happened after."

"After what?" Vanessa asked.

"After now, of course."

"You can see the future?" Michael asked.

"Not see. Remember. I have not yet lived in what you think of as the past."

"How is that possible?" Will asked.

"I come from a land that is the mirror of yours," the White Queen said. "You remember the past. I remember the future."

"They say Merlin was the same way, you know," Vanessa said.

"But that's just a story." Will paused and laughed. "You'd think I'd eventually get tired of saying that."

Vanessa grinned. "It does take some time."

"I have heard of the one you call Merlin from others of your kind," the White Queen said. "He is my descendant, or so I am given to understand."

"You mean an ancestor?" Will asked.

The White Queen reached to one side just as the hatter approached her with a cup of tea. Only after she took it did she glance at the hatter. He bowed three times before backing away. The queen looked back at Will.

"Of course not. A descendant, but that is not relevant just now. You wished to know about James Hook."

"How did you know?" Michael asked. "We haven't told anyone his name."

"You have, just not yet. What you haven't told me is why I should help you."

"Well, if you help us, I'm sure we can help you."

"Help me to do what?" the White Queen said. "You are my enemy."

"What? No, we're not. You haven't even met us before today."

The queen got up. Her gaze was as cold as ice. The dormouse looked up and squeaked before scrambling off its chair. It scurried across Vanessa's boot before disappearing into the tall grass. The hatter seemed to retreat into his seat. He whimpered as the queen's voice came out like a whipcrack.

"So you say, but I have known you a long time, and your crimes are many." She wrinkled her nose as if she was smelling something foul. "Three knights. Who needs three knights? Seize them!"

The creatures that came out of the woods could only be called reverse centaurs. They had the body of men and were clad in silvery white armor. If they had been human, they would have stood at least ten feet tall. Their heads, however, were those of horses. Each held a sword with a blade at least eight feet long. Their thick arms carried their weapons effortlessly, and they moved toward Vanessa and her companions. She tried to attack one, but it batted away her strike with a flick of its wrist. Such was the creature's strength that even that seemingly light blow sent pain shooting up her arms and knocked her weapon out of her hands. It flew through the air, and the hatter squealed as he avoided the blade. Her foe grabbed her with one arm and restrained both her arms. She tried to kick him, but her foot hit only armor. The other horse-man seized both of Will's hands in one meaty fist even as it captured Michael with its free hand.

"You have come to throw Wonderland into chaos and to incite it to resist the will of the Queen of Hearts. I will not allow that to happen."

"What?" Vanessa said. "I thought you came to fight the Queen of Hearts."

"I never said that." A patch of tall grass rustled, and the dormouse crawled out. It stopped at Vanessa's feet and looked up. "I said she came here because of the war. Both she and the Red Queen are allies of the Queen of Hearts."

"Thank you, my servant." She turned to the hatter. "You

might not have been a willing participant, but you are a very effective dupe. You have my thanks as well. As for you three knights, I can only assume one of you used to be a pawn." Michael struggled against the grip, and the queen laughed. "It's you apparently. What a poor choice. Well, my three knights, you will be locked up until you leave the land of the living."

16

The horse-men practically dragged Vanessa and her squires through miles of woods. They marched heedless of the underbrush, and before long, Vanessa's arms were covered in cuts made by thorns. In spite of being mostly human, the creatures smelled like horses, and that odor overpowered everything else.

After marching for nearly two hours, they came to a castle made of red stone. Roses surrounded the grounds, though their smell didn't do much to cover up the horse scent. Soldiers in the form of man-size cards patrolled the grounds. They were armed with spears with ruby points that looked like upside-down hearts. They gave the horse-men angry looks but averted their gazes from the White Queen.

A pair of the cards opened the massive cherrywood doors, which swung inward on silent hinges. Vanessa wondered if they would be brought before the Queen of Hearts, but instead, the White Queen turned down a side hallway and led them into a dark stairway. The horse-men barely fit, and they weren't gentle as they dragged the three Knights down the stairs. The one holding Vanessa gripped her so tightly that she wasn't sure if he'd broken any of her fingers.

The dungeon was dark, barely illuminated by the light from the doorway above. The wet air smelled of mold. The White

Queen opened one of the cells and the horse-men tossed them in, not even bothering to take their weapons. By the time Vanessa untangled herself from her friends, the door had been slammed shut. The horse-men had vanished, though Vanessa had no idea how creatures so big could move so quickly.

The White Queen scowled at them. "Do you have anything to say for yourself?"

"Why have you imprisoned us?" Vanessa asked. "We haven't done anything."

"But you will."

"You can't imprison someone for something they are going to do," Will said.

"I have done exactly that," the White Queen said, "as is my right. Goodbye, knights of a departed queen."

She turned and left, her footsteps fading as she went up the stairs. As soon as the door closed, they were plunged into darkness. Vanessa felt around the cell, trying to find some way out, but she felt only smooth stone and cold iron bars. Michael pulled out his phoenix feather and cast a dim illumination.

"Do either of you have any ideas?" Vanessa asked.

"I thought you said that if we followed the madness of this place, it would lead us to where we wanted to go," Michael said.

"It still might," Vanessa said, though she wasn't quite so sure of herself.

"This doesn't exactly seem like what we want."

"Neither did it seem right when we were captured by gremlins in Neverland's underworld," Vanessa said. "That turned out fine. Let's just wait and see what happens."

"That's your plan? Wait and see?"

"Unless you have a better idea," Vanessa argued.

Michael huffed and sat down in a corner. After a while, a three of hearts brought them bowls of mush.

"What are you going to do with us?" Vanessa asked. The card just put the bowls down and turned to walk away. "Let me speak to someone in charge!"

The card disappeared down the hall without saying anything. Reluctantly, Vanessa took a small bite of her food. She didn't get to eat much at the tea party, and her stomach grumbled from hunger. The substance was utterly tasteless, though it had a texture similar to sand. Will took a bite and shuddered before putting the bowl aside.

"Is this always what it's like?" Will asked. "Going to another world, I mean." He ran a hand along a bar. "Are you always taken prisoner?"

Vanessa laughed. "It doesn't happen every time, but it's actually not that uncommon."

"I would think you'd be right at home," Michael said.

Vanessa grinned, but Will gave Michael a level look. "Are you? Now that we're neck-deep in the chase for Hook, are you at home?"

"You don't know what you're talking about."

"He has a point," Vanessa said. "What is it about the hunt for Hook that has you so obsessed that you're willing to throw everything away?"

"How can you ask that after what he did?"

"I know Hook needs to be dealt with, but does it have to be *you* that does it?"

"Yes!" Michael practically yelled. "I invited him into our world. Without that, he would have remained trapped in Neverland."

"So would we," Vanessa said. "We would have been there while your wraith absorbed all of Peter's power, destroying him and Neverland itself. What do you think would have happened then? To Wendy? To Jane?"

"I don't know!" Michael said. "Maybe we would have found another way out. We might have convinced Mora to show us how, for one thing."

"Not without another deal."

"But it wouldn't have been Hook."

"There's no way to tell which would have been worse," Vanessa said.

Michael gripped the bars and stared through them. She knew him well enough to know he wasn't going to talk anymore, so she dropped the discussion. She wasn't sure how long they were there before sleep finally claimed her.

"Sleeping," a low voice said, waking her up. "None of the other prisoners did that. Of course, they all died, so perhaps it's not such a bad idea."

Vanessa looked around but saw no sign of the speaker. She caught a faintly sweet smell. "Is that tobacco?"

Both Will and Michael sniffed at the air. Will nodded. "I think so. Something more expensive than anything I ever smoked."

"Why of course. I only smoke tobacco of the very highest quality."

Something crawled on her leg, and she yelped. A blue insect thumped to the ground. At first, she thought she had killed it, but it got up and dusted itself off before looking up at her. "That was not a kind thing to do."

All three of them stared at the caterpillar. It was wearing a monocle. The sight was so ridiculous she almost laughed. "We seem to be rude to everyone today."

"Rude?" The caterpillar puffed on what looked to be a tiny hookah. "Did I say anything about being rude? I said you were unkind. That is very different."

"We're sorry," Will said. "Can you lead us to another queen or something?"

"A queen?" It blew out a smoky ring. "What would a queen want with you?"

"We are vassals of a queen," Will said.

"Who are you?" The caterpillar looked at them with curious eyes.

A smoky *U* drifted up from the caterpillar and grew until it was the size of Vanessa's head. She coughed as she breathed it in.

"Well, I'm Will. This is Vanessa, and that's Michael."

"Why?"

Will blinked. "Why what?"

"Why who?"

"What?"

"You already said what. The proper response is why where. Or perhaps why when."

"I don't understand," said Will.

"You are rather slow, aren't you?"

"Who's being unkind now?"

"You are."

"If I was really being unkind, I would squash you," Will said.

"Will," Vanessa interjected, "let me. What are you doing here?"

"Me?"

"Yes. Are you a prisoner?"

"Why?"

"Well, why else would you be here?"

"Just because I am here, you think I am a prisoner? That is unkind of you."

"Well, we didn't do anything to warrant being taken prisoner, either," Vanessa said. "It's reasonable to assume the same thing happened to you."

"I say the contrary," said the caterpillar. "If you had done nothing, then you should just leave."

It blew a puff of smoke through the bars, which cut it into

sections. One of the smoky sections shifted and looked a little like Vanessa. The other two became Will and Michael. All three were running, though the images faded after a second.

"Leave?" Vanessa asked. "How exactly do you propose we do that?"

"Simply walk through the bars."

Vanessa scoffed. "Well, if we were four inches tall, that might help us."

The caterpillar extended itself to full length. "Four? I am *not* four inches tall. I am three, and it is a very good height indeed."

Vanessa rolled her eyes. "Four, three. It doesn't really make a difference. We're still too big to fit through the bars."

"There is a very great difference between three and four inches." As it said each of the numbers, it blew out smoke in their shapes. The *3* and *4* hovered in the air for a second before dissipating.

"That doesn't change the fact that we can't fit through the bars."

"Because you are slow."

Vanessa groaned. "Forgive me for being slow."

"I do not forgive you."

"Then can you help us, being such a wise being?"

"I can."

She waited, but it didn't say anything. She heard someone chuckle, but she wasn't sure if it was Will or Michael. She let out a deep breath. "Will you?"

"Why?"

"Because I'll stop bothering you if you do?"

"That is a very good reason." It crawled across the floor until it reached the wall. Water dripped from the ceiling onto a pair of mushrooms. "One will make you grow taller. The other will make you grow smaller."

"The mushrooms?" Vanessa asked.

"Of course," the caterpillar said before it squeezed in the hole between the bricks.

"Which is which?" she asked, but no answer came. She looked down at the mushrooms, trying to distinguish one from the other, but they seemed identical. She brushed her finger on the cap. It felt smooth with small bumps all over. She brought her fingers to her nose and sniffed, but there was no distinctive smell. "Well, I guess we eat one."

Michael glared at her. "You can't be serious. You want to eat mushrooms you found on the floor of a prison just because a strange caterpillar told you to?"

"This is Wonderland," Vanessa said. "That's how things work here."

"That can't be your excuse for everything."

Vanessa plucked both mushrooms from the ground. They resisted a little but eventually came free. She examined them closely, but there was no indication they were anything other than fungi. She nibbled at one and scowled at the bitter taste. The next thing she knew, she was crying out as her head crashed against the stone ceiling. Will and Michael grunted as her bulk pressed them against the walls.

"That was the wrong mushroom," Will said.

"I can see that." Because she was so big, it was hard to bring the correct one to her mouth, and she ended up knocking both her companions off their feet. She took as small a bite as she could, and suddenly, she was as tall as Michael's waist. Michael and Will were picking themselves off the ground. Michael gaped, and she couldn't help but smirk.

"I told you it was the right decision."

"You're lucky it didn't change you into a pig."

"You're just never going to let that go, are you? I think I can

squeeze through the bars now." Putting the growing mushroom in her pocket, she held out the shrinking one to the others. Will carefully reached forward and took it. He looked at
Michael for a second before taking a nibble. His form melted
away until he was no bigger than she was. Michael took the
mushroom from Will. He shook his head and muttered something under his breath. He took a bite and shrank until he was
even smaller than Will and Vanessa. All three of them squeezed
through the bars. Once through, each of them took a small bite
of the growing mushroom until they returned to normal size.
They climbed up the stairs, but the cherrywood door at the top
was locked. Will pulled at it, but it seemed sturdy. He examined the lock.

"Does anyone have anything to pick this with?"

Michael raised an eyebrow. "Since when do you pick locks?"

Will shrugged. "I thought it might be a useful skill once I
joined the Knights."

They all looked for something but came up empty. Vanessa
bent down. She could just see light coming from under the door.

"Maybe we can get small enough to squeeze through the
cracks or something," Vanessa said.

"I'm not sure that's a good idea," Michael said. "Did you see
how many guards are out there? We'd be caught for sure."

"We avoided the mock turtle," Vanessa said. "Don't you
think you can do the same to a bunch of cards?"

"Don't be stupid," Michael said. "We got lucky with the mock
turtle. We're in a magical land. We have no idea what abilities
these cards have."

"Then what do you suggest we do?"

"Maybe leave from some direction other than the front door?"

"Do you have any other ideas?"

"We could leave the same way that the caterpillar did."

Vanessa narrowed her eyes. "After all the complaining you've done, you now want to follow a strange caterpillar into a hole."

Michael let out a long breath. Then, his eyes wandered down to a puddle at the base of the stairs, and he smiled and walked down to it. Vanessa followed him and saw her own reflection staring back at her. Her eyes widened as she realized what Michael was thinking. He met her gaze

"Is it possible?"

"I don't know. I couldn't get into Wonderland, but that was because it had been blocked. If the queens are here, though, there may not be anyone to block *that* way. I'm not sure we'd be able to get back in, though."

"The Lady did say the two places were more closely aligned," Michael said. "That should make crossing over easier."

Will looked from one to another. "What are you two talking about?"

"He wants to leave Wonderland."

"After all the trouble we had getting here, Michael, you just want to go home?"

"Not home," said Michael. He looked back at the puddle. "We're going through the looking glass."

anessa stared at that puddle for a quarter hour. Her heart raced every time it rippled, but it was always either Will or Michael taking a step or a drop falling from the ceiling. She couldn't even sense the barrier between worlds, probably because the two worlds were so closely aligned that the barrier was almost nonexistent—but if that were true, she should be able to pass through the puddle with almost no effort. When she tried that, though, she just splashed in the water with no effect other than her feet getting soaked.

"Maybe we should just try the caterpillar's hole," she said in frustration.

"We have to be missing something," Michael said.

"Obviously," Vanessa said. "I have no idea what that is, though."

Will stared into the puddle. "I remember the story of Alice. When she ate the mushrooms, wasn't she afraid she'd get so small she would disappear?"

"Yes, I believe you're right." Vanessa looked up and cocked her head. "What are you thinking, Will?"

"Well, maybe that's what we have to do."

Vanessa pursed her lips. It sounded like madness, but that was the nature of this land. "How did you come by that conclusion?"

"The White Queen said she could remember the future because everything was reversed in her world. Maybe if we disappear from this world, we'll reappear in that one."

"That's ridiculous," Michael said. "You can't get so small you'd disappear, and even if you did, you wouldn't just reappear in some other world."

Vanessa laughed. "I never thought I'd hear *Michael* telling *Will* that something is too ridiculous to be true." She stared deeply into the water. Her reflection winked, gave her a faint smile, and nodded slightly. She looked to the other two but they didn't seem to have seen it. She ran her fingers over the bumpy cap of the mushroom. "I think Will might have a point." Michael gaped. "Even if you're right, Michael, we're not really risking anything. At worst, we'll end up getting tiny and then have to take some of the other mushroom to restore ourselves."

Michael looked at the growing mushroom, which had several bites taken out of it. "We might not have enough to get out if we do that."

"It's this or the caterpillar hole," Vanessa said.

Before he could respond, she took a large portion of the shrinking mushroom and swallowed it. This time, the change wasn't instant. She felt herself shrinking. Her reflection grew. At first, she thought it was because her eyes were getting closer to the ground but soon, she was small enough that the puddle looked like a sea. Her reflection was still there, looking at her like some titan. She was still shrinking, though. Her head throbbed as thoughts that were too big for her body ran through her mind. She thought her head would split open. She knew that didn't make sense, but that didn't stop the pain. All at once, a cold gray fog rose all around her, stopping her from seeing more than a few feet in front of her. The air was colder, and the ground beneath her feet had changed. It was no longer stone, though even if she bent down, she couldn't see it. Just like Will had guessed, she had disappeared only to reappear in some other world, but it certainly hadn't been the one they'd intended.

"I guess it worked." Will's voice sounded far away.

"No, no it didn't!" Vanessa cried out.

"What if it's not really her reflection?" Michael spoke as if he hadn't heard her.

"Look at her." Will pointed at the puddle. "Who else could it be?"

"Will, there are a number of creatures that can take the form of another. Added to that, we're in a land where the normal rules don't apply. Even *our* rules don't mean a whole lot here."

"I still think we should do it."

"What if she's dead?" Michael said, worried.

"I'm pretty sure she's not."

"What are you basing this on?"

"On the fact that this is a story," Will said. "Isn't that what you told me in Neverland?"

"No," Vanessa cried out. "Don't take the mushroom."

Her voice sounded hollow, and the fog swirled around her. There was a long stretch of silence before Will spoke.

"I'll go first."

"No!" Vanessa yelled once more, hoping they would finally hear her.

A few seconds later, Michael appeared beside her. Will arrived shortly after. They looked at her and at the fog all around them.

"This doesn't look like the other side of the mirror," Michael said.

"No, it doesn't. I have no idea where we are." She thought for a second. "We have to be somewhere close to Wonderland, though, as far as other worlds go. The amount of magic it took to get here was relatively tiny."

"I don't know," Will said. "The mushroom seemed pretty powerful."

She waved that off. "From what the Lady has told me, transmutation of the body is one of the more complicated branches of magic, but it doesn't require a great amount of power. Plus, if native magic like the mushroom got us here, then it's not likely that it would take us far." She thought for a second. "I could hear you when you were talking about eating the mushroom. I take it you couldn't hear me?"

"No," Will said. "Your reflection was motioning for us to go after you."

"I was trying to stop you."

"So your reflection was doing the opposite," Michael said. "It makes sense, in a way, but it doesn't really help us. It does also leave us with a question. Where are we?"

Vanessa thought for a second. "I think we got halfway through the looking glass."

"What?" Michael asked.

"Will was right. The first time the Lady was here, she was afraid she would shrink so much she would disappear. That's what we tried to do, only we thought we could reappear on the other side of the mirror. We must have only made it halfway, though."

"We disappeared but didn't reappear?" Will looked confused. "Can someone tell us where we are . . . Vanessa?!"

Vanessa looked around. The fog had an odd uniformity to it, and as she studied it, she realized it was closer to blue than gray. It had a paleness to it that she knew she had seen before. A chill ran through her body, and all at once she remembered. When the skies of London had been filled with the ghosts Hook had awakened, the spirits had been that same color.

"I think we're in the underworld."

Will's eyes widened. "Wonderland has an underworld?"

"Everywhere has an underworld," Vanessa said, repeating what she had heard Peter Pan say once. "It's where the spirits go. The mock turtle told us that there have been a lot of spirits coming into Wonderland lately. The underworld must be closer to Wonderland than the Looking Glass Land."

"It's what the White Queen said, too," Michael said. "'You will be locked up until you leave the land of the living.'"

"So, we're dead?" Will asked.

"I don't think so," Vanessa said. "Things aren't that simple in Wonderland, especially not where magic is concerned. I'm pretty sure we should be able to find our way back."

"How?"

"I don't suppose either one of you thought to grab the growing mushroom before you disappeared."

Both of them shook their heads, though Will patted his pockets. "We should at least get away from here. I mean it's not like we haven't been stuck in the underworld before."

"We knew how to get out then," Michael said.

"No, we didn't," Will said. "I mean we knew that if we could get through the witch or find our way to the top of the mountain, or figure out how to breathe water, we would be able to get out, but none of those options were open to us." He shrugged. "If we had a magic mushroom, we could get out of here. It doesn't really help us, though." He pointed. "Let's go that way."

Vanessa raised her eyebrow. "Why that way?"

Will motioned around them. "It's the same in any direction. We may as well just pick one."

Vanessa stared at him for several seconds before shaking her head and chuckling. "You learned your lessons quickly. I'm sure any full Knight would have come to that decision. Eventually. Let's go."

18

Vanessa wasn't sure how long they walked through the pale blue mist. Time didn't seem to have a meaning in this strange underworld. In a way, it reminded her of sailing between worlds. She had done that on two occasions, going to and coming from Neverland. She didn't think this was the world of the dead, exactly. It was an in-between place, which made her feel a lot more confident that they could get back. Of course, if this place really was halfway between life and death, then it wasn't uninhabited.

A tremendous shadow passed in front of them, moving so fast the fog swirled in its wake. It made a sound like crashing waves. Vanessa couldn't make out its shape, but she knew it was flying rather than walking. She felt herself being pulled along after it. Michael had drawn his sword, and the weapon seemed almost more real than Michael himself was. After a few seconds, the roaring sound faded. The trio looked at each other.

"Does anyone have any idea what that is?"

"Some kind of ghost," Vanessa said.

"The ghost of what?" Michael asked. "A sea serpent?"

"I don't think there were ever any sea serpents in Wonderland. Plus, I don't think size there means the same thing here. In fact, size in Wonderland doesn't mean the same thing as it does anywhere else, not when eating mushrooms can make you grow or shrink."

"That doesn't answer the question," Michael said. "What was that?"

"A playing card, for all I know. Let's go after it."

"Go after it? Are you insane?"

"That's what I'm going for."

"I think you're taking this madness thing too far," Michael complained.

"Is she now?" a familiar voice said.

It would have turned Vanessa's blood to ice, except she wasn't sure she had blood in this ghostly place. She turned around. The man standing there was a head taller than any of them. Black hair hung to just past his shoulders. A greatcoat, vivid red in sharp contrast to the muted gray all around them, reached to his knees. On his right hand, a steel hook gleamed, though there was no light to reflect off it.

Michael raised his sword and centered his weight. He clenched his teeth, and his face twisted with rage. The fog retreated from him with such force that it dragged Vanessa and Will along with it, though whether in response to Michael's anger or for some other reason, she had no idea.

"Hook."

She felt as much as heard the name as the air trembled against her skin. Even Michael's sword pulsed with anger. Hook, however, only laughed.

"I'm surprised to see you, Michael. Normally, only the dead find their way here, and even then, it's mainly Wonderland's dead. How did you come to this place?"

Michael didn't answer. He just rushed forward, moving faster than Vanessa had ever seen any human swordsman move. His blade flashed, and though she didn't know why she thought it, Vanessa knew that his attack could have shattered stone. Hook gave him a half smile, and batted the weapon aside with his good hand, in the way a grown man might push away a willow switch wielded by a child.

"You come into this place, where I am strongest, and think you can defeat me so easily?"

Michael was no amateur fighter, and he knew better than to bandy words. He struck again and again. He was a skilled swordsman and had gotten even better since rejoining the Knights. Hook, however, treated him like he was a toy soldier, not even bothering to draw his own weapon or use his hook. He just brushed Michael's attacks away, either hitting the side of the blade or Michael's arm. Without needing to talk about it, both Will and Vanessa moved around the dead pirate. As one, they attacked as well.

No matter how powerful Hook was here, there were limits. Against three skilled opponents working together, even the best swordsman, living or dead, would have trouble. Hook, apparently, disregarded the laws of reality just as casually as he had those made by men. He moved with impossible speed, so fast that Vanessa almost thought he was in three places at once. He grabbed her sword and pulled it out of her hand even as he struck Will's wrist, causing his own weapon to fall to the ground. Michael's attack missed him by at least a foot, though there was no way that should have been possible.

"Michael, we have to retreat!" Vanessa said.

"No! Don't you understand? He can be destroyed here. He's even more vulnerable to attacks here than with wisp dust."

"We have to be able to hit him for that to be true," Vanessa said, picking up her sword. Frost had crusted on the blade, but she shook it off and moved in to attack again.

"Listen to the girl, Michael. You can't beat me here."

Again and again, Michael struck. Finally, Hook sighed. "I came to see who had intruded into this realm. I could destroy you with no particular effort, but I think leaving you trapped here would be a more fitting punishment. Goodbye, Michael Darling."

He rose into the air. The fog didn't obscure him at all. Michael followed, though Vanessa had no idea how he managed to fly here. Hook, however, was faster by far. He had gone so high that he appeared to be nothing more than a dot. A ship, three times as big as the *Jolly Roger*, was sailing through the sky above them. Hook landed on its deck and the ship quickly sped out of sight. Michael tried to follow it, but he had about as much success as one might expect a swimming man to have against a ship at full sail.

Cursing, Michael floated down to their level and glared in the direction of the ship. "That was a mistake."

"I know," Vanessa said. "You went after him, as powerful as he is here? And you call *me* insane?"

"That's not what I meant," Michael said. "It was a mistake to leave us here. Dead or not, I'm going to destroy him."

"We're not dead," said Will.

"What?" Michael said.

"We're not dead," he repeated, "at least according to Hook."

"He also said we're trapped," Vanessa said.

Michael scoffed. "And you believed him?"

"I believe he knows more about this place than we do," Vanessa said.

"About the world of the dead, maybe. We might have an advantage when it comes to Wonderland itself, though," Will said. "Think, Vanessa. How could we get out of here?"

"I have no idea." Then something occurred to Vanessa. "Michael, how come you could fly?"

Michael blinked. "I don't know. My pixie dust ran out months ago. When Hook took off, I just . . . went after him."

"Which suggests we can do the same things ghosts can do."

"I think it's more likely that the nature of this world is more mutable than ours."

"It amounts to the same thing," Vanessa noted. "My point is that ghosts can manifest in the physical world."

"As intangible shades," Michael emphasized. "I don't think it will work—"

"Why not?" Vanessa said, annoyed.

"Think of how much more powerful Hook is here than he is as a ghost in the physical world. If he had kept his full strength last time we faced him, neither you nor I would have survived. His energy has to go somewhere when he manifests into our world."

Vanessa pursed her lips. "You think he has to use most of his power when he comes to London."

"Yes . . . it makes sense. When you get right down to it, ghosts are a combination of both energy and various elements. If it takes more energy than we have to manifest, there might be nothing left of us if we tried it."

There was a roar in the distance, causing the fog to swirl and back away. Michael stared in its direction. His hand went to his hilt, though Vanessa doubted he realized it. She also looked toward the roar, and a plan began to take form.

"I think our best bet is to follow that."

"How could that possibly help us?"

"Maybe it could be an ally against Hook."

"Or maybe it will eat us," Will pointed out.

"I don't think Wonderland would have put us so near to the sound if it weren't relevant."

"That's thin logic," Michael said with a scowl.

"I know that it fits with the way this place works. I don't like it, but it's probably the best idea we're going to come up with."

The creature roared again. Vanessa almost thought she could understand what it was saying. She nodded once and motioned for the others to follow her. Michael frowned but nodded in agreement, and they went looking for the thing that the fog itself feared.

19

The creature was surprisingly easy to follow. Vanessa realized that if she concentrated, she could feel its effect on the land. It had a sort of weight to it that bent everything around it. Even the ground sloped toward it. Vanessa had an uncomfortable feeling due to its power. They headed in its direction, all of them keeping their swords drawn. Though there were no structures, they moved as they would when sneaking through a city, one moving forward while the others waited for them to signal it was clear. They never detected anything, though, other than an ever-growing sense of ominousness. Slowly, a shadow appeared in the distance, seeming more like a hill or a small mountain than anything living. They approached it as quietly as they could, and as they neared, it turned to them. Eyes like those of a cat stared at them from the center of a shapeless mass of shadows, and the creature roared. The sound hit them like a wall and threw them off their feet. Anger and power and desire for destruction filled its cry. Then the beast was gone. Even the sense of it had vanished.

Michael looked to Vanessa. "What do we do now?"

"We follow it."

"How?"

Vanessa pointed to where the creature had been. There was a barely perceptible motion in the fog as it swirled a hole in the air. Vanessa approached the disturbance. It formed a flat disc of solid gray and was as tall as her. She extended her hand and felt a vibration in the air. There was more to it, though.

"It's a gateway to another world."

"Isn't that awfully convenient?" Michael said. "Does it go to Wonderland?"

"Yes."

"You answered that quickly."

"I almost got us to Wonderland before, remember?" Vanessa said. "It has a certain feel to it that I recognize. Trust me, this will take us where we need to go."

"You've been wrong before," Michael said, indicating the fog that swirled around his hands.

Vanessa narrowed her eyes. "Michael, we're trapped in another world. We have a way out. Are you really going to turn away from it just because it's too easy?"

"There's something else to consider," Will interjected.

"What's that?"

"It's shrinking."

Vanessa looked back at the portal and realized he was right. It was, at most, three-quarters of the size it had been a few seconds ago, and she could see it slowly shrinking. It wouldn't be long before it got too small for them to get through it.

"Michael, we have to go now."

"You realize this is a trap, right?"

"Almost definitely, but we can't be sure we'll find another way out. Be ready for anything."

Michael nodded and dove in, sword first. Will jumped in after him and Vanessa followed right after.

She landed face-first on soft red carpet. The smell of fresh roses filled the air. There was murmuring all around her. She looked up to see a group of playing cards staring down at her.

They had the same heart spears that the ones at the gates had possessed, but these were all of higher values. She didn't see anything lower than an eight. Every one of them was a heart, though they apparently came from multiple decks. Each of her companions was held by a pair of tens. Two more of the cards held their weapons to Vanessa. One of them pressed the cold point into her shoulder, drawing blood.

The Queen of Hearts stared down from her ruby throne. There was only one of her, and as with all of the face cards, she had two faces: one at the top of the card and the other was her upside-down reflection. Her top expression was twisted with anger.

But the two people at her side were smiling. One was the White Queen. The other wore a dress the color of blood. It shimmered as she moved. Her scarlet hair was like fire, and her lips could have been coated in powdered ruby. Even her eyes gleamed with crimson fire. This could only be the Red Queen, counterpart to the White and one of the monarchs of the Looking Glass Land.

"The ghost was right," the Red Queen said. "They certainly don't look like a threat, but I don't see how we could use them."

"People are not so easy to use," a melodic voice said from the air. "Particularly humans. Particularly those."

A wide grin appeared in the air between Vanessa and the Red Queen. She couldn't tell which direction the smile was coming from at first, but soon the rest of the creature appeared. It was a cat, far bigger than any house pet Vanessa had ever seen. The thing had to weigh at least forty pounds, and it came up to Vanessa's chest. Its gray fur was striped with blue, and it stared at her in a way that made the hairs on the back of her neck stand on end.

Instantly, half of the tens turned their weapons on the

newcomer. It didn't seem to care, though. It turned and strode toward the queens, exactly as confident as every other cat Vanessa had ever seen. One of the cards thrust its spear forward, but the Cheshire Cat casually jumped over it and kept walking, as if its attacker wasn't worthy of notice.

"You were not summoned," the Queen of Hearts said.

The Cat turned its nose up at her. "It is not for you to summon or banish me, little card. The queens of the twin worlds have no authority over where I go."

The Queen of Hearts' top head flared in rage, but the Red Queen stood up and stepped forward, her eyes never moving from the Cat.

"What do you want?" she asked.

The White Queen cried out and jumped off her throne. She threw herself to the ground as the wall right behind where she had been sitting exploded inward, showering everyone in rock dust. Vanessa started to cough. The other two queens, who had been thrown to the ground, cried out and tried to get to their feet, but a pair of aces of spades jumped through the hole and seized both the Queen of Hearts and the Red Queen. The two monarchs screamed. Instantly, the eights and nines of hearts charged the newcomers. The aces released their captives and met the attacks with swords of black iron. Their weapons cut through the spear shafts like they were made of paper.

The jack of spades came through the hole. He quickly scanned the room and focused on the White Queen, who had retreated to the opposite side. He motioned in her direction, and half a dozen spades poured into the room. They moved toward the White Queen. Before the attackers got near, the two ivory horse-men burst into the room, bringing the smell of horse with them. A five of spades engaged one while a pair of threes fought the other. The White Queen moved toward the door but stopped after a few steps. She quickly ran back toward the center of the room as three tens and two sevens burst in through the door she had been heading toward.

"Full house," she said, "but all of the same suit. That's cheating."

The threes fighting the horse-man spread out and struck from two sides at once, closing in on their opponent. The horse-man managed to block one, but the other stabbed his thigh, causing him to stumble. That was all the cards needed, and they fell upon their enemy with a brutal savagery. The pair of threes then went to join their companion, taking down the second horse-man in short order. The remaining hearts had formed a protective circle around their queen as well as the Red Queen. The White Queen, however, was still free, and the spades surrounded her.

The jack moved to Vanessa and her companions. He examined them for a few seconds before his eyes went wide. He motioned to the tens at his side.

"Take them, too. Watch them closely. If they try to escape, kill them."

"What?" Vanessa asked.

"That wasn't the mission," one of the tens said.

"They are agents of a Looking Glass queen," the jack said, motioning to the others. "Not one of these. Another one."

"There are only two Looking Glass queens," the ten said.

"That was at the beginning, but someone else has taken a crown."

"Who?"

"That's what we're going to find out. I don't intend to be caught from behind by a third queen."

"An interesting development," the Cat said, heedless of the battle going on around it. "I wonder what will happen next."

The White Queen gave him a level look. "You will not be happy with the results, Cheshire Cat."

For a second, the Cat seemed rattled. Then it scoffed. "I will take my chances." It turned to Vanessa. "You should go with them willingly. You are going with them one way or another. It won't be pleasant for you if you resist. I don't think you would like to lose one of your friends as punishment."

"The Cat's right," the jack said.

Vanessa nodded once. The tens loosened their grip on her shoulders, and the other cards released her companions. All of them left the throne room, carrying the White Queen as their prisoner.

20

W hat do you want with us?" Vanessa asked one of the tens who prodded her with a sword.

"You were caught in the company of the Triumvirate," the jack said.

"Who?"

"The Queen of Hearts." The Cheshire Cat appeared in front of them. "The Red Queen and the White Queen."

They stepped through the front gate, which had been torn off the wall. The scent of roses hung heavy in the courtyard air. Vanessa was glad cards didn't bleed. Otherwise, she was sure the smell of their blood would have overpowered everything else. Hearts lay scattered everywhere.

"Have you finally chosen a side?" the jack asked the Cat.

"I have always been on my side," the Cheshire Cat assured him. "Unless I'm on the other."

"Just like Peter," Michael muttered.

"You know someone like me?" the Cat said as it casually walked over a facedown card. "Somehow I doubt that."

Michael rolled his eyes. "Yeah, you all think you're unique."

"Maybe I am," the Cat said, vanishing from one side of Vanessa and appearing on another. "Maybe I'm not, but you should consider what side you are going to be on."

"What sides are there?" Vanessa asked.

"The Triumvirate," the jack said, "or the House of Cards."

"One of those sounds a lot more stable than the other," Michael said.

"Not if it's built properly," the jack said as he poked the White Queen, forcing her out of the main gates and onto the road beyond. "Without her, the Triumvirate is only two, and with just two logs, it will fall."

"Without her, they are blind," the Cat said. "She is the one who could see into the future. She is the one who guided their effort."

The jack let out a breath of relief. "Then we've won."

They turned off the road and headed into the woods. Above them, birds sang. A cardinal hopped from branch to branch. It stared at Vanessa for a minute before flying away. The cards didn't slow. Vanessa tripped over a root, and when she stumbled, one of the cards behind her jabbed her with a sword. It stung, and she felt a wetness that might have been blood.

"Leave her alone," Will said.

"You were not given permission to speak."

"Leave it alone," Michael said. "We've both been through worse."

The Cat continued to speak as if nothing had happened. "The Triumvirate commands an army greater than any that has ever walked the ground of Wonderland." The Cat vanished again only to appear as nothing more than a grin. "You have won nothing. Now, however, you have a chance. If you can turn her to your side, you have a good one. If not . . ."

The grin vanished, and Vanessa felt a weight on her shoulder, where the Cat had reappeared. There shouldn't have been room, and even if there were, something that big should have been at least forty pounds, but it was almost weightless. She tried to shake it off, but the Cat seemed not to notice. She sneezed at its fur. The White Queen, however, was livid.

"Me? Join you? You don't really think it'll be that easy, do you?"

"Are you certain?" the Cat asked. It looked from Michael to Will to Vanessa. "They haven't even chosen a side. How do you know that it won't be the same one you have chosen?"

"Enough of this," the jack said. "Cat, if you are going to help us, then we welcome your aid. No one in all of Wonderland can move unseen like you can. If you intend to just annoy us, however, I would ask you to leave us alone."

The Cat laughed. "Well, that's rather foolish. If I had truly come to annoy you, what makes you think I would leave you alone just because you asked, little card?"

"Is there nothing you respect?"

The Cat looked at each of them and smirked, which looked decidedly odd. After a second, the grin returned. "Nothing that is here." He eyed the White Queen. "She comes closer than the rest."

"If you respect me, then aid me."

The Cat laughed. "I said you were closer than the rest, my dear queen. That is like saying a minnow who swims in the shallows is closer to the desert than a whale who dives into the deep ocean. They are both impossibly far."

The jack led them to a tree large enough to house a small building. The leaves were hearts, and like the castle grounds, they smelled of roses. The jack tapped it once near the roots and once more at eye level. Part of the trunk melted away into what looked like a doorway. On the other side was a verdant field with black-leaved bushes. A castle with high battlements and surrounded by a wide moat dominated the landscape. At least a thousand card soldiers, all of them spades, stood between them and it. Each held a black steel weapon. The jack motioned to the rest of their group, and the cards led them through the hole. Instantly, the temperature was at least ten degrees lower. Humidity hung thick in the air, so much so that Vanessa half expected the cards to wither. She looked over her shoulder, but the doorway they had come through was nowhere to be seen. It was merely a large rock.

"How do you suppose they managed that?" Michael asked.

"If I had to guess, I'd say it had something to do with crossing between worlds, but I didn't feel anything."

"The ways already exist," the Cheshire Cat said. "You can't detect their creation, because that happened long ago. You need only know where they are."

"And do you know the ways, Cat?"

The feminine voice was powerful and reminded Vanessa a little of the Lady. The Queen of Spades approached at the head of at least a dozen tens. She wielded a sword that shimmered in the afternoon light, looking more like obsidian than the black steel of the other spades. The cards around Vanessa and the others bowed. Vanessa tried to move, but a swift motion took her legs out from under her and she fell to the ground, biting her lip and tasting blood.

"Vanessa!" Will yelped.

Vanessa shook off the pain, slowly realizing what had happened.

"That's enough," the queen said. "Let them stand."

One of the cards moved its spear, which it had apparently used to trip them. Vanessa got up. The cards around her were flat on the ground, facedown, bowing before their queen. They looked eerily similar to the dead hearts in the Queen of Hearts' courtyard. The Queen of Spades, however, was an entirely different matter. She was almost as imposing as the entire Court of Camelot, and Vanessa had no doubt the queen could kill her without breaking a sweat.

"Interesting. You are agents of a Looking Glass queen, unless I miss my guess. Three knights. Perhaps one of them actually knows what she's doing."

"How do you know that?" Vanessa asked.

"It's obvious to anyone who has eyes to see," the queen's bottom head said. "The question remains. What are you doing here? Is there a third queen coming into Wonderland to conquer us?"

"No," Vanessa said. "We had no idea there even was a war until we got here. Our queen sent us here to pursue an enemy, the ghost of a pirate."

The Queen of Spades' expression hardened and the grass wilted under her feet. "James Hook."

Michael stepped forward. "You know of him?"

"Of course I know of him. He is the one responsible for all of this. He incited the Looking Glass queens to invade Wonderland and ally with the Queen of Hearts. If he is the one you are searching for, then we will help you."

"'We'?" Vanessa asked.

"The Queens of Clubs and Diamonds are at my castle. We are preparing a counterattack against the Queen of Hearts."

"They will be less able to resist us without her," the jack said as he pushed the White Queen forward. "Perhaps we can get something useful out of her."

21

What were you doing in the Court of the Queen of Hearts?" the Queen of Spades asked as they passed through the obsidian gates of the castle. As soon as they did, their steps echoed through the corridors.

"We ended up there by accident, Your Majesty."

The Queen of Spades scoffed. "Don't throw that title around at me. Call me Spade, or Lady Spade if you must use an appellation. How could you end up in one of the most heavily guarded locations in all of Wonderland by accident?"

"Well, we were having a tea party when she showed up and captured us." Vanessa pointed at the White Queen. "She threw us in the dungeon. Then a caterpillar showed us a magic mushroom that shrank us so much that we disappeared from the world of the living and ended up in some sort of ghostly realm." Vanessa shook her head. "I honestly can't believe I just said that. Anyway, we managed to find a hole back to this world. We didn't know where it went, but we didn't have a lot of time. As it turns out, it dropped us into the throne room just before your cards attacked."

The jack laughed. "If you're going to lie about it, then you should at least try for some originality."

Michael shook his head. "I'm not sure I could come up with something more original if I was lying."

"They do speak the truth," the Cat's voice said from the space just in front of Vanessa. The cards raised their weapons. The one behind Vanessa shoved her aside to have room to draw, though the Cat never appeared.

"We should trust someone who never even chose a side?" the jack asked.

"I am not so capricious as others. When I choose a side, you can be assured that I will stick to it."

"And I won't?"

The Cat laughed, and it echoed through the corridor so loudly that Vanessa's ears began hurting. She thought she saw it appear at the end of the hall, but it vanished before she could be sure. Its voice remained, however. The laughter went on for several minutes, not fading until they reached a large set of double doors at the end of the hall. A pair of sevens pushed open the doors, and they stepped into a large chamber. It was made of obsidian, though the uniform blackness made it difficult for Vanessa to tell how big it was. Light shone through windows near the ceiling and glittered across the polished ground.

Three thrones sat at the end of the room. The Queens of Clubs and Diamonds sat on two of them, and the Queen of Spades walked up to the middle one and sat down. The Cat appeared right in front of them and grinned at the jack.

"My dear paper-brained fool, you never had a choice about which side to choose. You go where your queen commands and do as she tells you."

The jack scowled and was about to respond when the Queen of Spades spoke in a whipcrack of a voice.

"Enough, jack. The Cat will do whatever it pleases. The wise just ignore it."

She proceeded to tell the other queens what Vanessa had told her. The Cat walked through the room, periodically stopping in front of a different person. Each one shuddered before the Cat's gaze. When it appeared before Vanessa, she felt her blood run cold.

Finally, the Queen of Diamonds spoke. "Can you do it again?"

Vanessa blinked. "Do what?"

"Could you go into the ghostly realm and reach the throne room?"

Vanessa stared at the card. "I don't have the slightest idea. Last time, we had magic mushrooms, but we weren't even trying to go there. We were fortunate enough to find a portal out. I doubt we can count on a situation like that again."

"Can you summon fairies here?" Michael asked.

"Fairies?" asked Vanessa.

"I was just thinking that if we could somehow get Rosebud here, her dust could probably get us into the ghostly realm. Maybe we couldn't take an army there like I assume the Queen of Diamonds wants, but it would be something."

"That's not a bad idea," said Vanessa. She turned to the queens. "What about it? Do any of you know of a way to summon the ghost of a fairy?"

"Mmm," said the Cat. "That sounds quite delicious."

"You could eat a ghost?"

The Cat's head appeared before them, wearing its ever-present grin. It floated across the ground, leaving footprints in the dust before its body appeared. "Of course. Where do you think I go when I am not here? Affecting a ghost takes no great effort."

"You can go into the ghostly realm?" the Queen of Clubs asked.

"Well, of course."

"Can you take others?" the Queen of Spades asked.

"Perhaps I could. Perhaps I could not. I have no desire to try, however."

"Why not?" the Queen of Clubs asked.

"That would place me firmly on your side, and I am not willing to make that commitment just yet."

"What if you don't take us?" Michael asked. "What if you just taught us how to get there?"

"You want me to teach you to go into the ghostly realm?" the Cheshire Cat asked. "Why, that is simplicity in itself." Its head faded, leaving only a grin that spoke one more sentence before disappearing. "You need only remove your head." Its head popped into existence, though its body vanished. "Or you could remove your body. Either way, you would soon find yourself a ghost."

Michael glared at the Cat. "That's not what I mean and you know it."

"Perhaps you could ask the Queen of Hearts. She may know. She sends people there often enough."

"By removing their heads," Michael retorted. "I would like to keep mine, Cat."

"I'll admit she sends most people that way, but by no means is everyone she sends dead."

"Oh, this is useless." Michael turned to the queens. "I don't suppose you have any magic mushrooms lying around."

"Regrettably, those are the creation of the caterpillar," the Queen of Clubs said, "and it is even more aloof than the Cat. As to your fairy friend, no, I don't think so. Perhaps we could summon her if we were already in the ghostly realm, but here? No, we are too far removed."

"Well, that is most regrettable." The Cat licked its lips. "Such a fairy would make a tasty snack."

"Is that all you think about?" Will asked.

The Cat seemed to bow. "One must follow one's nature."

"A shame," the Queen of Spades said. "It would have been

wonderful to strike directly at the heart of their territory with our full strength, but we have other means. You three are agents of another Looking Glass queen. I have heard of such a one. Alice, is that correct?"

That took Vanessa aback. "Yes, how do you know?"

"Do you think that someone could rise to the rank of queen without the rest of us knowing? She changed both Wonderland and the Looking Glass Land in ways I doubt you can imagine. If you are her agents, then perhaps you can be what we need to turn the tide of this war, provided you would be on our side. What do you say? Will you come with us?"

The jack stiffened and gripped his sword. He didn't say anything, though. Other cards had tensed as well. The Cat appeared on her shoulder again, wrapping its tail around her neck. Deciding to take the advice of the Queen of Spades, she ignored the Cat. Michael stepped forward, but he looked back at her before speaking. She nodded, and the Cat laughed.

"We'll go."

22

The Queen of Spades knocked on the boulder for the fifth time, but it remained solid. In frustration, the jack of spades swung his weapon at the rock. The stone shattered as if it were made of glass. Vanessa coughed at the dust, though none of the cards seemed affected. Instead, they all stared at the broken stone.

"That's not possible," said the Queen of Spades. "That stone was a gateway to the realm of Hearts. It might have been closed, but nothing so mundane as an ordinary weapon could break an opening, not unless the magic of the gateway has been completely undone." She turned to the jack. "Did you sense anything when you came through?"

"Nothing, though I am hardly a magician."

"I know a little about crossing worlds," Vanessa said. "I couldn't even sense the power of the gateway."

"They are too well woven into the fabric of Wonderland for most to be able to detect them. It would not be easy or quick to unravel, but if it were on the brink of collapse, you should have been able to detect *something*. We need to get some information."

"How far are the lands of Hearts in miles?" Michael asked.

"At least twenty miles," said the Queen of Clubs.

Michael, Vanessa, and Will all stared at one another. "Twenty miles? That's it?"

"Have you ever walked twenty miles?" said the card.

"A couple of times," Will said. "It's not pleasant, but it's hardly undoable."

The three queens talked among themselves for a few seconds before looking back at the trio. It was the Queen of Spades who spoke. "Perhaps you would consent to be our scouts."

"Of course," Vanessa said. "Just point us in the right direction."

The queens had provided them with fresh bread to eat on the way. Vanessa had no idea where they had gotten it—though given the peculiar nature of this land, she was a little afraid it would change their size when they ate it. But aside from being more filling than it should have been, it had no apparently mystical effects. Some of the cards went with them for a little while, but they fell behind after only a few miles, apparently exhausted. Neither of her companions, however, had the slightest bit of difficulty. The terrain was easy, and the cool air felt good against her skin.

"I guess that cardboard doesn't hold much stamina," Michael said. "Do we wait for them?"

Vanessa shook her head. "They'd only get in the way."

They moved on. The lands of Spades were different from the lands of Hearts, though it took Vanessa over an hour to identify what those differences were. The angles were harsher. The grass crunched under their feet and the wind carried the slightest bite of cold. Vanessa felt the urge to keep her sword drawn. At first, she thought that would be too conspicuous, but the few travelers they saw were cards that were all armed.

"Spades is the suit of war," Michael said. "In some countries, the fourth suit is the sword, not the spade."

"If the most warlike suit has trouble doing something as

simple as walking twenty miles, then they're in trouble." Vanessa pointed forward. "There, I think that's the border."

Flowers grew in a line. At least half of them were some shades of red. Some of them actually dripped paint from their petals. As soon as they stepped over the line, the sounds of their footsteps faded as the grass became softer. A cardinal flew into the branches above them and sang.

"It's going a little overboard with the red, don't you think?" Michael asked.

"You're going overboard with the judgment," the cardinal said. "Red is a fine color. I suppose you like brown."

Vanessa looked down at her coat. It was a serviceable garment, one well suited to travel. She glared up at the bird. "It's certainly less garish."

Michael blinked. "You understood him?"

"Well, yes," Vanessa said. "It's a talking bird, after all."

"It is?" He looked to Will who nodded. "Hmm. I guess I just got used to being the only one able to hear them after the dragon's-blood potion."

"Humph," the cardinal chirped. "You think you're so special just because you can speak to birds? Everyone I know can do that."

"Is everyone you know a bird?" Vanessa asked.

"Of course. They are the only ones worth knowing."

"Really?" Vanessa asked. "Well, then, I am pleased you decided to speak with us. I am Vanessa Finch."

The bird hopped from one branch to another, causing a leaf to fall and brush Vanessa's face. "Finch? Well, yes, I suppose you are. How can I help you, my lady Finch?"

Will cocked his head. "Because her last name is Finch, you think she's a bird?"

"She is a finch, is she not?"

"Well, yes, in a way."

The bird huffed. "I don't suppose you would understand. You don't even have wings."

"Neither does she!" Michael shouted.

"Of course she does. She's a finch."

"Michael, drop it."

He stiffened but nodded.

The cardinal sang a few notes. "At least you know enough to obey a bird."

"We do need help," Vanessa said before Michael could reply. "Perhaps you could aid us. We need to find the Queen of Hearts' castle."

"Why would you need me to tell you something like that?" the cardinal asked. "It's a rather large castle. You need only to fly high enough to see it."

"Hawks," Will said. "She's worried about hawks."

"Are you now?" The cardinal looked up and sang a few notes. Other birds nearby responded before it turned back to her. "I haven't seen one lately, but that doesn't mean there isn't one around. It is a sensible precaution." It flew to a tree that was just in sight. "Just beyond this tree is a road. Follow it, and it will lead you straight to the castle. Be careful, though. Some of the guards like to shoot things out of the air. I am sure they would love to hunt a finch."

"We will."

Vanessa resisted the urge to laugh. She and the others moved past the trees. The branches left sap on their skin as they pushed them aside. The path beyond wasn't exactly a road. It would be generous to even call it a trail, but then for a bird, it might well have seemed to be a road. They pushed through it, forcing their way through underbrush. Moving quietly was all but impossible, and dried leaves constantly crunched under-foot. All three of them were alert for an attack, but before long, Vanessa began to wonder if the cardinal had led them astray. She began looking for other animals to point her in the right direction, but the area was oddly deserted for a forest.

"Makes you long for the days when we had an animated shadow and an intelligent bird for companions, doesn't it?" Michael asked. "I could even go for a few fairies."

Sunlight shone through the branches ahead of them, though the forest was so thick they couldn't see more than about a foot. They moved a little faster. Suddenly, Will, who was in front, cried out and fell. Vanessa moved by instinct and grabbed his arm. He almost dragged her off the cliff, but she managed to hook a branch with her free hand. Before them, the ground simply fell away.

"Hold still," Michael said as he carefully crept forward.

He grabbed her arm and pulled back. Her shoulder ached as he dragged them up onto the ground. All three of them collapsed as soon as they were on solid ground again. Vanessa took a second to catch her breath before peering over the edge. At least a hundred feet down, the red stone of the Queen of Hearts' castle looked like a splotch of blood on the ground. The armies of the Triumvirate gathered beneath them. There were more cards than anything else, but Vanessa could just make out horse-men like the ones that had taken them prisoner.

"They're knights," Michael said.

"What?"

"Knights, like in a game of chess."

Vanessa stared for a second. "You're right. Horse heads. I should have realized it earlier."

"Does this help us at all?" Will asked.

"It might. At least it explains why they've been able to do

so much. The Lady always described the Queen of Hearts as letting her passion rule her actions, but in a game of chess, you have to think several moves in advance. The card queens assumed the Triumvirate was winning because of the White Queen's abilities, but that might not be the case."

"The queen is the most powerful piece," Will said, "but it isn't the most vital one."

"The king," Vanessa said. "You mean if we find the kings, we can overcome the Red and White Queens' armies."

Michael shrugged. "It's as good an idea as any."

"Where would we find them?"

"In a game of chess, the king is normally held back. If I had to guess, they would both be in the Looking Glass Land."

"Then we need to go there."

"We tried that, remember?"

Vanessa shook her head. "We tried that with a puddle of water and a magic mushroom. That's not how the Lady got there. We need a mirror."

"Where do you propose we find a mirror?" Michael said. "I haven't exactly seen one hanging on a wall."

Vanessa looked back down at the castle. "In there."

23

The top of the cliff was heavily wooded, and it took nearly half an hour for them to find a narrow ravine that wound all the way to the bottom. Night had fallen by the time they reached the base of the cliff. Fires could be seen in the distance beyond the castle, and Vanessa could make out cards huddled around them. She even saw someone that looked like a priest, though he couldn't seem to move straight ahead, instead always walking diagonally through the camp.

"It must be a bishop," she said under her breath.

Both her companions followed her gaze and nodded. The bishop joined several others of its kind. There didn't seem to be anyone between the cliff and the castle. They even waited several minutes in case there were patrols, but none ever came. It didn't take much effort to sneak up to the wall. They moved along it, trying to find a way in.

"This doesn't make sense," Michael said after they had gone most of the way around the palace. "In a castle this big, there should be at least a few servant entrances or kitchen doors. I would even take a drain, but there's nothing. Even the walls are too smooth to climb, so we can't reach any of the windows."

"How many castles have you snuck into like that?" Will asked.

"Seven," Michael said. "Those are pretty standard ways of doing things."

"Which makes sense why they wouldn't work here," Will said. "What is a crazy way to break into the castle?"

"Climb back up to the cliff and jump off it so we land in the grounds?" Michael asked.

"Not that crazy," Vanessa said. "This isn't like normal times. All we need is to find a mirror. Any one of the rooms should have what we need." She ran her fingers along the wall. It was nearly sheer, but only nearly. About ten feet up, there was a crack on the wall, and she could see a window just above it. It looked just wide enough to provide a handhold, though she doubted either of her companions would be able to use it as such.

"How about that?" She motioned to the crack. Michael gave her a skeptical look but brought his hands together to give her a boost. She ran forward and jumped, just barely catching herself. Her arm screamed in pain as she pulled herself up. The window ledge was only a little beyond the crack, and she barely managed to get hold of it. With a grunt, she managed to pull herself up to it. The window was locked, but they didn't need to be subtle. She swung her sword as hard as she could, and the glass shattered.

The room was garish in its opulence. Every surface had been covered in red silk or lace. Even the walls and ceiling were painted red. On a cherrywood dresser was a mirror rimmed in copper. The curtains were the long, flowing kind, and with a little effort, she pulled them off their rods and tied them into a rope long enough for Will and Michael to climb. Michael was first, and he did so with ease. Will, on the other hand, needed a little more help from Vanessa and Michael, though he did well enough for a squire.

"Well," Michael said, looking at the mirror, "that will either take us directly into the Red Queen's chambers in the Looking Glass Land, or it will do the opposite, mirrors being what they are. Do you think you can take us there this time?"

"Only one way to find out, but either way, we should hurry." She motioned to the broken window. "Someone probably heard that."

She walked up to the mirror and stared into it, trying to sense the way to the Looking Glass Land. There was a resonance, and she seized it, reaching forward and touching the mirror. It was just glass. Her reflection stared back at her. It might have been her imagination, but she thought her reflection smiled.

"Vanessa," Michael said, looking through a jewelry box. He picked up a ruby-encrusted pendant. On it was the symbol of a crown. "I think this is the Red Queen's chambers."

"Unless the Red King is here as well, that doesn't really do us any good." She banged on the mirror, but it stubbornly refused to let her through. She tried to sense something, *anything,* but there was nothing.

"We're in an enemy monarch's sleeping quarters," Michael said, "and you can't think of anything to do that would help us?"

"These aren't humans," Vanessa said. "We have no way to know what will poison them, even if we had anything to poison them with."

"I'll admit that would be the most obvious approach, but it's not the only one. We should at least look around. Who knows what we might find?"

"What do you think?" Vanessa asked. "We're going to find war plans just lying around?"

"Probably not," Will said as he opened a wardrobe. He gasped. "But how about the Vorpal Sword?"

He lifted a blade that was almost as tall as he was. The metal shimmered, glowing with its own inner light. His weight shifted into a perfect fighter's stance, something Will had always had trouble with. He held the hilt firmly and his center of balance was low. If Vanessa didn't know better, she would have thought he was a master swordsman. Of course, he did wield the Vorpal Sword. The Knights had spent more than a thousand years searching for magical artifacts and hiding them away where they could do no harm and be used only when necessary. They had found many magical swords over the centuries, but few were the equal of the legendary Vorpal Sword, which could cut almost anything, and which transformed anyone wielding it into a master of the blade. That sword, by itself, would make this excursion worthwhile, assuming, of course, that they could get it back.

"Is there anything else in there?" Vanessa asked.

Will's muscles tensed, but he relaxed after a second. He replaced the sword and moved away, never taking his eyes from the weapon. "See for yourself."

She stepped up to the wardrobe. It held dresses and robes of every design, all different shades of red. Jewelry hung from a hook on the side. The items in this wardrobe were worth a small fortune, and that was only what the Red Queen had brought with her to this realm. She didn't see anything to match the Vorpal Sword, but she extended her hand, touching everything and trying to sense anything out of the ordinary. When she touched the jewelry, something tingled against her fingertips. She examined them more closely and realized that the magic she sensed emanated from a watch. She picked it up. The gold chain was thin. Even the watch was small, as if it were made for a child, and she could make out only a faint ticking. Michael tensed at the sound but calmed down an instant later. She opened the watch case. The magic surged, feeling almost hot to her touch. Vanessa watched it tick a few times before gasping.

"This is one of the white rabbit's watches."

"So?" Michael asked.

"The white rabbit. The one that Hook killed to get to this world." She pointed at the mirror. "Or maybe to that one. I think this is what he used."

"I thought the power to do that was in the rabbit," Will said.

The tingle she felt was unmistakable. "So did I, but apparently it was the watch."

"You mean we can use this to go to the Looking Glass Land?"

"And probably to get home, too. Maybe to other worlds. This might be even more powerful than the Vorpal Sword."

Michael's eyes went wide. "We can use this to go into the ghostly realm to go after Hook."

Vanessa raised an eyebrow. "After what happened last time, do you still think that's a good idea?"

He pointed to Will. "With that sword, yes, I think it's a good idea."

Will nodded with an almost hungry look on his face. The door burst open, and a dozen hearts cards of different values rushed into the room, their footsteps oddly heavy on the plush carpet. They leveled their spears. Will stepped forward, and Vanessa found herself eager to see just what the Vorpal Sword could do.

24

Five of the cards rushed forward at the same time. Even someone as skilled as the Knight Protector would have had trouble with so many. Will, however, stepped forward with a grin that was totally out of character. His weapon sliced through the air in a maneuver that seemed at the same time casual and blindingly fast. It sheared through half of the spear shafts, making a *snicker-snack* sound and sending splinters of the cherrywood everywhere. Vanessa felt a few of the fragments sting her arms and face, though somehow they didn't even touch Will. The cards hesitated, but only for a second. The Knights, however, moved as one. Will danced around the incoming attacks. His sword sliced through one of the cards, reducing it to confetti. Another of them tried to stab Vanessa. She knocked the attack aside. A heartbeat later, Will had cut it down. They were laughably slow compared to him, and in a matter of seconds, all of the cards had been disabled or destroyed.

"That was incredible," Michael said. "I had heard rumors of the Vorpal Sword, but I never imagined . . ." He gave Will a sheepish smile. "Can I hold it?"

Will frowned, and his muscles tensed. He glared at Michael. She had seen looks that could cut steel before. The look he gave Michael would have melted that steel and then evaporated it. Michael saw it, too, and held his weapon ready, though the look on his face told her that he wasn't sure if he could bring himself to use it.

She spoke slowly. "Will, put it down."

He turned to her, and for a moment, she thought he would attack her. He blinked and let out a long breath. The tension seemed to flow out of him.

Michael moved to the wardrobe and pulled out a black leather scabbard lined with silver. He held it to Will. "Sheath the sword."

"What? Why?"

"Do it, Will," Vanessa said. "You know that many of the more powerful magical items have side effects. It's clouding your mind."

"No," Will said, raising the blade again, "I really don't think it is."

"Squire William." Vanessa spoke with all the authority she could put into her voice. "I am giving you an order. You will put the sword away."

He glared at her but took the sheath from Michael. He shoved the blade in, and instantly the rage vanished from his face. He looked at the weapon and then to Vanessa. "Well, that was incredibly unnerving."

Vanessa gave him a half shrug. "It's your first experience with a powerful magical item. They can be like that. It's why the Court is always so reluctant to let us use them. It may not be so easy to put it away next time."

He nodded and was about to put it on his belt but then hesitated before holding it out to her. "We're in the middle of a war zone, and you're the best with a blade."

As the Knight who had found the weapon, it was his right to wield it until they delivered it to the Court, but that also involved handling it responsibly. She met his eyes, and she saw her thoughts mirrored on his face. She nodded once and took the blade. The leather hilt felt oddly warm in her hand, and she felt an urge to draw it. Instead, she put it on her belt, opposite her normal one.

Commotion came from down the hall. Instinctively, Vanessa's hand went to her hilt, but she caught herself before she drew it. She looked back to the window. Going down the curtain wouldn't be easy, and it wouldn't be quick, but she didn't think they could escape through the castle.

Michael saw what she was looking at and nodded. She was the lightest, so she went down first. Before long, Will and Michael had followed. She could hear activity in the gathered army. At least some of them were coming this way. They had minutes, at most.

"Up the cliff again?" Michael asked.

"It's as good a plan as any."

The entrance to the pass had just come into view when a horse's cry came from the south. They turned to see three of the horse-men, two red and one white, running toward them. They were so heavy that the ground shook with each step. Behind them, banners had been raised and the army was preparing to march. A surge of joy ran through Vanessa, and it took her a second to realize it came from the Vorpal Sword. Her heart raced, and she closed her fingers around the hilt. It felt hot, so hot that it should have burned her, but somehow it didn't. She thought back to the look on Will's face. If she drew it, she might not be able to sheath it again.

"Run."

The path was steep but narrow. Though the horse-men could move faster, they had to squeeze through some of the narrower areas, which slowed them down considerably. Still, after a few minutes, Vanessa's legs burned with the effort. Michael and Will were falling behind. She realized her hand had gone to the hilt of the Vorpal Sword. The fact that it had done so without her knowing was more than a little terrifying. Still, it was their only option. She started to draw it when someone cried out ahead of her. She looked up and grinned.

The jack of spades stood there with a pair of tens at his back and at least a dozen other cards. She doubted they could stand against the horse-men on their own, but if they joined forces with Vanessa and her companions, they might just stand a chance. She managed to get behind and turn to face the attackers. She drew her sword—not the Vorpal Sword, but the curved weapon she had used for so long. Michael and Will caught up with her. Michael's face had gone red from the effort of climbing. Both he and Will were recovering quickly, however.

The jack and his soldiers stepped forward just as the horse-men reached them. The horse-men swung heavy maces, which the cards avoided even as they stabbed into their foes. The horse-men grimaced, but other than that, they barely seemed bothered by their opponents' attack. Will rushed forward. His blade, however, cut into a horse-man's leg. The horse-man cried out, spilling blood too bright to be human, before falling to the ground. The other two horse-men turned to Will, but Vanessa moved in, slicing into the red creature's side.

Black-tipped arrows sailed over them and pelted the horse-men. Most of them bounced off their thick hides, but a few of them stuck. The cards began moving forward. Vanessa joined them, but then the ground rumbled. At first she tried to ignore it, but after a few seconds the shaking became so violent that she lost her footing. Michael stood over her while Will helped her up, then the three stood back-to-back. The cards had all fallen as well and were scrambling to get up. The horse-men had gotten to their feet, though the one Will had cut limped heavily. What looked to be a wave of black bricks flowed around the horse-men and formed a barrier, reaching as high as the canyon walls. Michael stared at it. Will stepped up and knocked on the bricks to make sure they were real. Vanessa smirked.

"I guess that's a rook. I didn't expect it to be quite so . . . literal." She looked back up the path. The jack and both tens were staring at the wall. Vanessa stepped in front of the jack "Is the Queen of Spades nearby?"

The bottom face shook its head while the top one spoke. "She remained behind. We were sent to aid you should you need it." He looked at the wall. "Fortunate for you."

"I'm glad you were here. We should go to her." Vanessa held up the watch. "With this, we might be able to end the war."

25

The three queens looked down at Vanessa and her companions from their thrones in the Queen of Spades' castle. The queens' gazes no longer held the terrible weight that they once had the first time Vanessa encountered them—and with the Vorpal Sword at her side, she knew she had nothing to fear. Of course, it was the white rabbit's watch that held their attention. She hadn't given it to them; instead, she held it up by the thin chain.

"This seems too easy," said the Queen of Spades. "Why would they just leave the watch and the Vorpal Sword where anyone could just stumble upon them?"

"Hardly anyone," Vanessa said. "They were in the Red Queen's private chambers."

"Chambers that you got into easily enough," the Queen of Spades said.

"We left with an army chasing us."

"Only because you were foolish enough to actually break the window. Had you gone in more quietly, I doubt anyone would have ever known you were there."

Vanessa clenched her teeth so hard her jaw started to hurt. "We are pretty sure we know how to overcome the armies from the Looking Glass Land. They need to be dealt with or they'll tear you apart. We know how to get there. Are you saying that we won't use it?" She was practically shouting.

The Queen of Spades gave her a level look. "I'm not sure we should be hasty."

"We don't really have a choice," Vanessa said. "The Triumvirate's armies are marching. If they weren't slowed down by their own cards, they would have been here already. The three of you could defeat the Queen of Hearts' army, but it took a whole squadron to fight off three Looking Glass knights. There is simply no way you can fight off an entire army of them."

The Queen of Spades gripped her sword, and her voice was closer to a growl than words. "I hate to admit it, but you have a point. So then, what is your suggestion?"

"We go into the looking glass and eliminate their kings," Vanessa said. "If we do that, their armies will be defeated without our needing to actually fight them."

"When I joined the Knights, I never expected to commit regicide," Will said.

"It's happened before. You should search the archives for the Nome King when we get back," Vanessa said. She turned to Michael. "How many rulers have you killed?"

"Two," Michael said. "Three if you count Mordred's heir."

The blood had drained from Will's face, as he looked from one to the other, but the Queen of Spades spoke before he could say anything.

"The three of you can do it, then?"

"I don't know. If he were no stronger than the knights, we could, but the rook took us completely by surprise. I have no idea how powerful their kings would be, but if they have other defenses, we'll need help."

"How much help?"

Vanessa looked the cards up and down. They were so much

weaker than their Looking Glass counterparts. "As much as you can spare. This may be our only chance to really beat them."

"A clever plan," said a voice above them. They all looked up as the Cheshire Cat materialized, perched on a rafter. "If you can take out one of their kings, half their army would fall. It could be the break you need to win."

The Queen of Spades stared at the Cat. "Have you chosen sides now?"

"It was merely an observation."

"Have you gotten any information from the White Queen?" Vanessa asked.

"Do you have any idea how hard it is to question someone who already knows exactly what you're about to ask and vowed not to answer you? On top of that, she may be the strongest person I've ever encountered."

"It makes sense," Vanessa said. "The queen is the strongest piece on the board."

"I don't like it," the Queen of Spades said. "If she's that strong and can see the future, how were we able to capture her so easily?"

"Even she can't see everything," the Cat said. "It takes a mind far greater than hers to see every possible combination. It is entirely likely that you came at her from an angle she wasn't expecting. On the other hand, she may have seen that her presence would intimidate the card queens and make them afraid to invade her world."

"You mean she doesn't want us to go."

The Cat's body vanished. The head rotated until it was upside down, then floated down to the ground. Vanessa felt a weight on her foot and shook it away. The cat laughed but turned to the cards.

"My dear Queen of Spades, I would never presume to

guess your thoughts, much less those of a queen from another world."

"No, but it makes sense."

The Queen of Diamonds scoffed. "You want to outwit someone who can see the future by guessing at what they've seen and going against that? What makes you think she hasn't seen what you're thinking about and taken that into account?"

"If you don't plant your crops because you are afraid of what the weather *might* do," the Queen of Clubs said, "you'll never plant anything. We can't allow ourselves to be paralyzed by the White Queen's visions."

"Very well," the Queen of Spades said. "I don't believe there is anything more to be gained by more discussion. The question is do we use the white rabbit's watch to invade the Looking Glass Land with the intention of eliminating the Red and White Kings. Clubs?"

The Queen of Clubs scrunched her two heads in concentration. The bottom one sniffed her flower while the top one shook her head.

"No, the risk is too great. We would have to deplete many of our forces, and that would leave Wonderland undefended. I vote no."

The Queen of Spades inclined her top head. "Diamonds?"

The Queen of Diamonds pursed her lips and nodded. "Clubs is correct. The risk is great, but so is the potential gain. With this one move, we could end the war. I vote yes."

The Queen of Spades looked from one to the other before nodding. "We go. Sir Vanessa, do you know how to use that device?"

Vanessa closed her eyes and focused on the ticking. There was great power in the watch. It responded to her call, and its magic seemed to crawl up the chain and entwine itself around her hand. Compared to her previous attempts to cross between worlds, using this would be incredibly easy. The barrier felt paper-thin. She let go of the power and nodded.

"I can open the way as soon as you are ready."

The Queen of Spades raised her hand. Instantly, nearly a dozen rows of spades lined up behind her, each with a ten at the front and going down to an ace. The Queens of Clubs and Diamonds followed suit. In a matter of seconds, the three card armies had gathered.

Vanessa reached into the watch. It was just as easy as the first time, and after a few heartbeats, the magic had entwined around her wrist. She gripped it and forced the power out. She held up the watch and stared at her reflection in the golden object. It winked at her, but before she could react, the magic of the watch congealed and formed into a rectangular opening, nearly twice as tall as Vanessa and wide enough to fit all three armies side by side. The queens shouted and charged through the hole in the air with their armies right behind.

26

Vanessa felt like she had been plunged into freezing water as Wonderland melted away. She gasped, but there was no air to breathe in. She could see her own blood, muscles, and bones as her eyes inverted for a second. She tried to take a breath again. This time, it felt more like she was spreading herself out through the air rather than taking it in. Then, everything corrected itself.

They were in a wide chamber, larger than any Vanessa had ever seen. She could barely see the wall in front of them. The room's tiny windows let in light. The walls on either side were lost to darkness. Everything reminded her of smoke or fog. It was as if nothing was real. Everyone was on the ground. The cards were untangling themselves, but she and her companions got to their feet with little difficulty.

"Are we here?" Michael asked.

"I think so. Let's find a way out. We should be able to tell pretty easily."

The Knights and the cards scattered, and after a few minutes, Vanessa found that the wall on the left side was actually a massive stone door. She grunted and put her weight against it, but it refused to budge. After her failed attempt, the entire card army stepped in to help, but found little success. Will gave her blade a pointed look. It felt like a waste to use the weapon for something so plain, but after an hour of searching, they still hadn't found another way out. Vanessa clenched her teeth and drew.

It was nothing like she expected. There was no surge of rage or the desire for violence, and she wondered if the lack of an enemy had robbed the sword of its influence. She gave a pair of quick slashes, effortlessly cutting through the hinges before sheathing the weapon. The door fell outward, hitting the ground so hard that the earth trembled.

The building sat on a hilltop. There were other buildings around them, though they all had holes melted through their walls. She thought she saw something as big as a house move through the ruins, though she couldn't determine its shape. It started to approach, but then it squealed and moved away until it was out of sight.

"What was that?" Will asked.

Vanessa shrugged. "I have no idea, but it doesn't look like it's going to bother us."

She motioned them forward. Beneath them stretched a verdant valley surrounded by wide rivers. The valley itself was divided by hedges into squares, alternating between lighter and darker grass. She didn't have to count them to know there would be sixty-four of them. She turned to her friends. "This is it. This is the Looking Glass Land."

"Great," Michael said. "It looks completely abandoned, though. Where do we go?"

Vanessa pointed to one square. "In a traditional game, that's where the king would start off. Somehow, I don't think we're at the beginning of the game. Still, it's a good place to start. The square next to the king's would be the queen's, and I'd be willing to bet there's something important there, too."

"Very well," the Queen of Spades said. "We will take those

two squares. I don't suppose that watch can help us get to the other side quicker."

Vanessa was about to shake her head but then paused. "I'm actually not sure. I don't think it's meant to allow fast travel within a world, but we might be able to go back to Wonderland and then enter from another side. Though it should be easy enough to find out."

She reached into the watch, and once again its magic ran up her arm. She stared at the Queen of Spades as the power formed stars at her fingertips. Suddenly, the stars jumped off her hand and swirled in front of them, seeming to form a card, but it dissipated before it had completely formed. For a moment, Vanessa just stared. After recentering herself, she tried again, but no luck.

"I can't get back through." She held out the watch to the Queen of Spades. "Maybe you should try. I've never traveled to Wonderland under my own power. Perhaps the land isn't letting me in because it doesn't recognize me, but the same wouldn't be true for you."

"I've never heard of that kind of restriction," Michael said.

"Neither have I, but I'm grasping at straws here."

The Queen of Spades took the watch. The top head closed her eyes, but the bottom one glared at Vanessa. "How exactly are we supposed to use this thing?"

"Just concentrate on going home. If it works the way I think it does, the watch will do most of the work."

The queen grimaced. "I was never a sorceress."

Still, she closed all four of her eyes. Light flickered from the watch. Magic ran up the Queen of Spades' arm and tried to form a gateway in front of her, but it fell apart into a shower of black sparks. The queen shook her head. "It feels like there's something in the way. It's familiar. It's like my own power but not."

"The Queen of Hearts?"

"Perhaps."

"Oh no," Michael said. "Peter."

"What about Peter?" Vanessa asked.

"Peter could shut off access to Neverland."

"And?"

"And the rulers of realms can always do that."

"Peter is a god. The Queen of Hearts isn't."

Michael looked out over the empty landscape. A chill wind blew across the hill, and Vanessa even saw a tumbleweed roll across one of the squares. In spite of being vibrant, the land felt almost dead. He spoke in a flat voice. "The Queen of Hearts has the aid of someone who spent most of his life and death opposing a god, and one who knew enough to get here in the first place."

"I don't know, Michael. That feels like it's a stretch."

"It's also not relevant. If the Red and White Queens managed to bring an entire army to Wonderland, then there has to be another way to get there," the Queen of Spades said. "Let's take out whatever king is closest and then use their portal to get home. With half the Triumvirate's Looking Glass forces gone, we'll stand a much better chance of defeating them."

"It's better than nothing," Vanessa said, shrugging. "Let's go."

The hill was steep, and Vanessa struggled to keep her feet as they went down it. One of the cards in the rear tumbled forward, creating a domino effect. Before long, the collapse had caught the cards on either side. Nearly a third of the army tumbled down the hill. The others moved more quickly, but they couldn't go much faster without risking the same thing happening to them. No one was hurt, but they took quite a while to get back on their feet.

"There," Michael said. "I think that is the knight's square.

We should move over a few spaces to come directly into the king's."

Vanessa nodded and they tried to move over. As soon as they stepped beyond the square, however, the ground became gooey. Vanessa sank in to her knees after only a few steps. The substance seeped into her boots and under her clothes. The cold material sapped heat from her. It made a squishing sound as she moved through it. The farther she went, the deeper she sank, and before long she was waist-deep in the muck, having managed to get only about half a dozen feet.

"Michael, help me."

He nodded, took a spear from one of the cards, and held it out to her. She grabbed the shaft and he managed to pull her free. Surprisingly, Michael didn't say a word about having to help her. She started to brush herself off as she walked, but all the muck fell off her as soon as she was in front of the knight's square. She shook her head.

"We are knights," she said. "I guess that means we can only enter from the knight's square."

"Does that mean we have to do a knight's moves?" Michael asked.

"I'm not sure, actually. When the Lady came here, she just went forward. She was taking the place of a pawn, though. It's possible." She thought for a second. "Two spaces forward and one right for the first move. Then, one space right and two backward will bring us to the king's space."

"That's a roundabout way to go."

"Not if it's the only way."

She waded across the river of goo and stepped onto the knight's square. The sense of etherealness that she had felt since coming into this world vanished. Everything seemed real, though most of the squares around them were blurry. Only three were clear, the ones to which knights could travel. Apparently, there were no other pieces in the way because even the one normally occupied by a pawn was empty. Vanessa pointed toward the square that was to be their first move. The others nodded. As soon as they stepped off the knight's square, the world shifted around them. The rush made her feel like she was going to throw up. When everything stilled, they found themselves in their destination square.

There was a train station, though it was empty. Michael examined the tracks and frowned. Of course, he had been a train engineer, so perhaps he saw something she didn't. What concerned her was the object at the station.

"Is that a bed?" Will asked.

It was indeed a bed, covered with a white blanket. The frame was made of some pale wood, though it had six legs instead of the standard four. As soon as they approached, two compound eyes appeared at one end and an antenna rose from between them. It looked at them before scurrying away. The Knights and the cards stared at it.

"What was that?" Michael asked.

Will stared after it. "I think it was a bedbug."

"A . . . bedbug?" Vanessa was about to say something, but Michael shook his head. "No, I don't need to hear it again. This is a land of madness."

A bright yellow coat buzzed toward them. Will pointed, but Vanessa put a hand on his arm and shook her head.

"I wouldn't. I think that's a yellowjacket. Something that big would have a nasty sting."

"Correct," a familiar voice said.

Vanessa saw the telltale curl of blue smoke before she saw

the creature it came from. A bright blue caterpillar scurried across the ground. It stared at Vanessa, sneering at her in spite of their difference in size.

"What are you doing here?" Vanessa asked.

"You come into the lands of my people and ask me what I am doing here? Who are you?"

The smoke smelled sweet as she breathed it in. "I'm sorry. If I may ask, what do you mean when you say that these are the lands of your people?"

"You may not ask."

"I'm really beginning to hate you," Vanessa said under her breath.

"I began hating you long ago. I am not finished yet," the caterpillar said.

"Please forgive my companion's impertinence," the Queen of Diamonds said.

"I do not forgive."

"Of course. Will you consent to hear my request?"

The caterpillar moved around in a circle. It let out a large puff of blue smoke and crawled over to the Queen of Diamonds. When the smoke had passed over her, it became an exact duplicate of her before it dissipated. "Who are you?"

"I am the Queen of the Realm of Diamonds. I don't know if you were ever aware of it, but when I took the throne, I declared that you and your people would always be welcome in my lands."

"I am aware. I will hear your request."

"We are not able to return to Wonderland."

"That is not a request."

Though it seemed ridiculous, the Queen of Diamonds reddened. "Yes, well, I wonder if you know how we could return. Perhaps we could go by the same way you did."

"You cannot. The Queen of Hearts has sealed off the realm with the aid of her pirate friend. There are a few ways open, but you cannot take the way I took. I followed a worm, and you are far too large to fit through a wormhole."

"A wormhole?"

The caterpillar let out a smoke ring that grew until it was as large as Vanessa's head. "Your people do not even know wormholes exist yet." It puffed out some that formed laughing faces. "How foolish your people are. How can there be worms without wormholes?"

Vanessa opened her mouth to speak, but the Queen of Diamonds raised a hand, stopping her. "You mentioned other ways."

"There might be a rabbit hole or two hereabouts. The ends in Wonderland are doubtlessly sealed, but you might be able to burrow through, if you have a rabbit. Or a rabbit's key."

It stared at Vanessa, and then its eyes wandered down to the pocket of her coat. Vanessa pulled out the watch.

"You will not find Wonderland as you left it. The Cat has acted on its plans."

"The Cat?"

"Of course. Who do you think is responsible for all of this?"

"Hook," Michael said.

"The spirit known as James Hook came here to see the Cat. Were you ignorant of even that?"

"Why would Hook want to see the Cheshire Cat?" Michael asked. The caterpillar stared at him and he smacked his forehead. "Because the Cheshire Cat can cross freely from the ghostly realm to the physical one. That's what Hook wants. It's what he's always wanted."

"But the Cheshire Cat would not side with the Queen of Hearts," the Queen of Spades said. "It gives its allegiance to no one. I've tried for decades to recruit it. Even the caterpillar gives its word easier." She bowed her head to the caterpillar. "No offense intended, of course."

"I am quite offended." It puffed a smoke ring before burrowing into the ground.

"Wait," the Queen of Diamonds called out, but the caterpillar did not return. The Queen of Diamonds glared at the Queen of Spades. "The caterpillar has ever been a fickle ally, if it can even be called an ally, but it may be the wisest creature in all of Wonderland." She sighed. "There's nothing to do about it now. We need to find a rabbit hole."

Vanessa pointed behind them to the square that would hold a king in a normal game. One by one, her squires and the card queens nodded. Vanessa took a step in that direction, and once again, the world lurched. Vanessa shuddered as her senses returned to normal. There was a castle of white stone that reached to the heavens. She would have sworn that it hadn't been there a moment ago. Either it had come into existence once they stepped onto the square, or they simply couldn't see it from where they had stood before.

The ground was white marble, the exact same color as the castle, so that it was impossible to tell when one ended and the other began. There were no guards around the castle, nor was there an army pouring out through any rabbit hole. They approached the castle from the front, their footsteps echoing in spite of the fact that there was nothing for them to echo off of. They found the gate open and entered. The inside was all polished marble, and the air held a perpetual chill. There were white frames on the walls, but instead of paintings, they contained designs that had been carved directly into the wall.

It didn't take them long to find the throne room. Tapestries hung from the walls, but the designs were just varying shades of white, too similar for Vanessa to be able to tell what they were. Their footsteps echoed hollowly as they approached the throne. Both the chair and its cushions were pure white. A man who could only be the White King slumbered atop it. He had pale skin and ivory robes. His pearlescent crown sat crookedly on his head. Michael and Vanessa exchanged glances.

"It can't be this easy."

The Queen of Spades motioned to the cards around her. The nines and tens surrounded the throne, holding their spears at the king, who snored even louder as they approached. One of the tens brought the point of its spear to the White King's arm, spilling a drop of pale blood. Slowly, his eyes opened. When he saw he was surrounded, he gasped and stood on his chair.

"Oh dear." He had a high, squeaky voice. "What do you want?"

"We want your armies out of our lands," the Queen of Spades said.

"I do not command our armies."

"But your death might end their threat as well."

"You don't need to kill me for that. You have me captured. That will be enough."

"He might be telling the truth," Vanessa said. "A game of chess ends when a player can't take their king out of danger. That could be the case now."

"'Might be telling the truth' isn't good enough," the Queen of Spades said. "Take him."

The king screamed as the cards stabbed him. Their spears couldn't pierce too far into his skin. Still, he whimpered and tried to huddle into his chair.

"Wait! I can help you. I know how the White Queen took our armies through to your world."

"Hold."

The Queen of Spades spoke softly, but the cards stopped

their motion. The White King was riddled with wounds that oozed pale blood. With so much, it should have smelled, but it had no odor at all. The blood ran over his robes without staining. The White King's hands ran over his wounds, and he winced whenever he touched them. He looked at the Queen of Spades with gratitude.

"Oh, thank you. How can I repay you?"

"By giving us the information you just offered."

"Oh yes. Of course. She brought our forces to her castle. She had a white rabbit with her. Such a delightful creature. Pure white fur, you know. He opened a gateway, and they went through."

Vanessa sighed. "We need to go to the White Queen's castle, then? Moving one square over as knights. That's an annoyingly complicated maneuver. Three moves."

"There has to be a quicker way."

"What about him?" the Queen of Spades said, motioning to the White King.

"Yes, yes, I can do it." He stood up. His wounds had closed, and his blood had gathered at his feet. He stepped over the puddle. "I can take you there right now."

"Fine," Vanessa said. "Do it."

The White King's head bobbed up and down. He took another step and the world lurched. Suddenly, they were in front of another castle. It looked almost identical to the White King's, though the tops of the towers were more rounded. Vanessa looked around, but she saw nothing that would indicate a rabbit hole. Like the White King's castle, the grounds of this palace were pure white marble. There was no sign that a rabbit had ever burrowed through to another world from here. She looked at the White King. The Queen of Spades apparently had similar thoughts because her soldiers had once again surrounded him.

He was quivering and milky tears streamed down his cheeks. His voice was several octaves higher.

"I brought you here, just like I promised. Please let me go."

"You said there was a rabbit hole here that we could use to return to Wonderland."

"No, I didn't. I said there was a white rabbit here days ago, and that he opened a gateway. I said nothing about a hole still being here." He pointed at the gate to the castle. "He did something there. I don't know what it was, but when he was done, the gate opened to somewhere else. Wonderland, he claimed, though I have no way to be sure."

Some of the soldiers pressed their weapons into the White King's flesh, but Vanessa waved them off even as she stared at the gate. "I guess there's no reason a rabbit hole has to be in the ground. This one might be in the air."

She stepped forward and extended her hand, looking for the resonance that she had come to associate with traveling to other worlds. She thought she felt it, but it was faint. She tried to grab it, but it was like smoke. She clenched her jaw but remembered some of the Lady's lessons and forced herself to calm down. She reached forward more slowly. This time, she didn't grab it. Rather, she allowed it to flow around her fingers. She reached into the watch. Its power rushed into her like a dam had come down. It combined with the smoky remnants of the rabbit's gateway and exploded out of her with so much force that she was thrown off her feet. She hit the ground hard and slid several feet across the smooth marble.

Michael helped her up, and when she got to her feet, a gateway of gray smoke swirled in front of her. She tried to sense its nature. It had the same feel as Wonderland, though she wasn't entirely sure how she knew that. All three of the queens, however, stared at it with longing. The Queen of Clubs reached forward and pressed her hand into the doorway. A wave of plea-sure seemed to wash over her, and she began radiating heat. A heartbeat later, however, her wispy smile turned to a frown and then to a look of horror. She pulled back and hissed.

"What is it?" Vanessa asked. "Does it go somewhere else?"

"No, the White King was quite right. This does indeed go to Wonderland, but there's something off about it. Wonderland is in greater peril than I have ever seen."

"What do you mean?" the Queen of Spades asked.

"It's hard to say, but it's like the life is leaking away."

"You mean the armies are killing our people?"

"No." The Queen of Clubs paused. "Actually, that *is* likely, but that is not what I'm feeling. It's hard to explain." She turned to Vanessa. "You are aware that each of the queens of Wonder-land rule a different aspect, are you not?"

"Actually, I wasn't."

"Well, the Queen of Hearts is the passion, the anger, the joy, and all the emotions. Spades is the warrior. Her cards are the strongest in battle. Diamonds is the riches of the earth and the accumulation of wealth. I am the land, the growing things."

"I didn't realize that, but it makes sense," Vanessa said.

"Well, what I feel is the land dying. Something is happening to Wonderland itself. Whatever the Queen of Hearts is doing, it's killing the very essence of our home."

"We've only been gone a short time," the Queen of Spades said. "How could something like that happen so quickly?"

"Maybe it was already started," Vanessa said. "Time can pass differently in other worlds. I assumed it would be the same between Wonderland and the Looking Glass Land, but I never bothered to check."

"Of course it passes differently between the twin worlds,"

the Queen of Diamonds said. "Any joker could tell you that, but it doesn't pass that much faster. We need to go through right away if we're going to have any chance to reclaim what we have lost."

Vanessa turned to the White King. "What about your forces? Will they still be a problem for us?"

He stood up straight, though he was still trembling. "You will not have to worry about them. You have captured me. The white forces have been defeated."

The Queen of Spades suddenly looked uncertain. "Maybe we should go to the other side of the board as well. If we can capture the Red King, we could end this war here and now."

"That would be too late," the Queen of Clubs said. "Wonderland doesn't have that much time."

"Anyway, I don't think it would work," Vanessa said. She motioned to the portal. A faint wind blew out of it, carrying the smell of roses. It was fading quickly, though. "There was barely enough magical energy in the hole for me to open this doorway. If the one on the other side of the board is fading, too, it might be gone by the time we get to it, and we'd all be trapped."

One by one, the card queens nodded. This doorway was much smaller than the one Vanessa had created to get to the Looking Glass Land, so the Queen of Spades went in first, her army following right behind in a single file. The Queens of Diamonds and Clubs went right after, leaving the Knights to go last.

Will looked at the White King and fingered the hilt of his sword. "Are we sure that the White Queen's army won't be able to fight again once we leave him?"

"No, no." The White King backed up several steps. "It doesn't work that way. They would have to come back to their respective positions before they could act again, and without a white rabbit to lead them back, I daresay they would be stuck here."

"I think he's probably right," Vanessa said. The portal wavered. "We have to go now. We're just going to have to trust him."

Michael winced at that but went through without another word. Will followed a second later. Vanessa spared the White King one more glance before going through the portal herself.

27

This crossing was easier than others. One moment, they were in the Looking Glass Land, and the next, they were back on the shores of Wonderland. The waves crashed on the beach, and the air was filled with the smell of salt water. As far as Vanessa could tell, they were in the exact spot they had appeared in the first time they entered Wonderland. It was difficult to be sure, though. The landscape had completely changed. The blue waters of the ocean had given way to a pale gray, and the sand had gone black. Glowing blue clouds drifted across the sky, a shade of blue that Vanessa had gotten all too familiar with recently. Will touched her shoulder.

"The ghostly realm again?"

"No, I don't think so. It seems too solid, too real. I don't know what's wrong, though."

"This is not the ghostly realm," the Queen of Clubs said. Both her faces grimaced. "I have walked these lands long enough to recognize their feel under my feet. This is the same Wonderland we left. I told you it was dying." She spread her arms, indicating everything around her.

"I didn't realize a realm could be changed so completely so quickly," Will said. He knelt and ran his fingers through the sand.

"It can if its ruler wills it," Vanessa said, "or at least if the only remaining ruler wills it. We should have thought of that."

"There was no way we could have known," the Queen of Diamonds said. "None of us have ever been able to effect this kind of change, not even in our own lands. She can't have done this by herself."

"Hook," Michael said through clenched teeth.

"So it would seem," the Queen of Spades said. "We are in Hearts' lands right now. We need to get back to one of ours, mine preferably."

"There is a way to my lands nearby," the Queen of Diamonds said. "I don't believe any of Hearts' minions ever discovered it, so it might still be open. We should be able to get to your castle from there."

Spades nodded, and Diamonds led them to the same rock Vanessa and her companions had hidden behind when avoiding the mock turtle. It might have been Vanessa's imagination, but she thought she noticed a glimmer around the rock. When the Queen of Diamonds touched it, the glimmer became a shine. She moved her fingers in an S-shaped pattern, and the rock sank into the ground. The hole it left glittered with a myriad of rubies. The Queen of Diamonds smiled and jumped in as soon as the hole was big enough. The other card queens followed without a word, and Michael let out a breath before doing the same.

Will motioned for Vanessa to go before him. She gave him a slight inclination of her head before jumping in after the others. The sensation was similar to the first time she had tried to go into a rabbit hole. They fell for what felt like a full minute, passing an assortment of clutter. Then, all at once, they landed gently on the ground. A red road glimmered beneath them, though the landscape around them was as bleak as the one they had left. The lower head of the Queen of Diamonds frowned as she examined the road. Her foot moved along the glimmering stones, and she shook her head.

"The road is resisting the change, but I don't know how long it will hold out. As for the rest of my lands, I don't know. I fear there is little left. We should go to my castle. We can reach the lands of Spades from there, if we decide we need to."

She pointed down the road, and half her cards went ahead of them while the other half spread out behind. They started down the road, though no one felt the need to talk.

It was hard to believe that this was the same Wonderland they had left. The vibrant colors that had dominated everything were gone, and the fog of the ghostly realm rolled through the landscape as if it were native. In fact, as soon as the thought occurred to Vanessa, she saw a cloud of fog moving on stone wheels. She pointed it out to the others even as she wondered just how mutable Wonderland had become.

It was hard to tell how long they were on the road. The moments blended together, and though she never got sleepy or hungry, she wasn't entirely sure that she shouldn't have been feeling those things. Eventually, the shadowed form of a great palace came into view, though it was still several minutes before they got close enough to make out anything more than indistinct shapes.

The palace of the Queen of Diamonds seemed like a cross between those of the Queen of Spades and the Queen of Hearts. Rosebushes surrounded the castle, but the thorns seemed more important than the flowers. The angles were sharper, and the whole castle felt colder, though Vanessa wasn't sure if that was due to the nature of diamonds or the ghostly realm encroaching on Wonderland. She suspected it was a little of both.

A pair of tens saluted as they passed through the gate, though the Queen of Diamonds didn't acknowledge them. Instead, she led the group into her throne room. She didn't sit in her chair, however. Rather, the queens gathered in a circle, with the rest of the cards taking their places outside of the castle.

"What do we do?" asked the Queen of Spades.

"We strike back," the Queen of Clubs said, though it was her bottom face that spoke. "This insult to the land cannot be borne. If half of their Looking Glass forces have really fallen, then we may finally have a chance."

"Oh, do you?"

The walls trembled in response to that voice. A grin appeared in the center of the circle, followed by the Cat itself. The Queen of Spades didn't hesitate. She rushed forward, thrusting her sword at the creature. Its body vanished an instant before the blade would have pierced it. Instead, the dark metal sliced into the ground, throwing up a shower of sparks. The Cat's head smiled at her.

"Well, that was rather rude. Is it any wonder I never committed to your side?"

"This was your plan all along, wasn't it?" the Queen of Spades asked as she tried to tug her sword free of the ground. "You wanted to aid the Queen of Hearts."

The Cat's body reappeared, though it was standing on the blade. "Me? Aid her? Why, don't be ridiculous. What could she have to offer me?"

"Don't lie to us. The caterpillar told us that this was all your idea."

"Well, of course it was, but that doesn't mean I was ever on her side. Rather say that she was on mine, for a little while at least."

"What are you doing here?" Vanessa asked.

"I have come to offer you and your companions a way home."

Vanessa blinked. "Why?"

The Cat eyed the Vorpal Sword at her hip. "I hate that thing.

I would just as soon be as far away from that as I could be, so I give you this offer."

"Maybe I should just use it to kill you."

"Oh, don't be ridiculous. I don't deny that a weapon like that could kill me, but I would be gone before it ever got close. In any case, I will not permit you to take it with you."

"I thought you wanted to offer us a way home."

"Indeed, I do, but on one condition. You will take me with you and leave the weapon here."

"No," Michael said. "We brought an evil into our world once. We will not make that mistake again."

"Hook, you mean?" The Cat laughed. "Take me with you, and he will remain trapped here. That much is within my power to do."

"I thought he came here for your help," Vanessa said.

"Yes, he did, but I am under no obligation to help him. He is a treacherous ally, and I would just as soon not have him stab me in the back." It purred as it hopped off the blade. "Come now, it's not such a bad trade. Ask the queens. Before this incident, I existed in their lands peacefully for over a thousand years. I am nothing like the pirate ghost you unleashed."

"You're not offering us anything we don't already have." Vanessa held up the watch. "We can leave this realm anytime we choose."

The Cat blurred forward. Vanessa yelped as the watch was torn out of her hands so fast the chain tore off a layer of skin. The device shattered under the Cat's paw a second later. It hissed and its claws elongated. Its grin became an angry scowl that showed razor-sharp teeth.

"Do not mistake me for some whimsical pet, human. You will not leave here unless I allow it, and I will not allow it unless you take me with you."

180 GAMA RAY MARTINEZ

"And what of Wonderland?" asked the Queen of Spades, finally managing to pull her sword free of the ground. "Will you just abandon this land to the ghost?"

"What do I care what happens to this land? I have been here long enough. It is long past time that I leave."

"You're trapped," said Will.

"Yes." The word shook the walls and brought ruby dust drifting down from the ceiling. "Since before your order was founded, I have been trapped. I want my captivity to end."

"After what you did to this world, I will not unleash you on ours," Vanessa said.

The Cat roared, and instantly, Vanessa recognized it as the creature they had encountered the first time they had entered the ghostly realm. She remembered the malicious power radiating from it. There was only one thing to do. She drew the Vorpal Sword and struck. The world went red, and the weapon felt like it had no weight at all. She had never moved so fast. Her blade hissed as it cut through the air, but the Cat vanished before the sword cut into it. The sword made a *snicker-snack* sound as it sliced into the ruby ground. Unlike the Queen of Spades' blade, her weapon didn't stick.

Vanessa cried in pure rage just as Michael ran into her. He forced her to the ground, and the Vorpal Sword clattered away. Instantly, the haze over her mind retreated. She took a deep breath and looked herself over as she stood. She had bruised her elbow when she had fallen but otherwise was no worse for wear. Everyone else was staring at her.

"I'm sorry. I have control of myself."

"I don't think you should draw that again," Michael said. "Maybe you should let me hold it."

She slid the sheath onto the blade before she picked it up. "No, I don't think that's a good idea."

"My mind is as strong as yours, but it hasn't been exposed to the blade yet. If you draw it again, it might take you over even quicker."

She laughed. "Do you really want to get into an argument about whose mind is stronger? I seem to remember a certain someone walking into the Mermaid Lagoon in Neverland because he heard a mermaid's song." He blushed, and she laughed. "It doesn't really matter. It overwhelmed me so quickly that you wouldn't be able to stand against it for long. If anyone needs to draw it, it should be the one best with a sword." She looked at the shattered watch. "I guess we're back where we started. Does anyone have any other ideas?"

"How close is this to other ghostly realms?" Michael asked.

"What do you mean?"

"Do you think we could reach ghosts in Neverland?"

Vanessa's eyes widened. "Rosebud?"

"Can we get her here?"

"What good would that do?"

"Maybe it wouldn't do much, but I've never regretted having a fairy on my side, and in this situation, I can't think of a better fairy than her."

"This Rosebud," the Queen of Clubs said. "You have spoken of her before. She is a servant of the Queen of Hearts, I assume?"

"What?" Michael asked. "Oh, I see. Because of the roses. No, Rosebud is the ghost of a fairy who has aided us in the past, but she isn't from this realm."

The Queen of Clubs' bottom face scrunched her brow. "Now that we are essentially *in* the ghostly realm, I believe I can help you summon her."

Michael blinked. "You can?"

The Queen of Clubs leaped into the air. She flipped over so her bottom head was now on the top. Her arms and legs seemed to melt until they had changed shape so that she was once again standing on her legs instead of her hands. It shouldn't have made a difference. The card looked exactly the same no matter which side was on top. Still, she seemed darker and had a more ominous feel. Her gaze made shivers run down Vanessa's spine.

"Yes, I am well acquainted with the workings of spirits," the Queen of Clubs said.

"I thought your domain was life."

"When inverted, we become our opposites," the Queen of Diamonds said. "It's not a change we like to undergo, but we can if the need arises."

"And given all that has happened," the Queen of Clubs said, "I judge that there is a need. Diamonds, do I have your consent to continue?"

The Queen of Diamonds looked up to a stained glass window, whose pieces were different shades of red. Outside, Vanessa could barely make out a ghost floating past it. The Queen of Diamonds nodded once, and the Queen of Clubs motioned for Michael to stand before her. He gave Vanessa a quick glance before obeying. The Queen of Clubs raised her hands, and shadows swirled around Michael, howling and causing the temperature to drop several degrees.

"Speak the spirit's true name."

"Rosebud." Michael gasped. "No, that's not it. Michael Darling Rosebud."

Of course that would be Rosebud's true name. Fairies weren't born in the traditional way. When a human child laughed for the first time, that laugh became a fairy. Rosebud had been born from Michael's own laugh, and he'd always had a connection to her, though he hadn't realized it until he had met her ghost in Neverland.

The shadows swirled around Michael faster. More appeared in the air around him until they were all Vanessa could see. There was a musical sound in the air that she recognized as the fairy language. The darkness seemed to melt away until all that remained was a ball no larger than her fist. When that faded away, the lithe form of the ghostly fairy Rosebud appeared, glowing with the same pale blue light that had become all too familiar.

"Rosebud!" Michael cried out. "It's so good to see you."

The fairy bobbed up and down. Vanessa had studied some of the fairy language since returning from Neverland, but the fairy spoke too fast for her to understand. Michael, on the other hand, smiled and nodded.

"Well, I'm sure you'll forgive me. As you can see, we have a situation."

The fairy looked around. As if seeing Vanessa for the first time, she flew around her head, spurting out a quick series of words that she thought she caught the meaning of.

"Yes, I'm glad to see you, too," Michael said. "I don't suppose you know of a way to reverse a world that's started to turn ghostly."

Rosebud flew back to Michael and landed on his hand. She spoke quickly, and he laughed.

Michael told them, "She said that if she knew how to reverse something that's become a ghost, she wouldn't still be dead. Is there anything you can do to help, Rosebud?" He nodded as she spoke. "She doesn't know, but she seems stronger here, so there might be something."

Vanessa sighed. "So much for that idea. Unless anyone has anything better, we should at least see what's going on in Hearts' territory."

The fairy bobbed up and down again, and Vanessa smiled. "Yes, I guess that is something you can help with."

"Wonderland is divided into four quadrants," the Queen of Diamonds said. "The lands of Hearts are in the north. If you fly in that direction, you'll hit her palace."

Rosebud bobbed and flew north, moving straight through the wall.

The Queen of Spades looked to Michael. "That will be helpful. The birds were always too flighty to be consistent allies, and while the caterpillar is harder to talk to than most insects, they are often no greater help. It will be good to have someone who can scout through the air. How long will she take?"

"It's hard to say," Michael said. "I would guess no more than a few minutes, unless she gets distracted."

Almost on cue, Rosebud flew through the wall and bounced in the air in front of Michael. She spoke so fast that even he had to ask her to repeat herself. When she did, Michael went pale.

"What's wrong?" Vanessa asked. "Are the white Looking Glass soldiers still there?"

"She didn't see any Looking Glass soldiers at all, white or red. No cards, either."

"Then what's the problem?" Vanessa asked. "It sounds as if you're saying we have no army to fight."

He shook his head and took several deep breaths. "No, I'm definitely not saying that. Rosebud is no good with large numbers, but the new army stretched as far as she could see, covering almost all of Hearts' territory. It was made entirely of ghosts, and Hook was at its head."

28

T hen, James Hook rules the lands of Hearts," the Queen of Spades said. "It has been a long time since any of our lands were ruled by anything other than a face card. Even then, Wonderland was split between the two jokers. I don't even know the last time any part of this realm was ruled by anything other than a card."

Rosebud chittered something, and Michael translated. "He doesn't rule it. His army is like a hoard of locusts. It consumes everything in its path. Right now, it's in Hearts' territory, but it will spread soon."

"We couldn't defend against the Looking Glass forces," Vanessa said. "What are we supposed to do against an army even more powerful?"

She looked from one queen to another. All three of them looked as inanimate as the cards that they were. Even the Queen of Spades looked scared, and the sight left Vanessa with a bitter taste in her mouth.

After several seconds, Will stepped forward. "We attack them."

"Just like that?" Vanessa asked. "We just attack an army of ghosts?"

Michael patted the pouch on his belt. "He may have a point.

We have wisp dust. Ghosts are never as tough as they seem once you are able to actually affect them."

"Do you have enough dust for all the cards?"

Michael blushed. "I didn't actually give every magical item I found to the Court."

Vanessa made a mock frown. Technically, it was against regulations, but most Knights had an item or two squirreled away. "What do you have?"

He tapped the pouch with the wisp dust. "This is one of Saint Nicholas's bags. I spent over a month gathering the dust. I have a lot of it."

Both Vanessa and Will stared at him. It was several seconds before Vanessa could bring herself to speak. "You have one of Santa Claus's bags? How on earth did you get one of those?"

"Is that really important right now? We have enough dust for every card in the army. Even if we didn't, though, going after them has to be better than letting them come to us."

Both heads of the Queen of Spades nodded. "He has a point. Anything is better than just sitting here and waiting to be conquered."

"If that were true, why didn't you attack before?" Vanessa asked.

"Before, defeat was likely but not certain, and our world hadn't started changing into a haven for the dead." She gave Rosebud a slight bow. "No offense intended, Lady Rosebud."

The fairy danced around her for a second before returning to Michael. She sputtered something, and Michael let out a breath. "She's upset that I stole dust." Michael looked at the fairy. "I'm sorry, Rosebud. We all have to do what we have to do, and without this dust, Hook will win." He turned to the queens. "I'll go to the front gate. Have the cards go out in single file. I'll sprinkle them as they come out. We can go back through the portal we used to get here. We can strike at the center of the lands of Hearts from there."

Vanessa walked out with him, though she didn't say anything until they were outside the castle.

"Do you really think we can win?" she asked.

"Against an army of ghosts with numbers at least twice that of our own with forces so weak that they get tired if they have to go more than a few miles? Not a chance."

"Then why are we doing this?"

He looked toward the north, and Vanessa followed his gaze. The horizon glowed blue, and Vanessa shivered in a way that had nothing to do with the chill in the air. "Because we don't have to beat their entire army. All we have to do is get to Hook. You can fight him with that sword. Once we do that, I don't think the ghosts will be much of a threat."

"What are you basing that on?"

"On the fact that no ghosts we've run into have been very good at working together. Last time, we basically fought off an army with only a handful of people. Hook has to be the one holding them together."

"You're taking an awful lot on faith," she said.

He grinned. "Crazy, isn't it?"

She stared at him, but before she could say another word, the ace of clubs marched out of the castle. Like the Queen of Clubs, it had inverted itself, though what that meant in this card's case, she could only guess. Michael sprinkled the dust on it as it passed. One by one, the other cards filed out in ascending order and lined up outside the gate. Will came out with the jacks. The queens were last. Once again, the Queen of Diamonds took the lead. No one spoke on their march toward the portal to the lands of Hearts. The cards moved in an almost eerie uniformity, so much so that the sound of their footsteps was perfectly in sync.

The landscape was even grayer, and the road was only half as wide as it had been when they had come. It was weaker, too, and more than once, she felt it crack when she took a step. The large rock the Queen of Diamonds stopped next to was bright red, but it lacked the glimmer of the road. She drew a design with her finger and the stone melted away.

"Through there is Hearts' territory."

"Are you sure about this?" Vanessa asked. "Once we go through this hole, there will be no turning back."

"There's already no turning back," the Queen of Spades said. "We either do this, or we consign Wonderland to this gray death."

Each of the queens nodded. The jack of spades raised his sword and gave a battle cry. He jumped in, followed shortly by the rest of the spades and the queen herself. The other cards were more cautious, but none of them hesitated. Will nodded at both Vanessa and Michael before following.

"Half a league onward," Michael said and then jumped in himself.

This seemed like a terrible idea, but for the life of her, Vanessa couldn't think of a better one. She took a deep breath and jumped into the hole toward the lands of Hearts.

Once again, there was that strange falling sensation. This time, however, she didn't slow, and she slammed into the sandy ground. The impact knocked the wind out of her, and she coughed as she inhaled sand. Michael and Will apparently had the same problem, though the cards had no such issue. They got up and Rosebud flew back to Michael.

"Someone saw us coming," Michael said.

"That's impossible," the Queen of Diamonds said. "The paths connecting the realms don't move in traditional ways. We didn't actually fall through the sky. There was nothing for anyone to see."

"Well, however they found out, there's a full squadron of ghosts heading this way."

"I guess it's time to see how effective this dust of yours is," the Queen of Spades said. "Form up!"

The spades lined up, with their spears held forward. Vanessa's mind flashed back to the last time she had been recruited to face a ghost army led by James Hook. She let out a small chuckle. That was not something she had ever expected to happen twice.

The ghosts came over the horizon. They marched at a steady pace. It seemed like their footsteps should have made a sound, but they remained eerily silent. The Queen of Spades held her sword forward and shouted. The spade army ran forward as one unit, kicking up a cloud of sand. It made Vanessa think of a charging Roman legion. They slammed into the oncoming ghosts. Screaming filled the air, though Vanessa heard it as much with her mind as with her ears. Spirits exploded, so many that they released a wave of cold. Vanessa realized there were cards among the ghosts as well. Thin chains wound around them.

"They're not ghosts," she said. "They're specters."

"What's the difference?" Will asked.

"Specters are bound against their will, usually by a curse of some sort. They are easier to call up in numbers, from what I understand, but they're not as powerful as true ghosts."

"The cards are almost all hearts," the Queen of Clubs said as she struck with a dark metal mace, disintegrating a spirit. She pointed at one, a ten that was engaged against a four. "I recognize that one. The Queen of Hearts killed him almost twenty years ago for stepping on a rose." She pointed at a seven. "And

that one was executed fifteen years ago. These must be everyone the Queen of Hearts ever killed."

"But she's killed hundreds," the Queen of Diamonds said.
"Thousands. Every time she loses her temper, she calls for the
headsman. At least a full deck's worth are executed every year."

The Queen of Clubs nodded and spread her arms over the
gathered army. In spite of their numbers, the ghosts were being beaten back. The Queen of Spades mowed through them
like they were wheat before a scythe. Some of her cards had
fallen as well, but their numbers were only the smallest fraction of the ghosts that had been destroyed. The entire battle
lasted less than a minute, and the only reason the beach wasn't
littered with the corpses of their enemies was because ghosts
didn't leave bodies. As the cards fought the last few pockets
of resistance, another ghost came out of the ground. This one
was brighter and more solid than the rest. It had been human
once and carried the same curved sword as the pirates of the
Jolly Roger.

Michael noticed it, too, and he screamed and ran forward.
His sword almost seemed to flow into his hand. He didn't even
slow as he cut down the few ghosts that got in his way. The pirate noticed him coming. He flew forward, his own sword little
more than a white blur. The two met with such force that many
of the nearest cards were flattened by the sheer magnitude of
the impact.

Vanessa was one of the best sword masters the Knights
had. She was better by far than Michael, but she had no doubt
that if he had come against her, filled with rage, she wouldn't
have lasted long. She wasn't watching the techniques taught to
the Knights, or those of any mortal school of fighting, for that
matter. She was watching Michael Darling, friend of Peter Pan,
fighting a pirate who was in the service of Captain James Hook,

and it was like Neverland itself reached out to empower one of its own.

The two fought in a blur of motion. The rest of the ghosts had been cut down, but everyone, person and card alike, stared at the battle, though none dared to get too close. Even Rosebud drifted over to Vanessa and sat on her shoulder, muttering something too softly to be heard.

The ghost's sword darted forward, but Michael moved like lightning. His blade sliced into the ghost's side. The pirate screamed, and Michael pressed his advantage, delivering a series of powerful blows that knocked the spirit's sword away, which vanished as soon as it left its hand. The ghost was on the ground, fear evident in its face.

"Please, sir, mercy."

"Where is Hook?"

The pirate nodded and tried to scramble to its feet, but Michael took a step forward, forcing the ghost to stay down. "He's at the palace, sir. The Queen of Hearts' palace, I mean."

"What does he want? What is he doing here?"

"You don't know?"

"Besides turning Wonderland into a new home for ghosts."

The pirate laughed. "Home? You think this is home. Hook would never lower himself to call a place like this home." It scoffed at the black water. "It doesn't even have a proper ocean."

Michael pressed his sword against the ghost's throat. "Then what?"

"A body! He wants a body. He thinks he can get one here."

"There are literally billions of people in the world he could possess. Why would he come here for a body?"

The ghost got to its feet slowly. When Michael didn't react, it took a step back and calmed a little. "A possessed body isn't the same as having one of your own, boy. Sooner or later, a spirit has to leave a possessed body. Your own, on the other hand, you can stay in forever."

Vanessa and Will exchanged glances, but Michael kept his focus on the ghost. "Hook's own body died twenty years ago."

"I know. The mates told him it was madness, but Hook said this was the right place for it then."

Michael turned to look at Vanessa in disbelief before returning his attention to the dead pirate. "Fine, but what does that have to do with turning Wonderland into a dead wasteland?"

"Nothing, as far as I know, but that was the price the Cat demanded in exchange for his help."

"And what exactly is the Cat doing to help?"

The ghost stood up straighter, and Vanessa caught the faint smell of something rotten. "You don't really expect me to answer that, do you?"

Michael advanced with his blade forward, but the ghost didn't even flinch this time. It breathed in the fog, and a heartbeat later, it was twice as big as before. The huge ghost lunged forward, but Michael had been expecting it. He fell backward, thrusting his blade upward. It cut into the spirit as it soared over him. Michael rolled to his feet and gave three quick slashes. The ghost's leg came off, melting into motes of blue light. The ghost screamed in pain and crashed to the ground. Michael was already on it, moving so fast that Vanessa couldn't make out his sword. It looked as if he was cutting away the extra mass the ghost had gained, and after a few seconds the pirate had returned to normal size.

"You know, you might want to actually learn a little bit about fighting. Relying too much on special abilities won't get you very far." Michael smirked. "Though you won't be getting very far, anyway, at least not unless you can do us some good. Why does the Cat want this done with Wonderland?"

"Because once it's finished, the Cat can mold this world to its desires, and meld it with others so it can escape. It can even make Hook a body then. It can make one for us all. That was the price we demanded."

"That's not how it works. Maybe the rulers of a realm could do that, at least if they had any idea how, but you don't have one, do you? That's why your army doesn't have any cards. Living cards, anyway. The Queen of Hearts has abandoned you, hasn't she? I doubt the other queens will help you." Michael's eyes went wide, and he turned to the card queens. "Wait, unless the Cheshire Cat has some sort of authority over this world, too?"

"No," the Queen of Diamonds said. "There are only four realms. Most denizens of Wonderland owe their allegiance to one of the four queens, to one extent or another. The Cheshire Cat, though, has never sworn fealty to anyone."

Michael turned to Vanessa. "Would that be enough? Someone who isn't beholden to one of the rulers but who is an independent power?"

"I wouldn't think so normally." She gazed out into the sea. Even the smell of salt water was muted. "This world is changing, though. Who knows what it could mean as far as control over this realm? It might be possible."

The ghost took a slow step backward. "I've told you everything I know. Please, let me go."

The pirate screamed as a black blade erupted from its chest. It looked down at the weapon that had skewered it. All at once, the ghost collapsed into motes of light. The Queen of Spades stood there, weapon in hand. She glared at Michael.

"Why did you do that?" he asked.

"Look what it helped do to our lands. You may be mighty, Michael Darling, but you do not have the authority to pardon or condemn anyone here. It got what it deserved."

Michael opened his mouth to speak, but Vanessa put a hand on his shoulder. "Leave it alone. She does have a point, after all. At least, we have managed to take out one of Hook's lieutenants."

"Will he know?" Will asked. "I mean he probably only has a few of the stronger ghosts."

"He might," Michael admitted.

"He knew we were coming anyway, if they managed to sense us coming through the portal," the Queen of Spades said. "If anything, this is just a reason to move faster."

Vanessa didn't think that logic made sense, but the other card queens nodded. She had a feeling she wouldn't be able to convince them otherwise, but she had to try. Before she could respond, however, the cards were marching, leaving the three humans behind.

"They sure make their decisions quickly, don't they?" Vanessa said as the cards disappeared behind a sand dune.

Will started to say something, but before he could get a whole word out, the Queen of Spades came running back toward them with the other cards trailing right behind. She had inverted herself and looked more frightened than Vanessa would have thought possible for the warlike queen.

"Run!"

What they had faced a few minutes before had been a horde of ghosts. What came after them now was a sea. There were so many ghosts that Vanessa couldn't even see the land they were walking on. More than that, another horde marched in the air just above the first. They outnumbered the cards at least a hundred to one, and Vanessa did the only thing she could think of. She ran.

Vanessa, Michael, and Will quickly outpaced the cards, not that it would do any good. With that many ghosts, it was only a matter of time before they would all be overcome. A wisp flew out of the air and flew right through Michael. He brought his hand to his chest and gasped. They should have expected that. Wherever there were ghosts, there were always wisps. Vanessa glared.

"I told you not to antagonize the wisps!"

"Is this really the best time to be talking about that?"

"Well, we're probably about to die, so it's not like I'll get another chance."

"Can you get us home?" Will asked between gasping breaths.

"I don't have the watch anymore."

"You didn't have the watch the first time you tried to get us here. That almost worked."

He had a point. It probably wouldn't work, but she didn't have any better ideas. She tried to concentrate but her heart beat too fast, and she couldn't slow her breath or close her eyes in an effort to calm herself, not with the ghosts swiftly gaining on them.

"It's no use."

A wall of red light appeared behind them, and the cold that had been slowly seeping into her flesh vanished as the ghosts slammed into it. The ones in the front screamed as the barrier incinerated them, not even leaving the blue motes. Vanessa and the others stopped in their tracks. They looked around. Not far away, a man wearing a red robe stood with his hands held forward. They glowed red; he had obviously formed the wall.

It took Vanessa a few seconds to recognize him. "That's a red bishop."

Will nodded and looked toward the ghosts. "Men of faith do often have power over the dead."

"But a Looking Glass soldier?" Vanessa asked.

Will took a few seconds to catch his breath. "It makes as much sense as anything else in this land."

The bishop lowered his hands, and the wall extended behind him and disappeared over the horizon. He walked over to them. His hair was as red as flame, and though he had a smooth face, he seemed to walk with a great weight on his shoulders. "Please, come with me."

He scurried down the beach without waiting for them to answer. After a few seconds, he apparently realized they weren't following and turned to beckon them over.

"Are you serious?" Vanessa asked. "You're our enemy. Why should we trust you?"

"I just saved your life, for one thing."

"From your allies."

"No." He spoke so firmly that the barrier holding back the ghosts pulsed. "Those *things* are not our allies. We were betrayed. Now, my lady wishes to speak to you."

"So *she* can betray *us*," Vanessa said. "I don't think so."

The bishop lifted his hands. Red lightning ran up his fingers. Vanessa had no idea what god this bishop worshiped, but it apparently granted its servant a measure of power. Vanessa raised her hand, though she doubted she'd be able to counter anything he did.

"Wait! Why does she want to see us?"

"Because you're the enemy of the pirate, and now so is she. She wants to help you defeat him."

"We can't trust them," the Queen of Spades said.

Vanessa looked back. Cracks had formed on the wall and wisps of ghostly light leaked through. It wouldn't last for long.

"We don't exactly have a lot of choices."

The Queen of Diamonds nodded, but the other two didn't look too sure. Then, the wall shattered with the sound of breaking glass and a wave of cold washed over them. The bishop uttered a string of curses that Vanessa had never thought to hear from the mouth of a holy man.

"Go. A hundred yards down the beach, there's a rock formation. There, you'll find a cave. My queen is there along with what forces she could salvage."

"What do you mean?" Vanessa asked. "Aren't you coming with us?"

The ghosts howled as they neared. Red lightning ran through the bishop's entire body, filling the air with the smell of ozone. His eyes glowed, and his voice had an odd crackle to it. "I will hold them back."

A bolt of lightning shot from his hands, destroying at least a dozen of the spirits, but even that much was barely a drop in a very large sea.

The bishop looked back at them. "Go!"

The card queens were already running with their respective cards right behind them, though anything below five had trouble keeping up. Vanessa and her companions followed. Flashes of red light illuminated the sky as they ran. The ground shook, and Vanessa's skin tingled with the electricity in the air. A wisp shot through Michael, and he stumbled, but he managed to keep his footing. Rosebud flew behind Michael, and when another wisp approached, she stabbed it with a ghostly blade, causing it to wink out of existence.

Vanessa saw the rock formation ahead. Desperately, she hoped the cave wouldn't be hard to find, though she had no idea how a cave wall would protect them from hundreds of ghosts and wisps.

"Here!" a short stubby man in red called out as soon as they reached the formation.

Vanessa altered her path and headed in his direction. The cards were disappearing into a hole in the ground. A ghostly ace of hearts rushed forward, passing through two of the clubs. The cards withered, which only encouraged the rest of the cards to go faster. Another ghost passed through Vanessa, and she felt like all the warmth had been taken from her. She didn't even realize she had slowed until Michael took her hand and practically dragged her into the cave. One of the ghosts tried to come in, but there was a red flash and it was driven away. Curious, Vanessa extended her hands and tried to sense the nature of the shield.

"It's similar to the wards the Knights put around their safe houses, but those took months to put up. Unless the Looking Glass soldiers were planning to retreat here, this can't have been here more than a few hours."

"Yes," the Red Queen said from behind her, "my bishop put it up just before he went to find you. Given that there are so many ghosts out there that I can't even see more than a few feet outside the cave, I take it he won't be returning."

Vanessa turned and gave her a slight bow. The Red Queen's robes were in tatters, but they still looked finer than most things Vanessa had ever worn. "Yes, he sacrificed himself to save us."

"That is regrettable. His loss is a great one."

"You have others, don't you?"

"Some," the Red Queen admitted, "but none as skilled." She looked Vanessa and her companions up and down. "I hope you are worth it."

"He said you wanted to talk to us."

The Red Queen deflated. "Yes. The Cheshire Cat took control after the pirate raised the army of ghosts. They attacked the card queens and took back the White Queen. Then they turned against us."

Vanessa looked over her shoulder at the horde of ghosts pressing against the cave mouth. She gave the Red Queen a level look. "That much is obvious. What we don't know is how he was able to do *this* to Wonderland."

"It was the pirate's plan all along. Once the other three queens had left, he instructed the Queen of Hearts what to do." She looked at the three card queens. "We just needed to get you out of Wonderland. That was why I left the watch in my quarters."

"I wondered why that was so easy." Vanessa brushed the leather-bound hilt with the tip of her fingers. "Out of curiosity, why did you leave the Vorpal Sword there, too?"

"To be honest, I thought it would destroy you. No one else has been able to wield it without eventually turning against their friends. That's beside the point, though. I just want to go home."

"Home?" Vanessa asked. "You helped to unleash the ghosts of everyone who has ever died in Wonderland, and you expect me to help you leave this world?"

"You must! My people are dying."

"As are ours," the Queen of Spades said, drawing her sword.

There was murder in the card's eyes, and she moved to strike. Vanessa put a hand on the hilt of the Vorpal Sword. She could feel heat through the leather. The Red Queen hissed and backed up. The Queen of Spades backed up as well. Vanessa simply shook her head.

"She deserves it," the Queen of Spades said.

"Probably, but she's not your prisoner. In fact, she's the one who just saved us." Vanessa glared at the Red Queen. "If you want our help, you're going to have to return the favor. Where is James Hook?"

If possible, she looked even more frightened than she had been when Vanessa had touched the Vorpal Sword. "No, you don't want to go there. Hook is the most terrifying person I have ever seen. I think even the Cat fears him."

"He's the key to all of this," Vanessa said. "Tell us where to find him, or I will give you to the Queen of Spades." Once again, she looked at the cave mouth. "Or better yet, I throw you out into that."

"You don't understand. He'll know you're coming. I was able to escape when we were betrayed. The Queen of Hearts didn't. Neither did the White Queen. Hook probably interrogated her."

"I know a little about questioning that one," the Queen of Spades said. "He will not find it so easy to get information from her that she doesn't wish to give."

The Red Queen scoffed. "I am just as strong as she is, and trust me, the pirate would have no trouble breaking me. In fact, the White Queen would know that. She would know that her fall was inevitable and might well have cooperated to avoid the torture."

"Unless she also knows that we will rescue her before she

breaks," Michael said. "That might actually give her the strength to hold out even longer."

The Red Queen stared at him before bringing her hand to her forehead. "I hate this ability of hers. It always gives me a headache."

"Where are they?"

"They are in the Queen of Hearts' throne room."

"We know how to get there," the Queen of Spades said.

The Red Queen shook her head. "We found the passages you used and sealed them off. There is another way, though." She looked at Vanessa. "You know the path down the cliff that you used to get to the palace before?"

"Yes."

"Near the bottom of the path, there is a group of rosebushes."

"There are a lot of those around the Queen of Hearts' palace."

"Well, these are white roses that were painted red." Vanessa rolled her eyes but didn't say anything. The Red Queen sighed and kept speaking. "Beneath them, there is the entrance to an underground path. That leads directly to the Queen of Hearts' chambers. From there, it's not far to the throne room."

"What about defenses?" Vanessa asked. "If that's a path that leads into the castle, they won't have left it unguarded."

"The Queen of Hearts would never want anyone to know about her secret escape route, and without telling them that, she can't have it guarded."

"How do you know about it, then?"

The Red Queen raised her eyebrow. "I was an ally to the White Queen, and she has access to more information than you would believe." She waved to the cave mouth, which was still flooded with ghosts. "Getting through that will be a greater challenge."

"We still have the wisp dust," Michael said.

Vanessa shivered. Whatever magic the bishop had used to block out the spirits apparently didn't prevent their cold from seeping into the cave. She shook her head. "That's like trying to dry yourself with a towel in the middle of a thunderstorm."

Michael considered for a second before his eyes wandered down to the Vorpal Sword. His hand twitched, and Vanessa thought he would ask for it again. Instead, he met her gaze. "You can do it."

"What?"

"You can get through them with that."

"I'm not sure I can protect any of you if I do. The sword might go after you, too."

"Then go alone."

She ran her fingers along the hilt and shivered. "Michael, I can't use the Vorpal Sword like that. If I hold it for more than a few seconds, I'll lose control."

"That's an easy problem to get around."

She blinked. "It is?"

"Yes. Just don't lose control."

She gave him a level look, but her expression softened after a second. She looked to the horde of ghosts and then to the card queens. Even the Queen of Spades looked frightened.

Vanessa sighed. "I'm not sure I can make it."

"I wasn't sure I could fight off the wraith with a broken arm, remember?"

"You remember how that ended with us trapped in Neverland, right?"

"We got out, though." Michael gave her a smile that only lasted a second. "Vanessa, there's no other way. We'll come after you as soon as we can, but in case we can't, you have to go save the White Queen."

Vanessa looked out of the cave. The ghosts were as thick as

ever. They weren't trying to come in anymore. They were just moving past the cave mouth. Could there really be so many, or were they just circling around? She had no way to be sure. The sword at her side quivered. It seemed eager to be used. She walked to the cave mouth and took a deep breath. Ice crystals had formed on the stone, and her breath steamed as she exhaled. She drew the Vorpal Sword.

The ghosts outside suddenly didn't seem like so great a threat. She had been treated by wisp dust, but somehow, she knew she would have been fine even without it. She lifted the sword, and it practically hummed with power. She cried out and ran forward. As soon as she cut into the first one, the sword made that distinctive *snicker-snack* sound. After the first half dozen had been cut down, some of them tried to flee, but her blade found them before they got out of range. The spirits wailed as they melted away before her assault. There were so many, but she didn't care. The Vorpal Sword was hungry, and she charged forward, intending to feed it its fill.

30

Vanessa was a whirlwind of death. The ghosts came at her from all sides. She had studied enough battle doctrine to know that only in stories did one person fight so many and live. Of course, in places like Wonderland, stories were the stuff of reality, and the craziest plans were the ones that often worked. The Vorpal Sword seemed to move of its own accord, dragging her arm along with it. Its magic spread to the rest of her body, too, as her legs moved in maneuvers she had never learned, giving her a grace that was far beyond what any human could possess.

She wasn't sure how long she walked, nor was she entirely certain she was going in the right direction. At one point, she noticed the ground beneath her feet had changed from grainy sand to the packed dirt of a road. She still couldn't see the landscape around her through all the ghosts. A slight weight landed on her shoulder, though she had no idea how it had gotten through the attacking spirits.

"It's the finch. What are you doing?"

She managed a glance to one side. The cardinal sat on her shoulder. Its bright red feathers were a stark contrast to the gray landscape, and it looked calm in spite of the chaos around it.

"I'm trying to get through these ghosts."

"You seem to be doing okay, but there are a lot of them. Do you want help?"

One of the ghostly spears grazed her forearm before she cut down its wielder. There was a flash of cold where her flesh had been pierced, but it vanished a second later.

"I don't really think you can help me here."

"Sure I can. Do you want help or not?"

The spirit of a crane flew down and stabbed its beak into her arm before she decapitated it. "Fine, yes. Do whatever you can."

The cardinal chirped and flew away. Another ghost slashed across her leg before she cut it down. The cold didn't fade anymore. She was faltering, and even the magic of the Vorpal Sword had its limits. She wouldn't last long. The screaming ghosts drowned out everything, everything except for the caw.

The sound cut through the wailing, and a black streak burst the spirit of a giant bug just before it bit Vanessa. She would have stopped and stared, but the sword's blade dragged her along, fighting even though her body screamed at her to stop. More streaks of black cut down the ghosts, and in a few moments everything was silent. The air was filled with motes of ghostly light, and the ground was covered in ravens.

She stopped and nearly fell to the ground, exhausted. The sword's magic waned inside of her, its bloodlust apparently sated, at least for now. She managed to put it in its sheath. Exhaustion washed over her, and it was all she could do to remain standing and look to the nearest raven. It hopped forward, and for a moment, stories of the birds plucking out eyes filled her mind. Ravens were symbols of death, and it was said that their beaks could be used as potent weapons against the undead, though she had never seen any evidence of that until now.

"You helped me," she said.

"Yes, the cardinal said a finch needed help, and we birds need to stick together in times like this." It cocked its head. "You don't look like any finch I've ever seen."

"She told me she is," the cardinal said as it fluttered to a nearby branch. "I can tell when someone is lying to me, you know."

The raven bowed, "Of course, your eminence."

"'Your eminence'?" Vanessa asked.

The raven cawed and seemed confused. He looked over at the red bird. "Certainly. He's a cardinal. Cardinals are holy people. Even a finch should know that."

Vanessa blinked and looked from one bird to another. Not for the first time, the idiosyncrasies of Wonderland made her shake her head in frustration. Still, it was better than the alternative.

"The castle," she said through heavy breaths. "I need to get into the castle."

"Yes," the raven said. "There are people going in and out of the castle all the time. They use doors, which are a lot more trouble than they are worth. Much easier to just fly in."

She managed to calm her breathing. "The ghosts hurt me. I can't get off the ground right now."

The raven looked her up and down. "Well, you're much too heavy for us to carry. Do you know the cliff that overlooks the palace?"

"Yes, though I'm not sure how to get there from here."

The raven flapped its wings once but didn't take off. The gesture caused a gust of wind to brush against her face. The bird cawed.

"Why, that is simplicity in itself. We can lead you there. Then, you need only go to the top of the cliff and jump off. We will catch you and slow your fall."

Without waiting for her to respond, the raven took off. The rest of the birds followed. watched them go, brushing a black feather off her face before turning to the cardinal.

"I'm just supposed to jump off a hundred-foot-tall cliff and trust that they will catch me?"

"Oh, don't worry about that. They know that if they don't, I'll scold them quite severely."

Vanessa raised an eyebrow. "You'll scold them?"

"Yes, my scoldings can be quite harsh. They wouldn't want that."

She pursed her lips. "Maybe I should just try the secret passage."

"I guess if you want to try the slow way."

"That might be best."

She was feeling a little stronger and managed to get to her feet. She was still tired, but she could move forward. She was even more aware of the Vorpal Sword than before. The cardinal returned to her shoulder while the raven kept hopping from branch to branch, showing her the way. She knew she wasn't far from the castle. When they had been captured, it hadn't taken them long to reach the palace, but the bird apparently took her on a roundabout route because it took her an hour to finally reach the top of the cliff. She looked down at the castle, and her heart fell. In spite of what the Red Queen had said, the entire perimeter of the castle was being patrolled, including the area where she'd find the secret passage. Most of the soldiers were cards, though there were a fair number of ghosts as well. She could probably get to the painted rosebush, but she'd never be able to find any secret passage before she was spotted. That left only one choice. She looked up, but the sky was empty. There was no raven in sight. Even the one that had led her here had vanished. She turned to the cardinal.

"Where are the ravens?"

"They don't like being seen, especially now. Ghosts are their enemies, you know, and there are so many of them here that it wouldn't be wise for the ravens to make themselves too obvious."

"But you're sure they'll catch me?"

"Oh yes. They are nearby. You can trust me on that."

She stared down between the castle and the cliff face. The patrols were too regular and the interval between them was too small. There was no way she'd be able to get in that way. That only left the cliff. This was madness, which actually made her feel a little better when she considered it. She crept up to the edge of the cliff. The ground seemed impossibly far away. This wasn't going to get any easier if she put it off, so she backed up several steps. Then, she ran forward as fast as she could. Just before she reached the edge, she jumped. It took all her self-control not to scream as she started her fall. Something grabbed on to her left shoulder. An instant later, something else grabbed her right. Four ravens had grabbed her and were flapping fiercely. Her fall had slowed, but the ground was still approaching with alarming rapidity. She was moving forward almost as fast as she was going down, though. She cleared the wall, and the ravens brought her toward a tower. She screamed, thinking she would crash into the wall, but the ravens moved her around it until she saw a window. With impossible coordination, they dropped her inside.

She rolled as she hit the ground. She slammed into a wall and cried out, tasting her own blood. The world didn't stop spinning for several seconds. When she could finally stand up, she felt like her entire body was bruised. The tower room was empty. A crack spread across the wall she'd crashed into, but she had no idea if that had been there before or if that had been caused by her impact. A wrecked table leaned against the wall, having been worn down by exposure to the elements. She found a trapdoor in the floor, and she grunted as she pulled it open to find stone stairs leading down. She drew her sword, the normal one, and started down.

Hurt as she was, it was difficult to move silently. The stairs groaned under her weight, though they grew quieter as she descended. The door at the base of the tower had long since rotted away. She walked through the doorway and found herself in an old and dusty passageway. It was obvious no one had been here in a long time. She didn't know which way to go, so she picked a direction at random. Her movements swirled up a cloud of dust that sent her into a fit of coughing. Once she recovered, she listened, but it didn't seem like anyone had heard her, so she crept forward again. After a few seconds, she thought she heard something up ahead. She moved as quietly as she could manage until the hall intersected with another passage. A pair of cards passed her, but they didn't see her. She waited, but the patrols inside apparently weren't as regular as the ones outside because it was a full half hour before any more cards came. They didn't see her, either. She waited five minutes before following.

The castle wasn't as complex as other palaces she'd been to. Apparently, this was the main passage, and before long, she found herself in more populated areas. There were mostly cards, but there was also the occasional ghost. She thought she recognized one as a member of Hook's crew, but she didn't dare get close enough to be sure. Now that she was in the main area, she had to be sneakier. Thankfully, she also overheard people talking and soon learned exactly where the throne room was. Something was off about the hallways, and it took her a while to figure out what that was. The whole palace had a run-down feel to it. It wasn't just that the valuables had been looted, tapestries torn down, and stone pedestals overturned after whatever had been on there had been stolen. There were cobwebs in almost every corner, and the floor creaked under her feet, despite its being made out of stone. She even caught a hint of salt water in the air. Nearly all mystical realms were mutable to one degree or another, but the speed at which Wonderland changed never ceased to surprise her.

It didn't take her long to make her way to the throne room. There were a number of side entrances, and she pushed one of them open slowly enough for it to not make a sound. She couldn't see anything, but she could listen.

"You have what you want," Hook's voice said. "It's time you gave me what you promised me."

"The world has not fallen yet," the Cheshire Cat's melodic voice said. "There are still pockets of resistance."

"It's fallen," Hook said. "Trust me. It hasn't hit the ground yet, but it has definitely fallen."

"Then let it hit the ground and break into a thousand tiny pieces. Once that happens, I'll create bodies for you and the rest of your men. What is your hurry?"

"You haven't been dead for two decades."

"And you haven't been trapped for nearly two millennia. You will wait until I am free."

"Then let's get the rest of what we need from her to shatter this place."

"You will not find getting information out of me as easy as you expect," the familiar voice of the White Queen said.

Vanessa stepped into the room and moved behind a large pillar before peeking around it. Spirits floated around the room. The Cheshire Cat hovered a dozen feet above the ground. Hook stood at eye level with it; on the ground, held by ghostly chains, was the White Queen. She was looking right at Vanessa and smiled before looking back at her captors. For their part, neither Hook nor the Cheshire Cat noticed what she was looking at. At first, she worried that the ghosts might see her, but these weren't Hook's crew. Rather, these were the wispy specters that she had seen earlier. They had no will of their own, and as such, they weren't likely to notice her unless Hook did first.

"I admit," the Cheshire Cat said, "you have a stronger will than I expected, even for a queen. Still, I have no doubt that even you will break, given the right pressure."

"Perhaps," the White Queen said, "but there is much that I know that you do not, and that knowledge gives me power to resist you. You would have done better to summon me than capture me. Then, I might have been inclined to aid you. As it is, I do not think so."

"Summon you?" Hook said.

"Of course. The hall at the end of the valley in the Looking Glass Land can be used to summon all Looking Glass queens. It could even draw me away from your tender mercies if it were to be used properly."

"Interesting," Hook said, "but not particularly relevant. Where is the Red Queen? What happened to the ghosts we sent after that incursion? Was it the other card queens?"

Hook was right. That was interesting knowledge, especially because it wasn't relevant for him. To someone who wanted to rescue the White Queen, on the other hand . . .

"That would be convenient for you, would it not? For all your enemies to line up for you to knock them down, but this is not that sort of game. No, James Hook. I'm afraid most of your ghosts were destroyed by simple birds."

"Birds?" The Cheshire Cat seemed interested.

"Ravens, specifically."

The Cat made a hacking sound. "I despise ravens. Curse Merlin for ever allowing the creatures into Wonderland."

"Did he now?" the White Queen asked. "Those animals that guard the borders between realms have a habit of going where they were never intended. I'm not sure my descendant could have stopped them if he had tried."

The Cheshire Cat purred, its body fading in and out of existence as it circled the queen. "Your descendent. I had forgotten. Tell me, my dear White Queen, have you had the child that will eventually lead to that wizard being born?"

"In a way I have," the White Queen said. "In a way I have not."

"Because your past is our future, you mean? Interesting."

"What is it?" Hook asked.

"Just that I might have another way out, even if I did not realize it."

Hook ground his teeth. "We had a deal, Cat."

"Yes, indeed we did, but do you think that I would be so foolish as to trust you, James Hook?"

"Treacherous animal."

The main doors burst open. Eight red pawns rushed in, bearing heavy clubs. They struck at the ghosts. Caught off guard, most of the spirits were destroyed before they even had a chance to act. The pawns closed in on Hook, but the pirate ghost moved like the wind, dodging and weaving through their attacks and occasionally cutting down one of them on his own. Vanessa stared for a second, but another battle cry came from the door. Michael and Will came in with Rosebud hovering above them. After them entered two red knights and the Red Queen. In the hall behind them, Vanessa could make out fallen cards, all of them hearts. The standing ones, on the other hand, were all spades.

Not having a reason to stay hidden, Vanessa charged in to join the battle as well, drawing her ordinary sword. She had cut down three ghosts before anyone noticed her, but though she didn't wield the Vorpal Sword, she was still a master of the blade. It was practically an extension of who she was, and against specters like these, that was more than enough. She fought her way to her friends, and the three stood back-to-back.

"How did you get here?" Vanessa asked.

"The ghosts disappeared a little while after you left," Michael said. "At first, we thought they all came after you, but we saw black feathers all over the ground. We found a writing desk that told us that her cousins had destroyed the ghosts."

"Cousins?" Vanessa asked.

"How is a raven like a writing desk?" Will asked. "The Lady asked us that, but she never told us the answer. Apparently, the two are related, though."

"So then, you took the secret passage the Red Queen told you about? How did you get past all the guards?"

Michael shrugged as he fought off a pair of ghostly cards. "The Queen of Spades made a distraction near the front of the palace. The Red Queen knew exactly where it was, so we didn't need much time. Once we got to the Queen of Hearts' chambers, it was easy enough to get here."

"Impressive," the Cheshire Cat said, "and yet you have already lost."

Vanessa looked up. The Cat stood over the White Queen, its razor claws extended and touching her throat. Vanessa almost attacked, but somehow, she doubted she would be able to do anything before that creature spilled out the White Queen's lifeblood.

"What do you want?" Vanessa asked. "Why are you doing this?"

"After all I've told you, you still don't know?" The Cheshire Cat vanished, though its claws remained in place. Its face appeared not far from Vanessa. "I want to be free. It's the same thing I've always wanted."

"How will destroying Wonderland free you?"

"Isn't it obvious? Wonderland cannot hold me if it does not exist. Then, I will be free to enter the Looking Glass Land."

Michael and Vanessa exchanged glances. Michael chuckled and Vanessa smiled so wide her face hurt. Even Rosebud bobbed up and down in the air as if laughing.

"Wow," she said. "I didn't think it would be so easy to get the Cat to divulge its evil plan. We barely even tried."

"I guess it doesn't really have experience with this sort of thing."

The Cat hissed and leaped toward Michael. He raised his sword and managed to cut off its right paw. The Cat yowled in pain. It landed and spun to face him again, but it didn't attack. Michael grinned.

"I was starting to wonder if you were related to ghosts. At least it's close enough for wisp dust to affect you."

Ghosts rushed Will, who was holding his own against them, and the Red Queen's knights had engaged the remaining hearts cards. Hook had managed to take down half of the pawns that had attacked him, but he hadn't done so uninjured. His hook had snapped off, and that arm hung limply at his side. He still held his sword and was managing to keep the pawns at bay, though only barely. Half a dozen spades came through the door as well, engaging the enemies that were still unoccupied. Vanessa didn't bother to take in many details. Her attention was focused solely on the Cheshire Cat.

In spite of its wound, the Cat didn't bleed. It looked at its severed paw and held out the stump, as if expecting it to materialize there. It didn't, of course. The Cat glared at Michael, who raised his sword. In that second, Vanessa decided that if the Cat jumped again, she would catch it with the Vorpal Sword. It didn't, though. It just stared at Michael.

"How dare you come into my realm. This place is mine, and you are not welcome here."

Michael scoffed. "Last I checked, it belonged to the four queens. You may have one of them held prisoner somewhere, but that still leaves three others, and they will not follow you."

"The queens, leaders of this world?" The Cat laughed even as it sharpened its claws on the stone floor, leaving gashes. "They are newly come, barely a score of decades. That is nothing to me."

"So what?" the Red Queen asked. "You were here before they were? Before us?"

It spoke in a low voice that made the ground vibrate under Vanessa's feet. "I was here when the foundations of Wonderland were laid. I saw this world come into being, while my other half was trapped on the other side of the mirror."

"My lands?" the Red Queen asked.

The Cat laughed. "Don't look so surprised. This is a small world. It cannot hope to hold something like me at my full power. Soon, the boundary between worlds will fall, and I will be able to cross over and claim what was taken. Then nothing will be able to stop me."

"What are you talking about?" Vanessa asked.

The Cat glared at her. "Now, you don't expect me to tell you that, do you? Not after you mocked me for doing just that."

Michael sighed. "Spoke too soon?"

"So it would seem," Vanessa said. "How about we just kill it?"

Michael grinned. "Works for me."

"Go," Will said, having dispatched the few remaining spirits. "I'll guard your backs."

Vanessa and Michael had done this type of attack before, though never with Will as the third man. As one, they rushed forward, swords slashing. The Cheshire Cat vanished before they reached it, but acting on impulse, Vanessa slashed at the severed paw, which still lay on the floor. The Cat had displayed an ability to disconnect parts of its body before and yet still remain linked to them. She only hoped that still held true. Her sword sliced through the paw, and the Cat cried out, appearing halfway between Vanessa and Michael. It hissed and then leaped, not for any of them, but for the Red Queen.

Its remaining claws sank into her scarlet robe and it bit into her. She screamed, but as in chess, the queen was one of the strongest pieces on the board. She quickly recovered and delivered a powerful blow with her fist right into the Cat's head. It wasn't prepared for the ferocity of her attack, and its head collapsed inward. It melted away, its substance almost seeming to seep into the queen.

Hook gaped as the remnants of his former ally disappeared. He glared, first at Michael, then at Vanessa and Will.

"Through the window!" Hook called.

At first, Vanessa had no idea what he was talking about, but a second later, a pair of ghosts came out of the ground near the White Queen. Each grabbed on to her chains and dragged her into the air. Will cried out and tried to grab her, but they were already out of reach. The ghosts flew through a window near the ceiling, which shattered when they pulled the White Queen through it. At a motion from Michael, Rosebud went after them. Then Hook fled, flying out of the door the others had come in through. Michael started after him, but Vanessa grabbed his arm.

"No, this is obviously a trap."

"No, it's not. We've beaten them. Now he's on the run."

"Michael, think. Hook is not half so foolish. If he really wanted to get away from us, he would have fled through a wall or out of the ceiling. The only reason he ran through a door was that he wants to be followed."

"We can't just let him get away."

A ten of spades stepped between them. "Wonderland is not big, Sir Vanessa. Hook will not be able to hide for long." It bowed to Vanessa and turned to Michael. "His strongest ally is dead, thanks to you, and this world is not so easy to leave if all the queens are against him. He's trapped here. He has no resources. We will be able to find him eventually, but your friend is right. Going after him now would be beyond foolish."

Michael looked like he was about to respond, but Vanessa put a hand on his shoulder. He tensed at her touch but relaxed a moment later. He looked into her eyes and nodded once before returning his attention to the gathered queens.

"She's right," the Red Queen said after several seconds of uneasy silence. "Right now, we need to consolidate our forces and figure out how to rescue the White Queen."

"I have an idea on that," Vanessa said. "I was hiding, but she knew I was there. She mentioned that all the Looking Glass queens could be summoned from the hall at the end of the valley in the Looking Glass Land. She specifically said that it could even be used to summon her out of Hook's grasp."

"That makes sense," the Red Queen said. "Yes, I should have thought of that before. In fact, that may have been part of the Cat's plan to get there."

"Why would the Cheshire Cat want to go there?" Will asked.

"Isn't it obvious?" the Red Queen asked. "It wants to get its body back."

"Its body?"

"Why yes. The Cat is a spirit. Didn't you know?"

All three Knights exchanged glances before Vanessa answered. "No, we had no idea."

"How else could it cross so easily between this realm and the ghostly one?" The Red Queen looked around. "Though, I suppose the two are not so far apart at the moment. It is a spirit that knows how to manifest itself."

"And its body is in the Looking Glass Land?"

The Red Queen stared at them as if that were the stupidest question she had ever heard. Even the other queens looked incredulous.

"Its body is the most fearsome creature to ever walk the lands of the other side of the mirror, and even that is with it acting only on instinct. If it had a mind and soul of its own, especially one as cunning as the Cat, it would be a power unmatched in your world or mine. The Jabberwock."

The magical blade at Vanessa's waist vibrated at the sound of that name. She glanced at it before looking back to the Red Queen. "The Jabberwock? Are you serious?"

"Yes. That sword was crafted with the express purpose of killing it, though its power was never tested."

"What is a Jabberwock?" Will asked.

"'Beware the Jabberwock, my son! / The jaws that bite, the claws that catch!'" Vanessa said. "'And, as in uffish thought he stood, the Jabberwock, with eyes of flame, / Came whiffling through the tulgey wood.'"

"I don't understand," Will said.

"You're not supposed to. From what the Lady taught me, the Jabberwock is the sort of creature that will drive you mad if you know too much about it."

"An Old One?" Will said. "I didn't know those actually existed."

"The truth is we're not entirely sure." She pursed her lips. "If the Cat really is a Jabberwock, or something resembling it, that might actually explain a lot about both Wonderland and the Looking Glass Land. This might all be the Cheshire Cat's nature given form." She shuddered. "That fight could have been a disaster."

"We still need to rescue the White Queen," Michael said.

"How long will Rosebud be gone?" Will asked.

As if summoned by her name, the ghostly fairy drifted through a wall. She spoke quickly, and Michael's shoulder slumped.

"She lost them." He kicked at the ground. "The White Queen is too powerful to let someone like Hook have her. We need to get back to the Looking Glass Land."

"We don't have the watch anymore," Vanessa said.

"There is another way," the Red Queen said. "I made sure there was a way left open to us in case the ghost should turn against us."

"You mean you didn't trust him?"

"I was ambitious." She laughed. "I was not a fool. The way out of Wonderland lies in the very center, where all four realms meet."

"That is a dangerous area," the ten of spades said. "Normal rules don't apply there."

"It sounds like the rest of Wonderland," Michael said.

"The rules of Wonderland make sense," the card said. "The center doesn't. It is insanity given form."

"A land of madness in the middle of a land of madness?" Michael asked. "That doesn't sound promising."

"Maybe we'll get lucky, and what these people see as madness will be completely sane to us," Will said. "Like the eye of a storm."

Vanessa looked at the broken window through which the White Queen had been taken. Pale blue clouds swirled outside. She let out a long breath. "I get the feeling it won't be so easy. I don't suppose your queen knows of another way out of Wonderland."

"If she did, we would not have needed the watch," the card said. "The Queen of Diamonds knows more about the ways through Wonderland than anyone, but I don't believe even she knows how to leave this place."

"Normally, I'd say we should check with her to see if there's a way to avoid the danger, but Wonderland is even worse than Neverland was when Peter was captured," Michael said. "There's not much time left."

"The center it is, then," Vanessa said. She turned to the Red Queen. "Lead the way."

The Red Queen inclined her head and led them out of the palace. As before, everything but the road felt transient. The ground looked more like fog than earth, and the road ran through it like a stream of blood. They walked on it for three hours. Strangely enough, even the ten of spades kept up with them without apparent difficulty. As they neared the center, the land grew wilder. The ghostly nature of the world lessened, as if the center could somehow resist Hook's influence even better than the rest of the land. Abruptly, a gust of hot air brought a thick cloud of fog, and when it faded, they saw a tower reaching to the sky a few yards in front of them. The side closest to them was made of interlocking stone hearts. The tower was only ten feet wide.

Vanessa moved around it. Each side was made of a different suit, but there was no way in, as far as she could tell. She turned to the Red Queen. "How exactly are we supposed to get through?"

"The wall will let you through if you are meant to," the queen said.

She placed her hand on one of the hearts and pressed. It glowed under her touch, and there was a hum that made the air vibrate against her skin. She pushed harder, but the wall resisted, and the Red Queen scowled. "It wasn't like this last time."

She tried each of the sides, but none yielded to her touch. Michael and Will did the same, but for them, the stones didn't even glow. When Vanessa touched the hearts, they quivered a little, and she thought she felt excitement from the sword at her side. The sword would be able to break through. She had no doubt about that, but still she hesitated. Michael seemed to read her mind.

"Can you control it?"

"I don't know."

"Perhaps I should try," the ten said.

It reached forward. As soon as it touched the hearts, a spark of energy came out of the wall and threw the card back. It slammed into a tree and folded around it. For a moment, Vanessa worried it had been killed. She touched it and it stirred. It blinked and let out a breath as it stood up. A small tear had formed at the top of it, though the injury seemed not to bother the card.

"Let me try again."

"Are you sure?"

"Not entirely, but serving your purpose serves my lady."

It moved around the tower until it came to the spade side. This time, when it touched the wall, the spades parted, revealing a field that was far wider than should have been contained by the walls. The ten backed up.

"This is as far as I go."

"What about serving your queen?" Will asked.

"I can best serve her from here."

"Are you sure?"

It stared into the field for several seconds before respond-ing. "Again, no, but here I will remain."

"Fine." Vanessa turned to the Red Queen. "What can we ex-pect in there?"

"I don't know. Last time, it was a red-and-black board. All the pieces were flat, and the rules were completely different."

She shivered but Michael laughed. "Checkers? They gave you a checkerboard, and that unnerved you."

"You don't know what it was like."

"So what can we expect?" Michael asked.

"I've heard of places like this," Vanessa said. "They're shaped by perceptions. Neverland is like it a little, but even that is mostly shaped by Peter. Something as fluid as this, though, can be confusing the more people that go in. It could be anything."

"We should wait for the guide," the Red Queen said.

"What guide?"

"I believe she is referring to me," a singsong voice said.

A card with a clown painted on it stood up. It danced around a little, and the ten backed up even more. "Have care, my friends. Jokers can be unpredictable."

"A joker?" Vanessa asked. "I understand you used to rule this realm."

"Once, long ago, but the past is the past, at least it is if you are not her counterpart." He bowed to the Red Queen. "You wish passage again?"

"Yes," the Red Queen said. "We wish for you to guide us within the center."

"Come with me," the joker said. "You should probably hold hands. If you get separated, you may not find your way out again."

"The Red Queen first," Vanessa said.

"How very brave of you."

Vanessa gave her a level look. "You're the strongest of all of us, and you know it."

"I don't wield that blade."

Vanessa looked down at the Vorpal Sword and smirked. "Do you really want me to draw this in there, where getting separated is apparently a danger?"

The queen frowned and moved toward the opening. She took Michael's hand. Will went after him. In spite of her words, Vanessa took the back, feeling that she would be best able to deal with any danger that came from behind. The queen crossed into the field, practically dragging the rest of them through. The air rippled as they each crossed the border. Vanessa held her breath. Cold washed over her, not unlike the other times she'd crossed between worlds. Her hand came free as she realized Will was gone. So were the rest of them. Only the joker remained. It twisted around and smiled before continuing. As it took a step, the landscape morphed. Instead of a field, she was now in a plain white hall. It was completely featureless. There was no apparent source of light. The joker moved forward on silent feet, not even pausing to make sure she followed.

"Wait." Her voice echoed for several seconds. "Where are we?"

"We are in the center." Its voice was flat. "I should think that was obvious."

"Where are the others?"

"They are also in the center."

Vanessa made an exaggerated motion of looking around. "Where?"

The joker shrugged and kept walking. "The center is a complicated place, not meant for mortal understanding."

He wasn't inclined to say more, so she just followed. She had difficulty keeping track of time. Rather, she found herself in a mental haze. Suddenly, there were people in suits all around her. She couldn't quite make out what they were saying, but she had the sense that it was something very businesslike. She realized she was in a suit, too. One of the people, a matronly woman with steel-gray hair, turned an iron gaze on her.

"What do you think, Vanessa?" she asked in a voice like a whipcrack.

"Think about what?"

The woman huffed and turned to her companion. "See? I told you. She's no good."

Anger welled up in Vanessa. "As if I wanted to belong to your world."

"And why should you? You would never fit in here, just like you can't fit into the world you have chosen."

"What are you talking about?" Vanessa asked. "I fit in with the Knights perfectly."

"Oh, do you? If you had done what Michael has done, you would have been expelled without a second thought. Instead, the Court gave him a second chance, with a punishment that was barely a slap on the wrist."

"They made him a squire again."

"That rank is in name only, and you know it. As soon as you are done with this mission, he'll be a full Knight again. They would never want to lose someone like him. You, on the other hand, what are you? A foolish woman who once survived a gargoyle attack." She scoffed. "Many people survive their first encounter with the supernatural. That does not make you special. That does not make you one of the Unveiled."

Vanessa's breath caught in her throat. She didn't know how she had gotten here nor how the old woman had known those words, but they stung. Michael was Unveiled: someone who had encountered the supernatural as a child. That wasn't really all that rare. Many children did, but most learned to forget about such encounters and eventually convince themselves it had only been their imaginations. All of Michael's siblings save Wendy had. Michael hadn't. He had grown up knowing full well that there was a world out there that most knew nothing about. He had been a natural recruit for the Knights of the Round and had excelled ever since he had joined. Vanessa, on the other hand, had encountered it as an adult. She'd had to learn a lot of what someone like Michael had known all along. The Court placed a high value on Knights such as him. Vanessa's shoulders slumped, and the woman sneered at her.

"Turn back and return the way you came, Vanessa Finch. This is no place for the likes of you."

Vanessa thought about it. Had the woman said another word, she might have, but as she was about to turn, she caught sight of the joker. He hadn't slowed. The crowd parted for him, seemingly without even knowing they had done it. They even left a path for her. The joker was almost out of sight. Vanessa's mind sharpened, and she took off after it. The old woman cried after her, but her words slid off Vanessa as if they were made of water. She grabbed the card's arm. It was slick, as if covered in oil, and it slipped out of her grasp.

"You almost left me there."

"I did nothing of the sort. I told you. You must follow. If you do not, that is no fault of mine."

"What if I had turned back?"

"You can never return to where you have been. Time changes all things. You would not have gone back. You would have been elsewhere."

"But where?" Vanessa asked.

"Somewhere that is not here and not where you intend to go. Do you really need to know more than that?"

She resisted the urge to reach for her sword. A part of her

recognized that the anger had come from the weapon itself. For the first time, she realized that she wasn't sure the Vorpal Sword would be enough to overcome this card, at least not here. There was a sense of power about the card that she hadn't felt since she had stood before Mora, the witch of Neverland. She took a deep breath and moved to follow. The card had never stopped walking and was now almost out of sight again. Vanessa ran to catch up with it just as it turned a corner. The hall ended, and the sounds of the crowd behind her vanished. Hanging on the wall was a large mirror. Vanessa gazed into it and realized that Michael, Will, and the Red Queen were all in the reflection. All were staring back at her in awe. Vanessa looked around and realized that they were all around her.

She blinked and asked, "Where were you?"

"The joker took me . . ." Michael shuddered, as did Rosebud, who was sitting on his shoulder. "I wouldn't even know how to explain it."

Will nodded. "Me neither." He turned to the Red Queen. "What about you?"

The Red Queen looked visibly shaken. "It was disturbing. Let's just leave it at that." She motioned to the mirror. The people looking back at them didn't look quite right, though it took Vanessa several seconds to identify what was different. A few strands of hair in her reflection were out of place, and Michael's eyes were a slightly different shade. There were other minor differences as well, but she would have had to study the reflection for a long time to identify them. The Red Queen touched the mirror, and its surface rippled under her fingers, causing her reflection to vanish. She pushed forward, and her hand disappeared, followed by the rest of her. The other three exchanged glances. The joker nodded and turned to go.

"Where are you going?" Vanessa asked.

The joker didn't turn as it spoke. "I have no desire to leave this world. I leave that to you."

It rounded a corner, and the sound of its footsteps vanished. Vanessa turned back to the mirror. Michael was already pushing through. As soon as he vanished, Will motioned for Vanessa to go first. She bowed her head and pressed through. This time, the crossing was a lot easier. It was like walking out of the sun and into the shade. Once again, she found herself in a wide room. She wasn't sure if it was the same hall that they had been in before, as it was a nearly exact duplicate. There was even a door at the end of it that had fallen down, though it took Vanessa a second to realize it was on the opposite side from the door she had cut down earlier. They stepped on it as they walked out. Vanessa looked over the valley, which looked like the same chessboard as before. The Red Queen was walking down the hill, heading for the queen's space. She was halfway there before Vanessa and her companions followed, not that the Red Queen noticed. She crossed onto the queen's space, and only then did she stop. When Vanessa and the others crossed into it, it was like walking into a warm summer day. The Red Queen glowed with a radiance so bright that it almost hurt to look at her. Her power seemed to permeate everything. Vanessa could feel the Red Queen's will writhing inside of her head. It made her shiver, but the queen only smiled.

"Shall we go?"

"There's something I don't understand," Vanessa said. "Last time we came here, we were on the white side. We certainly didn't see any hall to summon queens. Doesn't this mean it's on this side?"

"Of course not. The hall is at the end of the board, not the beginning. We have to cross to the other side."

"But it's not on the other side."

"Of course it is. It's always on the other side. Come."

This time, a lot more of the spaces were clear, which made sense, considering how far a queen could move as opposed to a knight. The Red Queen somehow encompassed them in her power. There was the rushing sensation as they moved across the board. This time, however, the movement came to an abrupt halt. Suddenly, there were a line of pawns before them, stout men dressed in white, each bearing a spear and shield. The Red Queen screamed and grabbed her forehead. She fell to the ground. Vanessa ran to her side. The Red Queen's skin was burning up, and blood had rushed to her face. Her eyes bulged, and her screaming made Vanessa think her ears would bleed. In spite of that, the pawns remained stationary.

"Help. Me." The Red Queen held tight to Vanessa, her voice weak and full of desperation.

Then the Red Queen fell on the ground. Vanessa tried to help her up, but the queen's body went stiff. Her eyes erupted in red flame. She screamed once more, and the fire streamed out of each eye. The flames swirled around each other and formed into a wide grin. The Red Queen had become nothing more than an emaciated corpse that could have been dead for weeks. Meanwhile, the grin widened, forming a cat's head. Its body popped into existence a second later.

"Thank you. I don't think I could have gotten out of Wonderland without your help."

"You possessed her," Vanessa said.

The Cat laughed. "Do you think it's such a simple thing to destroy a spirit as old as I? Merlin himself could not do that. All he could do was separate me from my power. Thanks to you, that is undone."

"The Jabberwock," Michael said. "It's here somewhere."

As if on cue, a roar pierced the air. Vanessa looked behind

her. A . . . thing, a blob that looked like nothing more than eyes and teeth, rushed toward them. Bones and weapons seemed to have been stuck into its hide, and it left burned grass in its wake. Vanessa recognized it as the same thing she had seen around the melted buildings the first time she'd been here. The Cat laughed and leaped toward the creature. It looked impossibly small next to it and dove straight in. As it had done with the Red Queen, the Cat seemed to melt. The Jabberwock's skin rippled and the whole creature shrank until it once again was in the shape of a cat. It smiled.

"Now, that is much better."

Michael's hand rested on his hilt. "Now what?"

"Now, I break out of the twin worlds and find one better suited to my tastes." The Cat's grin grew even wider. "That is after I have fun in the world that Merlin so loved."

"I've seen cats play with their food," Vanessa said. "We can't allow that."

"My dear girl, you cannot prevent it."

The Cat leaped at her, moving so fast her eyes couldn't follow. She tried to draw the Vorpal Sword, but the Cat sank its teeth into her arm before her hand had even moved the few inches to the hilt. Michael slashed at it, but the Cat grabbed his blade in the air with a hand that hadn't been there a moment before. The limb had just grown right out of the Cat's head. Michael struggled to pull it away, but the skeletal arm held fast. Will tried to cut it free, but his weapon bounced off of the arm, releasing a shower of sparks.

The Cat laughed and let Vanessa go. It jumped to the ground, and she felt a line of pain flare up on her side. She looked down and saw that the Cat had cut her belt away. The Vorpal Sword's sheath fell to the ground. Another hand emerged from the Cat's body, and it tried to draw the weapon. The hilt hissed as it touched it and filled the air with the stench of rotting flesh. The Cat jumped back, and its body morphed. It still stood on four legs, but everything else had changed.

It had grown until Vanessa and the rest only came up to half its height. Its hind legs were at least three times the size of its rear ones. The substance of its body was the most disturbing. It was made of tremendous worms, each as thick as her arm. They wiggled and writhed, making Vanessa feel like she was going to throw up. Two of them formed circles in the spots where its eyes should have been. It spoke in a voice like wet paper.

"How did you do that?"

Vanessa blinked, and it was all she could do not to take a step back. "Do what?"

"The weapon is protected."

Michael dove to the ground and picked up the Vorpal Sword. He drew it and slashed in one fluid motion, cutting into one of the worms. Black blood spilled out with a stench that drove Vanessa back. Michael, however, stood tall, the power of the Vorpal Sword coursing through him. The Cat roared, but when Michael slashed again, it backed up, right into a quartet of pawns.

As if they had been waiting for it, the pawns stepped forward and stabbed at the Cat's wormy body. Their spears, however, slid off the worms and sank into the spaces between them. The Cheshire Cat flexed, and all four shafts shattered. The Cat turned to its new attackers, and with one slash of its paws took out all of them. The queen's bishop, which had stood behind one of the pawns, raised its hand. A beam of white light moved diagonally and illuminated the Cat. With a hiss, one of the worms burned away. In the same instant, the queen's knight rushed forward and slammed its heavy mace into the creature. There was a splat, and more black fluid leaked from where it had hit. The Cat, however, looked at them like mice. It didn't even bother to raise its hand against the knight. It simply rolled over the horse-man until it stood right in front of the bishop. It looked the holy piece in the eye, and the air around it warped. The bishop screamed, its robes becoming black, before the whole thing collapsed to ash.

Michael was already running forward again. The Vorpal Sword shone so brightly Vanessa couldn't look at it. The Cheshire Cat roared, and the force of the sound knocked Michael off his feet. The Cat charged, but Rosebud interposed herself between them. For a second, the Cat stared at her, amused. Then, something passed in its face. It sniffed and turned away. It took a few steps before looking over its shoulder and shuddering. Then it leaped away, crossing the horizon in a single bound. The three Knights looked at one another. Michael had a hungry look in his eyes. The Vorpal Sword quavered in his hands. Will walked up to him, and Michael turned to face him.

Then Vanessa rushed forward and delivered a quick strike to his wrists that made him drop the sword. He blinked and took a deep breath as Vanessa carefully sheathed the sword. She managed to tie the belt where it had been cut and replaced the sword on her waist. Then she glanced at the horizon. "Well, that was odd."

"Just like the wraith in Neverland," Michael said.

"That, at least, made sense," Vanessa said. "Rosebud and the wraith both came from you. As far as I know, you have nothing in common with either the Cheshire Cat or the Jabberwock." She looked in the direction it had fled. "We still need to do something about that."

"I'm open to suggestions," Michael said.

"The White Queen," Will said.

Vanessa nodded. "She supposedly knows more than anyone.

If we can get to the hall and figure out how to summon her, she might be able to help us."

Michael looked toward the end of the board. The white defenses now had a gaping hole in them. Once again, only a few of the spaces were clear. One of them held the White Queen's castle. If there was a hall, it made sense that it would be there.

Vanessa took a step, and the three of them rushed to that square. It looked different from the last time they had been there, but Vanessa was hard-pressed to say what it was. They reached the gate, and she raised her hand, trying to sense where they created the portal earlier, but the air seemed dead. She shivered as she walked through it. Inside was a single room with a great white throne at the end of it. It glimmered, and if Vanessa had to guess, she would say it had been carved out of a single pearl. A long table took up most of the room. Three of the chairs near the center had names written on them. *Vanessa, Michael,* and *William.*

"That's creepy," said Will.

"The White Queen can see the future," Vanessa said. "She must have known we would be here eventually."

"So what do we do?"

"We sit, obviously," Vanessa said.

She walked over to the chair with her name on it and plopped down. A band of energy ran through the table as she settled in. She motioned to her companions, and they sat next to her. The table began to glow, and Vanessa smelled something rotten. Suddenly, the body of the Red Queen sat across from Vanessa. The table hummed and the White Queen appeared beside her.

"That is curious," she said. "I did not see that coming."

"You didn't?" Vanessa asked. "You're the one that told us to come here."

"Of course I did. That isn't what I was speaking of." She turned to the Red Queen. "That I did not see her death. There aren't many things that could block my sight. I take it that the Cat has been reunited with its body?"

"Yes."

"Then that is why there is an army of ghosts about to come into my hall."

"What?"

The hall doors burst open, filling the chamber with a pale blue light. Hook stepped inside, looking almost solid. His very presence robbed the heat from the air. The wounds he had taken in the previous fight had been healed, and even his hook had been restored. Some of his pirates came in with him. All of them wore wicked grins and carried ghostly weapons. Behind them, a myriad of ghosts covered the landscape outside, filling up the entire grid. Wisps hovered above them. Rosebud flew into the air, prepared to meet their attack, though she would be hopelessly outmatched. Worm creatures crawled in through the top of the doorway of the hall, and after a few seconds, the Cheshire Cat formed on the ceiling.

"I believe you will find us more evenly matched this time."

"We weren't exactly beating it last time," Michael said under his breath.

"You will not find this battle as easy as you believe," the White Queen said to the Cat. "We have allies of our own."

The Cat laughed. "Yes, I've seen your allies. I ate a number of them."

The White Queen laughed as well. "The pawns and others you destroyed were not allies. They were subjects. No, you will find our allies to be much more formidable foes."

"Oh?" Hook asked. "And where would these allies be? Are you going to just magically summon them?"

The pirates beside him laughed. Even some of the ghosts did, too, though Vanessa guessed they only mirrored Hook. The queen, however, joined in their laughter. It took the ghosts several seconds to notice, and one by one, they stopped laughing and stared at the White Queen.

"Magically indeed. You did realize this hall would summon the Looking Glass queens, didn't you?"

"Of course I did," Hook said. "The Cat told me. Ripping you out of Wonderland is what weakened the barrier. Without that, I could never have brought an army through."

"You misunderstand," said the White Queen. "This hall summons *all* the Looking Glass queens."

The air in the chair next to the Red Queen's body shimmered and then parted. A robed figure appeared there. Gray strands of hair tumbled out of the hood. Vanessa felt the smile form on her face as Alice, the Lady of the Knights of the Round and a Looking Glass queen in her own right, stood up to face the army of ghosts.

31

S ir Vanessa," the Lady said. "Would you care to tell me what I am doing here?"

"To tell you the truth, Lady, we summoned you by accident."

The Lady looked around. She winced at the sight of the dead Red Queen, but then her eyes fell on the ghosts. "Ah yes. Now, I see. Captain Hook, had you faced me instead of Michael last time, I believe the confrontation would have ended quite differently."

Michael stepped forward, but the Lady raised a hand. As brash as Michael was, even he wouldn't stand against a member of the Court who was prepared for battle. The Cheshire Cat dropped from the ceiling. Its form became fluid in the air, and when it landed, it was right side up. It sniffed at the Lady.

"Alice. I remember you."

"And I remember you. You were not an evil creature the last time I saw you."

"I am what I am. I was no different then. I only have more options now. You, on the other hand, have changed much. You were not half so mighty before."

"Humans change, Cat, unlike whatever you are."

She raised her hands, and azure flame formed around them, driving back the cold of the ghosts. The Cat grinned, but rather than attacking it, the Lady threw the fire at Captain Hook. The pirate sneered and sank into the ground. The fire passed through the space he had been in and impacted against one of the other ghosts. For a moment, its chains flashed brightly. The spirit screamed, but did not collapse into motes of light as Vanessa had seen before. Instead, this one exploded into half a dozen streaks of energy. Each one hit another ghost. The process repeated itself dozens of times before the spell fizzled out, leaving a bare handful of spirits. The Lady smirked. Her eyes wandered upward, and the wisps fled. Then, the Lady returned her attention to where Hook had disappeared.

"Your minions are not particularly strong, are they?"

Hook rose out of the ground right in front of the Lady, his sword moving in a white blur. The Lady caught it on her hand, which shimmered with gold light. She said a word in a language Vanessa didn't know, and the ghostly weapon snapped. Hook backed up, shock painting his face. The Lady threw back her head and laughed. It was an unearthly sound that echoed back and forth through the hall. Strangely enough, the echoes didn't soften. Rather, each one was a different volume. Vanessa felt an almost irresistible urge to laugh herself. The magic in the sword at her side quivered, though even it felt restrained. Will was laughing, and the White Queen didn't quite manage to suppress her smile. The ghosts behind Hook had erupted in hysterical laughter. Hook himself shimmered, and cracks spread through the skins of his lieutenants. The Lady stopped laughing, and the urge to giggle faded from Vanessa. The ghosts, however, did not stop chortling. Several fell to the ground, clutching their stomachs.

"What are you doing?" Hook asked. Strain showed on his face. He stood in front of one of the laughing ghosts. "Stop it. I command you. Stop."

The ghost in front of him exploded. Hook screamed and backed up. One by one, the other ghosts did the same until only a half dozen pirates were left. The Lady gave Hook a level look.

"When you attacked London, we were caught unawares. I swore it would not happen again."

"She has you cornered, Hook." The Cat laughed. "I don't think you're getting away this time."

"We needed that army," the pirate said.

"We needed that army to lay siege to this world until its borders weakened enough for me to cross out of it." It sneered at the Lady. "Her coming, however, accomplished the same thing. You have my thanks, Alice."

"You don't think I would let you get away so easily, do you?"

The Cat's laugh shook the ground. "Merlin could barely stop me, little girl. You won't even be an obstacle."

"You might have almost defeated Merlin, but you never tangled with the Lady of the Lake."

Ghostly chains shot out of the wall, wrapping around the Cheshire Cat. For a moment, it smiled as the worms writhed, but then its smile faded. It struggled against the chains, but even the worms that weren't restrained seemed paralyzed.

The Lady grunted. "It's stronger than I expected. I can't hold it and fight Hook at the same time. Sir Vanessa, you and your squires destroy the pirate if you can. Keep him busy if you can't." She gave Michael a small smile. "This is what you have been waiting for. I will handle the Cat. Do what you need to do."

She pointed, and a bolt of blue lightning shot out of her finger and struck the Cat. It yowled and tried again to break out of the chains. This time, darkness congealed around the bindings. The Lady shuddered as one of the links shattered. The Cat leaped at her, but a wall of blue light appeared in front of her. It bounced off the wall with a flash of energy.

Hook shot forward, once again armed with a ghostly blade. Michael lifted his sword and parried the attack. The two exchanged half a dozen furious blows before Vanessa got there. She tried to attack from behind, but another spirit, a stout man with a large nose, rose out of the ground and intercepted her attack. Vanessa took a step back.

"Smee."

"I bet you never thought you'd see me again."

"I rather hoped you had been destroyed." She slashed, but the dead bo'sun moved faster than he ever had in life. He sidestepped her strike and slashed into her side, sending a wave of cold through her, and half her body went numb. Will threw himself at the pirate. Vanessa half expected him to pass through the ghost, but the wisp dust had still not worn off, and he took the spirit to the ground. He untangled himself, managing to get a few cuts in before getting to his feet. Vanessa moved to stand next to him, but before they could close in, two other ghosts came at them. Will nodded to Vanessa and moved to intercept them while Vanessa crossed swords with Smee. The dead pirate seemed to be enjoying himself. If she hadn't been numb from her attack, she would have destroyed him easily. "You've improved. You were never a warrior."

"Yes, well, you'd be surprised how quickly you can learn when you're not bound by flesh."

"You were always a fool, though."

"What?"

A spear of white steel cut into the spirit. Smee's jaw dropped as he looked down. For a moment, he couldn't believe what he was seeing. He touched the point gingerly with his fingers before collapsing into motes of light. The White Queen smiled as she turned her weapon against another ghost.

Will had acquitted himself well. Only one of his enemies

remained, and it was clear that Will was the more skilled. Michael, on the other hand, wasn't doing so well. Ice chips had formed on his clothes where Hook's sword had cut into him, and he favored one leg. Vanessa and Will approached from different sides. The three struck at the same time. Hook caught Vanessa's sword on his hook even as he batted aside Michael's blade with his own. Hook twisted, catching Will's weapon with Vanessa's. He ripped the weapon out of her hand before cutting at her stomach. Vanessa cried out and jumped back. Her knees felt weak, and she felt like throwing up.

Michael tried to take advantage of the distraction, but Hook moved like the wind. Michael had gotten in a lucky blow when they had faced off in the catacombs of the Knights. He had managed to cut into Hook's throat with a sharp rock. Before that, only Peter Pan himself had been able to stand against Hook in single combat for more than a few seconds. Since the closest thing to a god here was the Cheshire Cat, Vanessa doubted that would do any good. They needed an edge, and the only one she could think of hung at her waist.

She drew the Vorpal Sword. She couldn't help but smile as the euphoric power rushed into her. She slashed. Hook tried to parry, but her weapon made that *snicker-snack* sound and sheered through his blade. Hook flew back just in time to avoid the worst of the blow. Vanessa pressed forward, enraged beyond reason. Another of the pirate ghosts tried to get in the way, but her sword flickered forward and dispatched it without any effort. For the first time, Hook's jaw quivered in fear. He rose up, but the Lady could apparently spare some attention from her battle with the Cheshire Cat. A ball of light splashed against the pirate and he fell to the ground. Hook scrambled to his feet and leaped into the air, but he came crashing to the ground before he had gone a few feet.

"What did you do to me, witch?"

The Lady flew through the air, shrouded in blue fire. She crashed into the Cheshire Cat. The flames reduced some of the worms to cinder, while the others flew in every direction before coming together again. The Lady gave Vanessa a look of desperation.

"Hurry, the binding won't last for long."

The sword hummed in her hand, and the world went red. All she could see was Hook, and she ran forward, screaming. Her weapon came down. Hook moved to one side, and the sword took a piece of his coat. He lunged forward, but she shifted her grip, bringing her sword between them, and Hook skidded to a stop. He threw himself to one side just before she would have split him in two. He turned and ran. Vanessa laughed before following. Hook stopped to face her, but before she got close, he turned and ran again. Vanessa was vaguely aware of Michael calling out to her, but the sword hummed too loudly for her to make out any words. Hook jumped to one side and landed on a raised platform. It pricked something in the back of Vanessa's mind, but she didn't care enough to try to remember what it was. She brought the sword down in a two-handed blow, but once again, Hook jumped aside.

"No!"

The Lady's cry cut through the red haze just as the Vorpal Sword cut through the table that had been used to summon the queens. There was a blinding flash of light that left red dots in Vanessa's vision. When her sight returned the table had been reduced to rubble. White bands of energy ran through it, and the air was almost alive with the dissipating energy. Hook stood atop it, but he no longer looked afraid. Vanessa slashed. He avoided the attack, but this time stood with full confidence, moving aside just enough to avoid the attack before thrusting with his own sword.

His strike caught Vanessa in her combat arm. The Vorpal Sword fell to the ground point first. It stabbed into the earth and sank in to the hilt. The wounds, combined with the energy the sword had required of her, had sapped her of her strength, and she fell to the ground.

Hook didn't even bother to finish her off. He just walked around her and approached the White Queen. She raised her sword, holding it in a stance that suggested she was much more skilled than Vanessa would have thought. The White Queen and the pirate exchanged a series of blows, and surprisingly, she seemed to be holding her own. More than once, her sword left a shallow cut on the ghost. Hook didn't look afraid, but he had lost much of his confidence.

Michael was moving around them, but the two combatants were an order of magnitude more skilled than either him or Vanessa. If he tried to interfere, he could just as easily get in the White Queen's way, and he knew it.

The White Queen made a mistake. It was so slight that Vanessa couldn't even be sure it actually *was* a mistake. She took a step that was just a little too big, causing her to overreach a fraction of an inch. If Hook had been armed with only a sword, the motion would have been insignificant, but the old pirate stepped in close. His hooked hand slashed across her stomach. The queen staggered. She tried to lift her weapon, but the strength drained out of her arms. Her sword started to fall, but it hadn't even left her grasp before Hook's weapon sliced into her neck. The queen went stiff. Ice crept across her body, and her eyes froze. She managed a whimper before falling. Her body shattered when it hit the ground.

Everything went silent. Even the Lady and the Cheshire Cat stopped their battle to stare at the remnants of what had once been the White Queen. Hook seemed unable to believe what he had just done. He threw back his head and laughed. The Cat chuckled as well, effortlessly avoiding an energy blast from the Lady. Hook jumped, and there was the sound of glass shattering. He rose into the air and flew out through the ceiling. The ground shook so hard Vanessa was thrown from her feet. A pale figure caught her, and she realized it was the White Queen. She stared at the monarch and then at the pieces that the queen had left when she had shattered. It didn't make sense, but the queen looked alive and well even as she stood next to the shattered remains of her own body.

"What's going on?"

"She lives backward," the Lady said. "For her, the past hasn't happened yet, though I don't really understand how she was here before Hook killed her."

"And your small mind wouldn't be able to," the Cheshire Cat said. "Not that it matters anymore."

It extended its claws and slashed at the air, leaving three bright green lines. The Lady screamed and threw her hands forward. Energy shot out, but before it reached the Cat, it vanished into the holes in the air before they faded away. The Lady rushed to where the Cat had disappeared and ran her hands over the air. Power cracked in the spot the holes had been. She cursed and did something to the air. It rippled but then the effect vanished.

"It's no use. It's gone."

"Gone where?"

"Our world."

"We have to go after it."

The Lady shook her head. "We can't. We don't exist in that world anymore."

Vanessa blinked. "What do you mean? That can't happen to us. We're not fairy tale characters."

"We may as well be. Don't you understand? Hook killed the White Queen."

"She seems to have gotten better," Will said.

"She lives life backward. For her, it hasn't happened yet."

"I still don't understand how that makes us not exist."

"She was Merlin's ancestor," the Lady said.

"Yes," Vanessa said. "She told us, but I don't understand how that works, either."

"She had just had her baby when I was here the first time, so for her, giving birth to her child hasn't happened yet. That child, like her, would have lived backward. At some point even further in the past, that child would have had a child of their own with the same peculiar relation to time, all the way back to Merlin himself."

A chill ran down Vanessa's spine. "No, you can't be serious."

"Very serious."

"What is it?" Will asked.

"Merlin founded the Knights of the Round," Vanessa said. "By killing the White Queen before she had her baby, Hook essentially prevented Merlin from ever being born. No Merlin means no one to guide Arthur. No Arthur, no Camelot. No Camelot, no Knights of the Round. Wonderland and the Looking Glass Land allow us to exist here." She waved a hand. "But out there? The world has changed, quite probably more than we can imagine. We might have never been born, and even if we were, we wouldn't be Knights." She turned to the Lady. "Is that why Hook came here? To destroy the Knights entirely?"

"It doesn't make sense," Michael said. "I mean I'm sure Hook would love to kill us all, but he had the White Queen as a prisoner for a long time. He could have killed her whenever he wanted."

"That wouldn't have been what the Cat wanted, though," the Lady said.

"I don't follow," said Michael.

"This world is still here. Merlin created it to exist outside of time, so eliminating the White Queen then wouldn't have done anything—though now that the Cat has escaped, it's falling apart."

The ground shook, and Vanessa was nearly thrown off her feet. She wasn't sure she understood what the Lady had said, but this wasn't the time for discussion of the theories of time and magic. "Lady, how do we stop the Cat if we can't even get to where it is?"

"It's not there yet," the Lady said. "It can't use the rabbit holes. The twin worlds were constructed explicitly to contain the Cat, so none of the normal entrances and exits will work for it."

"Contain the Cat?" Michael asked. "How would they do it?"

"I have no idea how," the Lady said. "The magic of creating realms has been lost for centuries. As to the why, however, there are old beings out there, creatures so great and powerful that the mere mention of their true names could drive you mad. I always believed the Cheshire Cat was one of those. It always had a tendency to warp the world around itself. Hence, we have Wonderland. The Looking Glass Land was constructed to contain its body. That kingdom is based on a game with very rigid rules, and only by understanding it can one win. That is almost the opposite of Wonderland."

"And we let it escape."

"It can't go down a rabbit hole," the Lady said again. "The

Cat has to burrow its way through, and that will take some time, but not much."

"So what do we do?" Vanessa asked.

The Lady closed her eyes and mumbled something in a musical language. It sounded a little like the fairy tongue, though Vanessa didn't understand any of the words. Just then, the ground shook. A crack formed at her feet and she backed up. Sickly yellow light bled out, and the acrid smell made her gag. The Lady clenched her teeth and brought her fists together. The light shifted from yellow to blue, and the crack in the ground closed up. The shaking stopped. For a second everything was calm, though the Lady was doubled over. Her face was red from exhaustion, and she was breathing too heavily to speak. Vanessa moved to her side to help her, but she waved the Knight away and stood up straight, taking a few seconds to compose herself.

"I won't be able to do that many more times," she said.

"What exactly did you do?"

"I held the Looking Glass Land together. It won't last, though. It's like trying to hold together broken glass."

"You need glue."

"What?"

Will cleared his throat. "Glue. You need something to hold the pieces together."

The Lady gave him a half smile. "If only it were so easy. The trouble is, young squire, that some rather large pieces are missing. When Hook's army tore into the world, they caused much damage, and we have nothing to fill the holes with."

"Wonderland," Vanessa said. "Whatever they did to Wonderland had made it mostly a ghostly dimension. What if you jam the pieces of Wonderland into the holes of the Looking Glass Land?"

For a second, the Lady just stared at them. Then, she laughed.

"If this were anywhere but a land of madness, I doubt it would work, but here? Why not?"

The Lady shifted her stance and started speaking in that same flowing language. This time, Vanessa thought she recognized a few words. She couldn't be sure, but she thought . . .

"Is that Atlantean?" Michael asked.

"I think so."

"I didn't think anyone spoke that," Will said.

"Neither did I."

There was a twinkle in the Lady's eyes at that, but she continued speaking. Waves of blue energy rolled out from her. The land shuddered, and Vanessa smelled roses and mushrooms and horses as Wonderland was drawn here. The land itself seemed to cry out in response to what the Lady was doing. Wonderland resisted, but the Looking Glass Land melded in response to the commands of a Looking Glass queen.

Everything lurched. Vanessa was thrown from her feet, though when she landed, the ground was soft, almost like a bed. It was only when she heard the voices that she realized it was a bed, or at least close enough to one to count in this world.

A dandelion bit her arm and roared. Vanessa yelped and got up. The other flowers in the flower bed growled. Their petals had been arranged to look like a lion's mane. She looked at her arm. The bite had broken the skin, though only barely. She stepped around the rest of the flowers, some of them shouting insults at her, before returning to the others.

They were no longer in the hall, though she saw signs of it. Two of the walls were still standing. The table was back, though it was made of wood. It took Vanessa a second to recognize it as the table the hatter had taken them to.

The Lady was having trouble standing. Sweat drenched her face, and it looked like she had aged a decade. Michael and Will stood at either side of her. She looked up at Vanessa and smiled. "I don't think I've ever done anything quite so big."

"Did it work?"

"I believe so. I couldn't fill in the holes in the Looking Glass Land with Wonderland, but I did manage to do the opposite. It's not entirely stable, but then Wonderland never really was."

"So how do we stop the Cat from making it to our world?" Vanessa asked.

"I'm not sure we can," the Lady said.

Vanessa let out a long breath and tried to hold in the sigh. Had it all been for nothing, then?

"Why?" a strange voice asked.

The word surprised all of them. They all looked around for the source of the voice, but the Lady simply smiled and looked down. There, at her feet, was the smoking caterpillar. Rosebud landed in front of it and chittered something, but it ignored her.

"You will forgive me, Caterpillar," the Lady started.

"I will not forgive."

"You misunderstand me. I was not asking you a question. I was telling you what you will do."

"Rude."

"And yet, you will forgive."

The caterpillar gave a petulant look. "I will."

"Do you know how to stop the Cheshire Cat from reaching my world?"

"I do know."

"You will tell us."

The caterpillar's face twisted in concentration, as if trying to find an opening that the Lady had left, but such a simple command had left none.

"You must summon it."

"We need a reagent to summon a being that powerful," the Lady said.

"Yes, you do."

"You will tell us where we can find a reagent."

"The creatures of the mountains have it."

Vanessa looked to the north. The mountain range stabbed into the sky like a series of knives. She couldn't tell how high it reached, but it was definitely huge. It was also miles away. They didn't have time, not if the Cheshire Cat was really on the verge of reaching their world. The Lady apparently thought the same thing.

"We can't get there soon enough."

"No, you cannot."

"You will give us some of the growing mushrooms."

"Why?" As before, a smoky letter *Y* came from its mouth, growing as it approached the Lady, though it dissolved before it reached her.

"Because if you do not, Wonderland will fall."

"Yes, it will."

"You would have to go to our world."

"I could manage that."

"In our world, caterpillars don't smoke. No one would sell you any tobacco."

The caterpillar let out a thick stream of smoke and Vanessa coughed as she breathed it in. "How horrid. Your world is a place for barbarians. It would never do for one as refined as I."

"You wouldn't have to go there if Wonderland survives."

"I would not."

"So you will give us growing mushrooms."

"I shall."

"And some of the shrinking ones."

The caterpillar nodded. It crawled through the grass, through a series of mushrooms that Vanessa could have sworn hadn't been there a moment before. The Lady smiled and picked one up.

"How do you know that will make you grow?" Vanessa asked. "Last time we shrank so much we disappeared."

The Lady chuckled. "Did you? I wasn't sure that could actually happen. Well, I'm certain now because if this mushroom does shrink us, the caterpillar would end up with all of us being three inches tall, and it wouldn't want that."

"No, I would not," the caterpillar said. "Three inches is a most excellent height. It is not for unmannered barbarians like you. This will make you as far as it is possible to be from three inches."

"You will also give us the other kind so we can return to normal."

The caterpillar sighed and crawled through another batch of mushrooms. The Lady took some of those and put them in her belt pouch. She then handed them each a mushroom. "Shall we?"

32

Vanessa had no idea how tall they were, but she wasn't
sure there was a building in the whole of England to
match her. The Tower of London wouldn't even come
up to her waist, and Big Ben might reach her shoulders. Michael said that Rosebud hovered around them, but she was too
small to see. At this size, Vanessa's steps ate up the miles on the
way to the mountains.

"I didn't know you could just tell the caterpillar what to do,"
Vanessa said. "If I had, that might have saved us a lot of trouble."

"The truth is, I wasn't sure it would work," the Lady said. "I
just knew it always gave me a headache trying to be polite to
that one."

"What lives in the mountains?" Vanessa asked.

"I have no idea," the Lady said. "The mountains marked the
border of Wonderland. I never made it that far."

The mountains grew swiftly closer as they strode through the
land. It was an odd sensation, being so big and yet still dwarfed
by the massive peaks. In a few minutes, they were at the base of
the range. They were the strangest mountains Vanessa had ever
seen. Gray stone rose at an angle from the grass and continued,
as far as she could tell, all the way to the peak. There was no
vegetation or even loose rocks. It was smooth stone as far as she
could see.

"It's like a child plopped down a toy mountain in the middle of a field," Michael said.

He tried to climb it, but he got only a few feet up before he slipped back down. He shook his head. "They are completely impassable."

"Of course they are," someone said in a voice that was like stone grinding against stone.

What Vanessa had mistaken as a large boulder uncurled itself. The being stood just as tall as they were. It had gray skin and a white beard that went all the way to the ground.

Will looked shocked. "Is that a dwarf?"

The being scowled. It ran forward and kicked him in the shin. Will yowled in pain.

"Dwarf? I used to be a dwarf, but not anymore. I am over three hundred feet tall. Have you ever heard of a dwarf that tall?"

"I can't say that I have," Will said after he had regained his composure.

"Of course not. It's preposterous."

"You have something we need," the Lady said.

"Oh? And what is that?"

"I'm really not sure. Something belonging to a cat, I suspect."

The giant dwarf scowled. "If you think I'm going to give you my lucky cat's foot, you're fooling yourself."

"Wonderland is dying. You must know that."

"Why should I care? Wonderland abandoned me nearly a thousand years ago. Just because I got taller than my brothers, they cast me out and branded me with the name Eilifr. I care nothing for Wonderland."

"'One who lives alone,'" the Lady said. "How fitting. If you really don't care, however, why do you need a lucky cat's foot?"

"Do you have any idea how hard it is to find enough to eat when you're this size? I need all the luck I can get."

"How did you get that big anyway?" Vanessa asked.

"I stepped on a bug. A caterpillar got mad at me and told me to eat a mushroom. Instantly, I became this size."

"If it was mad at you, why would you do what it says?"

"It's like they always say, when a blue smoking caterpillar tells you to do something, you do it."

"Who says that?" Michael asked.

The dwarf rolled his eyes. "Everyone."

Michael looked at the others, and the Lady only shrugged. She stepped forward. "I've had some dealings with your people. You are traders. Everything has its price with you. What do you want for the cat's foot?"

The dwarf laughed. "What do you have that you think I would want?"

"Maybe a way to get small again," the Lady said. "Then you could go back to your people."

Eilifr took a slight step back. "My . . . people." He shook his head. "No, they cast me out. I am done with them."

"Loyalty to the clan above all," the Lady said. "Isn't that what Dvalin said?"

"Alviss," the dwarf dragged out the name, smacking his lips as if tasting it.

"What are you two talking about?" Will asked.

"Dvalin and Alviss were ancient leaders among the dwarves," the Lady said. "Some even say Alviss was the first king, though no one is really sure about that."

"Dwarves haven't had a king in a long time," the dwarf said. "At least the ones here haven't."

"Nonetheless, your people honor tradition, and the words of Alviss are at the very heart of that."

He walked over to the mountain and ran his fingers on it. The motions produced sparks, and Vanessa wrinkled her nose at the smell of smoke, but he stopped before anything caught fire.

"Yes, they are," the dwarf said, "but Alviss's words aren't enough. If they were, my clan wouldn't have cast me out in the first place." He shook his head. "No, I will certainly not trade my lucky charm for a return to people who hate me."

"Then what?" the Lady asked. "What is your price?"

Eilifr smiled. "Let's start with the destruction of Wonderland. Give me that, and I'll be your ally. You can have anything that is mine."

Michael scowled. "Hook. Hook got to you, didn't he?"

"Is that the ghost's name?" The dwarf shrugged. "He never told me. Yes, if I keep the cat's foot from everyone, he will destroy this world. I was worried he would betray me, but he's making good on his part." He sniffed at the air and glared at them. "You have the smell of that other land on you. Did you have something to do with this world surviving?"

"I did," the Lady said.

The dwarf roared and rushed forward. He didn't have any weapons, but his hands looked like boulders. He slammed one fist into Michael's stomach. Michael doubled over and fell to the ground, crushing several trees as he struggled to get to his feet. Will charged the dwarf, but his sword only clanked against the dwarf's stone skin. Eilifr turned to him and grabbed the blade in his hand. He squeezed for a moment before dropping the weapon, the metal having been twisted out of shape. Vanessa took a step back as the Lady raised her hands. Green light surrounded them. The dwarf rippled as if, for that moment, he was more mud than stone. Hoping it was what the Lady intended, Vanessa stormed forward and struck. Her blade sank in. When she pulled it back, she saw a narrow gash. The dwarf didn't seem to notice and lunged at her. His body slammed against her with all the force of a freight train. She tumbled to the ground, certain that he had broken at least a few bones by his impact. The dwarf put a foot on her neck and pressed down. He was impossibly heavy. Any second, his weight would snap her neck or crush her windpipe.

Will threw himself at Eilifr, but he just bounced off, though the dwarf rocked a little, which made it even harder for Vanessa to breathe. The Lady once again brought her power to bear, and the ground under Vanessa turned to mud. She sank a few inches in. The rapid change threw the dwarf momentarily off balance. Vanessa grabbed him by the ankle and pushed. He stumbled back rather than falling altogether, but it was enough for her to get free. She rolled to her feet, struggling to catch her breath.

"You've dealt with dwarves before?" Vanessa asked.

"Many times," the Lady said.

"How are we supposed to beat this one?"

"I generally talk to them rather than fight them."

Vanessa raised an eyebrow. "Generally."

The Lady inclined her head. "There were a few times where the conflict couldn't be resolved by diplomacy. For those instances, hammers work better than a sword."

"We don't have any of those."

"Then, perhaps you should improvise some."

Vanessa nodded and quickly glanced around. Though the mountain was bare of any loose rocks, there were a few stones on the ground. Though as big as she was, "boulder" was probably more accurate. She grabbed the largest one she could find. It was vaguely triangle shaped, and she shoved it into the base of a particularly thick tree, which she then pulled up. It didn't look much like a hammer, but the Lady walked up to her and whispered a word. The weapon in her hand shifted. The tree smoothed itself out and the rock took on the shape of the head of a hammer. Vanessa nodded in thanks before rushing into the battle again. She slammed her weapon into the dwarf's arm with a loud *crack*. The impact sent vibrations up her arm. A rock chip came free, and the dwarf grunted.

Michael, who had resorted to backing away from Eilifr until he was far enough away to throw boulders, did the same thing Vanessa had done with a tree and a rock. The Lady transformed his weapon as well, and the two of them moved to come at the dwarf from either side while Will stayed near the Lady.

The dwarf looked from one to the other and sneered. "Just because you found a way to hurt me doesn't mean it will be easy."

He rushed at Vanessa. Michael ran up behind him and hit him in the back of the head before he reached her. That didn't slow the dwarf by more than a second, but it was enough. Vanessa brought up her own weapon and slammed it into the bottom of the dwarf's chin as he ran. The force of the blow lifted him off the ground a few inches before he went down. He fell so hard that he shook the earth and sank into the ground a little. As before, the Lady worked her magic to turn the ground to mud, but this time, as soon as he had sunk most of the way in, she reversed the spell, changing it to stone. The dwarf grunted and tried to get up, but he couldn't move so much as an inch.

"Now," the Lady said, "perhaps we can revisit our previous discussion. I will trade you the restoration to your normal size. In exchange, you will give us this cat's foot."

The dwarf struggled to get free, but it was no use. He narrowed his eyes. "I already told you no."

"Then we will leave you here. Perhaps we can tell your clan where to find you. Wouldn't that be something? I imagine they will want to come see the great and mighty Eilifr held here as a prisoner. Children will probably play on you. Maybe even slide down your nose and use your hair to swing on. I'm sure they would enjoy that."

"No," the dwarf said.

"I will not free you," the Lady said. "At least not directly, but if you return to normal size, this trap will not be able to hold you. You need not return to your clan. Wonderland is failing. Its borders are weak. You could burrow to another world if you so choose."

The dwarf blinked. "I could?"

"Yes. The Cheshire Cat escaped that way not long ago. Do you really think a cat could burrow where you could not?"

He struggled against his bindings. A small crack formed near his right cheek, but he still couldn't move. "Of course not! No cat can dig better than a dwarf."

"Then make the trade," the Lady said. "If you care nothing for Wonderland, then whether it lives or dies should make no difference to you."

The dwarf pursed his lips. He struggled for a second more before sighing. "The rock stops me from moving my head, but I was trying to nod. You have a deal. Shrink me first, and I will give you my lucky cat's foot."

"Very well."

"Wait." Vanessa grabbed the Lady's wrist as she reached toward him. "How do you know you can trust him?"

The Lady raised her eyebrow, and Vanessa felt her face heat up. She let the Lady go.

"He's a dwarf. They could no more break their word on a trade than you could turn your blood blue or grow wings."

She reached into her belt pouch and pulled out a mushroom. She held it to the dwarf's mouth. He looked at her for a second before opening. She dropped it in. Almost instantly, the dwarf shrank until he was so small Vanessa could barely see him. The

Lady extended her hand and the dwarf jumped onto her middle finger. He rummaged around in his vest before pulling out a cat's foot on a chain, the same one that Michael had severed from the Cheshire Cat. The Lady nodded, and he handed it over.

"You have my thanks."

Eilifr said something, but his voice was too soft. He started digging, seemingly into the air itself. There was a flash of light, and then he was gone. Vanessa looked at the Lady.

"How many creatures get to other worlds by digging?"

"A surprising amount, actually. It's one of the more common ways to cross over. We should go to a place where the Cat might be contained before we summon it." She held up the claw. It looked diminutive in her hand. "I can use this, but one spell will expend its power, and it would not do to summon the Cat only to have it immediately dig its way out again."

"Where could we contain it?" Vanessa asked. "Even when it was trapped in Wonderland, it could still go freely from there to the ghostly realm."

"The center. The joker's domain. It's subject to it even more than most realms are to their gods. Without the joker's guidance, that place could hold practically anything."

"Really?" Vanessa asked. "I wouldn't think that to be a particularly effective prison."

"It is. Believe me. The magic of the center is the same type of magic that held the Cat prisoner in Wonderland all those years, only it is a hundred times stronger."

Vanessa looked south. She thought she could see the center from her height. It didn't seem that far away, and they would probably get there in a few minutes. She motioned for the Lady to lead the way, and the trio followed her. It wasn't long before they came upon the Queen of Hearts' castle. It appeared to have come through the melding of worlds with little harm. Cards patrolled the area around it, and Vanessa wondered how the other queens were doing and if they were still in this castle.

"The ground is moving," Michael said.

He was right. It writhed. She bent down to get a closer look, but the Lady grabbed her shoulder. "No! Those are ghosts."

Vanessa was so big that she hadn't been able to see the ghosts. There were so many that they hung over the grass in a transparent sheen. As one, they rose up to the faces of the giant Knights. They were comically small, like the ghosts of fleas or some other insects, but the Lady reacted as if they were venomous animals. Blue fire surrounded her hands. Ghosts screamed as she incinerated them, but they were too many, and they swarmed her. One headed right toward Vanessa's mouth. She felt a chill as it passed through her lips. There was a slight sensation, too, as if it were dragging something in with it. There was a bitter taste on her tongue, and the next thing she knew, the ground rushed up to meet her. It took a second to realize what had happened. Hundreds of ghosts had converged on the Lady, and some must have gotten into her pouch. The mushrooms were small when she was at normal size. As big as she had been, the mushrooms became microscopic. It was no great challenge for a ghost to drag the fungi in between her closed lips.

The ghosts grew relative to her until soon they were giants instead of her. They must have given her more than one mushroom to shrink her so much. Now she was the size of an insect. Tiny critters were slowly approaching. Several ants and one beetle were dragging something that looked like a cannon.

Suddenly, the ground shook, and something that would have made mountains seem small crashed into the ground near her. It shrank rapidly and in a matter of moments, a tiny Michael stood beside her.

"They got you, too?" Vanessa asked.

Michael looked himself up and down. "Obviously."

"What about the Lady and Will?"

Michael looked up. The grass was tall enough to look like a forest, and it gave them a heavy canopy. Vanessa cried out in surprise when Rosebud, now twice as big as they were, drifted down. She said something, and Michael nodded. Then, the fairy flew away.

"She's going to try to find them." He looked at the beetle pulling the cannon. "I think that's a bombardier beetle."

"You will surrender, in the name of James Hook," the beetle said.

"Oh, you can't be serious," Michael said. "What could Hook possibly offer a bunch of insects that would make them follow him?"

The beetle snorted and stamped two of its feet. "Well for starters, he doesn't look down on us."

Michael smirked. "Somehow, I find that hard to believe."

The beetle's eyes bulged. "People like you are what's wrong with the world. You think that just because you're normally bigger than us, you're more important. Well, you're our size now. That means you have to play by our rules. Now, will you surrender?"

Michael looked at Vanessa and chuckled. "No, I don't think so."

The ants scrambled in a circle for a few seconds. "You must." They spoke in unison. "We have you surrounded."

"Maybe we should be a little more careful," Vanessa said. "Ants are really strong for their size."

"And you would be wise not to forget it," the ants said. "Surrender, and your deaths will be quick."

"That doesn't really encourage us to do what you say," Vanessa said.

One of the ants moved forward, but Vanessa slashed at it, taking off a piece of its antenna. It scrambled back and the other ants clicked at her. The lead one would have no doubt turned red if it wasn't already.

"How dare you?" the ants said.

"You threatened us first."

"Well of course we did. You are our enemies, but that's no excuse for you to attack us."

"I'm pretty sure it is," Vanessa said. "Now, let us go, or you'll lose more than antennae."

The ants clicked. "This is your last chance. Surrender or we'll fire."

The bombardier beetle stamped its back legs. The cannon adjusted itself, aiming directly at Vanessa. The sword at her side hummed with power, and she could barely resist the urge to draw it, not that she expected even the Vorpal Sword to do anything against a cannon. Michael eyed her and nodded.

He stepped forward. "If that one fires, you will all be dead before the cannon hits."

The ants clamped their mandibles together. "You cannot get to us that fast."

"Do you have any idea how many impossible battles I've fought against foes who thought they could squash me"— Michael smirked—"like a bug?"

The ants hissed. Michael didn't wait for them to speak again. He rushed forward, slashing at an ant's abdomen. Greenish ichor spilled from the wound. Other ants surged toward him. Michael's sword was a blur as he cut into the attacking insects, but Vanessa knew he wouldn't be able to hold them off for long. She rushed at the ants from behind. She didn't bother trying to kill them. She just slashed at their back legs. The first two fell backward. The third one saw what she was doing and turned to face her, but Michael took off its head. There was a loud boom as the cannon fired. Vanessa half expected the ball to tear through her, but when she turned toward the beetle, her jaw dropped.

Will was on top of the beetle, driving his sword into it.

Nearby, a winged horse fluttered into the air and landed on a blade of grass. The ground rumbled beneath them as the Lady fell out of the sky, drifting down as if she was a dandelion seed. She looked at Vanessa and Michael. "I can't leave the two of you alone for five seconds, can I?"

"It's her," one of the ants said.

"It's Alice."

"Lady Alice."

The ants backed up. Michael was still standing, though his right arm looked bloated, possibly from an ant bite. He smiled but stumbled. Instantly, the Lady was at his side, chanting a few words. She shook her head. "That will help a little, but I was never a healer. I'm not sure how bad it is."

"How did you get here so fast?" Vanessa asked.

The Lady waved up at the blade of grass where Will's horse had landed. Another one fluttered above it, its wings flapping so fast that the wind pushed Vanessa back a step. Rosebud hovered in front of it and demanded that it stop, though the bug ignored her.

"Horseflies," the Lady said. She saw the look on their faces. "Yes, horseflies look like actual horses here. Anyway, it didn't take much to convince them to help. Your fairy led us here."

"Of course not, Lady Alice," one of the ants, the first one to speak individually, said. "You are a queen, and all insects respect a queen."

"You mean ants, termites, and bees and the like," Vanessa said.

"Yes, the important ones."

"I don't think horseflies recognize a queen."

"Oh, they recognize one," the ant said. "They just generally refuse to serve one. They are not opposed to a favor every now and then, though."

The Lady nodded. "I'll have to pay them back, but I've made deals with such beings before, and it's no great burden." She turned to the ants. "Why were you attacking my friends?"

The ants exchanged glances. A different one spoke, though it seemed to have trouble speaking on its own. "Well, you see, Lady Alice, the one you call Hook said both the Red and White Queens were dead. There was no one to lead the Looking Glass Land except for him." It looked at Alice. "At least there wasn't anyone except you. We had no idea the third queen had returned."

"Then you will help us?"

"Of course, my queen. Our entire colony is at your disposal, though I am saddened to admit that most of us were destroyed when the world tore apart. What you see is all that we have left."

"Well, that's okay. As long as you don't attack us, we should be fine. Now, I don't suppose you have any of the smoking caterpillar's growing mushrooms."

"No, it never deigned to speak to any of our kind. It said we lacked original thought."

"I wonder why," Michael said.

The ants spoke to each other in a high-pitched tone that made Vanessa's head hurt. A winged ant whispered to the leader, who gave a smile that almost made Vanessa draw her sword. The Lady raised her hand, though, and Vanessa relaxed. The leader of the ants stepped forward. "We have gathered some of the growing cake, though."

The Lady stood up straight. "Really? That will certainly be useful. Can you bring us all that you have?"

"We had hoped to eat them ourselves," one of the ants said. "Food has become so scarce."

"Do not speak to the queen like that," the leader said. "Of course you may have it. Bring it at once."

The winged ant flew off, and Will spoke. "What is the growing cake?"

"It was one of the first things I ate when I came here the first time. It made me grow enormous, though I never learned where they came from."

The ant returned a few minutes later with a piece of bread nearly as big as it was.

The Lady sighed. "Is that all you have?"

"Yes, Your Majesty."

"It won't be enough to get us as big as we were, but it should return us to normal size." She took a handful and looked to the others. "There's no point in taking more than this."

Vanessa nodded. The three of them each took a handful and ate. It tasted of honey and had a gritty texture. In a few seconds, they had returned to normal size. They were in the courtyard of the Queen of Hearts, though Vanessa could barely recognize it as such. Patches that she had seen in the Looking Glass Land littered the grounds, and the ghostly nature of Wonderland had started to encroach on them. There were no ghosts nearby, but a raven perched on a nearby rosebush provided ample explanation for where they had gone.

"They are here!"

Vanessa looked around. The jack of spades was headed for them with a pair of tens following. They formed a triangle around the four Knights and scanned the area. After they had made sure there was nothing threatening nearby, they put down their spears. The Queen of Spades approached. Somehow, Vanessa could tell she was still inverted, with her death side up.

"We've had scouts out looking for you in case you should reappear. I take it by the state of the world that your journey into the Looking Glass Land did not turn out as planned."

"Unfortunately not." Vanessa waved at the Lady. "We have a new ally, but I'm afraid both the Cheshire Cat and Captain Hook escaped from us."

The queen looked at the Lady, and all four of her eyes went wide. "Yes, I have heard of you. Alice, one of the few to defy the Queen of Hearts and live, and one who rose to the rank of Queen in the Looking Glass Land. You, I believe, will be happy with our development."

"Oh? And what is that?"

"We have captured the Queen of Hearts' castle. The queen herself is a prisoner there."

"Now that is good news." She looked at Michael. He still looked weak, and his arm had grown even bigger. It was red and there was a growing smell of rot in the air. "We will go there straightaway, but could you send someone ahead of us? Our ally has been wounded, and he requires the aid of a healer."

The jack of spades bowed. "Of course. My counterpart in clubs is quite skilled. I will go get him myself."

33

They were only halfway across the courtyard when the jacks returned. The jack of clubs wore a sash that had a number of small pouches. He reached into one and pulled out a green powder, which he rubbed on Michael's arm. It released a sharp smell that reminded Vanessa of cinnamon. Though Michael didn't say anything, the softening of his expression told Vanessa that the poultice had taken away a great deal of the pain.

The jack examined the wound more closely. "Giant ants. Nasty creatures."

"They weren't giant ants, exactly," Vanessa said.

The jack huffed. "I've seen enough of these to know that this kind of wound only comes from an ant the same size as you. That means a giant ant, unless you have some other explanation."

Vanessa opened her mouth to argue but saw no point. It was close enough to the truth, anyway. Michael was certainly looking better, and that was all that mattered.

"How did you ever manage to capture the Queen of Hearts in her own castle?" Vanessa asked.

"It actually wasn't too difficult. Once Hook and the Cat were gone, most of their minions fled. We found the Queen of Hearts in the dungeon. She had not been treated well once they didn't need her anymore." The Queen of Spades laughed. "They had put her in a leaky cell. Her ink had started to run."

"Do you think she'll turn against them?" Michael asked. The swelling in his arm had disappeared. "I can't shake the feeling that this is all part of Hook's plan."

"Michael, I think you're seeing connections where there aren't any," Vanessa said. "Hook was outwitted by the Cheshire Cat, and now he's on the run. I don't think it's any more complicated than that."

"Maybe not," Michael said, "but then a cornered animal is more dangerous."

"He may be right, Vanessa," the Lady said. "However, that does not change our plans. We need to summon the Cat before it makes it to our world. Our realm may not have the strength to resist it, especially with the Knights of the Round gone. We need to summon a place where the Cat can be contained."

"Then why did we go to the castle at all?" Michael asked. "I'm grateful to the jack for helping me, but we don't really need to go there. We should go directly to the center."

"The Cheshire Cat will be the better part of a day in reaching our world," the Lady said. "We shouldn't rush ahead. The Queen of Hearts was on Hook's side, and I have never yet encountered a situation where I regretted having too much information. Lady Spade, I take it you have questioned her."

"Yes, of course, but we haven't gotten much out of her."

"Did you try turning her over and questioning her inverted?"

The queen blinked and stumbled, though she managed to keep her footing. "What?"

"Turning her over," the Lady said again. "In her traditional form, she is focused emotion. Passion. Anger. If she is inverted, however, she becomes emotion uncontrolled. You might be able to make her so afraid that she'll give you more information."

The Queen of Spades stopped in her tracks. "I had never considered that. We flip our aspects when the need suits us, but I never thought of doing it to another queen against her will. I don't know, Queen Alice. It's barbaric."

The Lady extended her hands. "More barbaric than what has been done to this land? More barbaric than summoning the ghosts of everyone you killed? The Queen of Hearts has been more barbaric than anything we are considering."

The Queen of Spades' lower head gave a slow nod. It was several seconds before the top one did the same. They walked the rest of the way in silence. The other card queens were waiting for them just inside the gate. The Queen of Clubs looked happy to see Michael well. Diamonds smiled but didn't say anything. The Queen of Spades led them inside to a chamber near the back of the palace. A pair of nines stood guard. They saluted the Queen of Spades and stepped aside, and she drew her weapon and pushed open the door. The Queen of Hearts sat on the bed of the richly appointed chamber. Her wardrobe sat open with its contents spilled and scattered throughout the room. Heavy boards had been nailed to the fireplace. Vanessa raised an eyebrow, but the Queen of Spades shrugged.

"The Red Queen told us of a secret passage leading to this chamber. That's where it comes out."

"Wouldn't it have been easier to just hold her in another room?"

"Probably," said the Queen of Spades. "But we only knew of the secret passage here because we were told. Who knows how many others there are in this castle? She may even know a way out of the dungeon, now that ghosts aren't patrolling the grounds. Better to hold her where we can be sure we've blocked the only way out."

Vanessa tugged at the boards, but they felt sturdy. "Makes

sense." She stepped closer to the Queen of Hearts. "Help us. Your allies have abandoned you. Even before that, they held you prisoner. You don't owe them anything anymore."

The queen stood up and looked her in the eye. Her irises were red, and for some reason, that unnerved Vanessa. "Perhaps not, but I owe you even less."

"What did they promise you that you would sacrifice all of Wonderland?" the Queen of Spades asked.

The Queen of Hearts looked at the Lady. Even the white parts of the card became red, though the Lady returned her gaze with casual indifference.

"Her," the card said. "She is the only one to ever escape my wrath. I wanted her head."

The Lady laughed and stepped forward until her face was only a few inches from the queen's. "I escaped you when I was a child, but I came back to Wonderland several times. You had plenty of opportunity to capture me. What stopped you then?"

"A powerful wizard. You would not have been so easy to take."

"And somehow, you thought it would be easier to get me this way? Instead of one person escaping your wrath, you have two who have destroyed your kingdom. Is that really better?"

"You turned me into a laughingstock."

The Lady laughed. "I'm sure people were laughing at you long before I came here, but imagine how much they will laugh at you now." Her face brightened. "That actually sounds like a good idea. I may not be able to cross back into my world, but I believe I can still send a message. How would you like that? What if everyone in my world, and in every world that I can reach, were laughing at you?"

"No. You can't."

"*Yes, I can.* It wouldn't even be particularly difficult."

A tear formed at the queen's upper eye. Even the hearts on her card wilted. "Please."

"Flip over."

"What?"

"Flip over. I want to speak to your other side."

The queen scowled but the Lady brought her fingers to her lips. A blue light appeared on her fingertips. She started speaking.

"No," the Queen of Hearts said. "Please don't."

"You know what my price is," the Lady said. "Tell us what you know."

The queen looked at the glowing light. "Fine. You win. I will tell you what you want to know."

Rather than jumping and flipping upside down, as the Queen of Clubs had done, she simply folded over. For a moment, she stood on her hands. Then, her hands transformed into feet even as her feet transformed into hands. She slumped onto the bed.

"Was this Hook's plan?" Michael asked. "To destroy this world in exchange for the Cheshire Cat's help in getting a body?"

"Yes."

"Was that all of it?" Michael asked. "Hook didn't have a backup plan?"

"Not as far as I know, but . . ."

"But?"

"They are scoundrels, Hook and the Cat both. Each planning on betraying the other."

"How do you know?" the Queen of Spades said.

The Queen of Hearts wilted before Spades' glare. She was in tears when she spoke. "You may be the best warrior among us, but I understand the passions that drive the world. Believe me. Neither of them was faithful to the other."

"Did Hook know that the Cat was going to betray him?"

"Almost certainly," the Queen of Hearts said. "Only a fool wouldn't, and that one is as devious as any spirit I have ever seen."

"He would have had a backup plan."

"Very likely," said the Queen of Hearts. "Unfortunately, he didn't discuss his plans to betray his compatriot with his prisoners."

"Perhaps we were his backup plan," said the Lady. "He might well have planned to help us defeat the Cat's spirit only to turn on us when we were done."

Michael pursed his lips. "I hate to think he could have been using us, but you may be right. He might have planned to manipulate us, knowing that he could return to our world afterward and we wouldn't be able to follow him."

"So do we contact him?" Vanessa asked.

"No, we shouldn't play into his plans. Let him come to us if he wants. We should go to the center."

The Lady raised an eyebrow. "Giving commands now?"

Michael rolled his eyes. "The Knights don't exist anymore. I'm no longer under your command." He looked at Vanessa. "Or hers, for that matter."

"Maybe not," said the Lady, "but I still know far more about both Wonderland and the Looking Glass Land than you. Plus, I'm the only one who may actually stand a chance facing either Hook or the Cat."

"She has a point, Michael," Vanessa said. "You're not going to do this without help."

The Lady laughed. "I do have to admit, Michael, you are right about one thing. We do need to get to the center as quickly as we can." She turned to the Queen of Hearts. "What help can you give us?"

"I told you what you wanted to know."

"The ghosts," Vanessa said. "They still follow you, don't they?"

The Queen of Hearts hesitated. "Some of them."

"Command them to help us."

"Vanessa," the Lady said, "necromancy is forbidden."

"We're not using it. She is."

"That's a fine distinction."

"We need all the help we can get if we're going to stop the Cat."

The Lady scowled, but after a second, she turned to the queen. "Command them to aid us, and I promise I will never reveal how your allies betrayed you and held you prisoner in your own castle. You can even tell people that you outwitted me into helping you get back at your betrayers. I'll even confirm it if asked, so you'll get everything you want."

The Queen of Hearts ground her teeth. "Duchess!"

A ghost came out of the ceiling and hovered above them. It was a woman with a head that was at least three times bigger than a normal one. A large nose dominated its face, and its grin made Vanessa want to draw her sword. There was a line across its neck that dripped ghostly blood.

"Yes, my queen." The ghost had a voice that was like nails on a chalkboard.

"Speak to my generals. You will command them to obey the Lady Alice in all things as long as she is moving against James Hook or the Cheshire Cat."

"As you command." The duchess bowed once and rose up into the ceiling.

The Lady watched her go. "She was your friend, the last I heard. When did you kill her?"

The Queen of Hearts waved her off. "A few years ago. I forget why. I believe she beat me at a croquet match, but who can keep track of these things?"

The Lady let out a breath and shook her head. "It's a wonder your people didn't rebel against you long ago. We should go."

34

They moved as quickly as they could. Like last time, the cards couldn't keep up with them, and before long, they had left them behind. Vanessa worried that they wouldn't be able to open the way to the center without a card, but the Lady didn't seem concerned. In a few seconds, the wall of hearts came into view, and shortly they were standing in front of it. Unlike the rest of the landscape, the wall had retained its vibrant color. Vanessa pressed her hand against it, but it was as unyielding as the first time. She started to move around it, but the Lady raised a hand.

"Don't bother. I spent a great deal of time studying this place. Those entrances only work for cards. We'll have to get in another way."

"You're saying this is magic strong enough to hold a godlike being, and we should just find another way in?" Vanessa asked.

"Of course. It won't be terribly difficult."

"It won't be?" Vanessa suddenly looked very confused.

"No. I will simply summon the Cat without using a binding circle."

"Doesn't that mean you'll have no control of where it appears and what it does?"

"Not *no control*, just not much. I don't need a lot, though. I just need to ensure that it is summoned in front of me." She smiled and stood so close to the wall that her nose was nearly touching it. She reached into her pocket and pulled out the severed cat's paw. It warped the air around it, as if it were giving off heat. Vanessa suspected the only reason she hadn't seen that before was because she had been too big. Both Michael and Will were staring at it, though neither said anything.

"Duchess," the Lady said, "guard us. I doubt our enemies will stand by and allow us to do this unopposed."

"By your command, Lady Alice," the duchess said as the ghost rose out of the ground. Everyone but the Lady jumped back in shock as spirits of cards and animals appeared all around them. Their very presence leeched warmth from the air, and ice crystals began to form on the grass. Vanessa's breath steamed in front of her. Up above, a wisp appeared. It dove at Michael, but Rosebud got in its way and fought it off.

"You know, Michael, you're really going to have to do something about that."

"They're fairies." Michael nodded toward Rosebud. "With very few exceptions, they can't hold a thought for more than a few days. Odds are, they will all have forgotten about me by the time this is taken care of."

"'Taken care of'?" Vanessa asked. "Michael, you realize that the Knights never existed? Even if we destroy both the Cat and Hook, we have no way to get home."

"It will work out," Michael said. "It always does."

Oddly, in the light of such a hopeless situation, he had lost much of the pessimism that had shrouded him ever since Hook had escaped from him the year before.

"Where do you get that idea from?" Vanessa asked.

The Lady chuckled. "He gets that from being a friend of Peter Pan. For all I know, he may be right. There could be avenues we haven't considered yet, but none of that alters our immediate plan."

She turned to face the wall and started chanting. The air thrummed against Vanessa's skin. The magic the Lady was working was far too complex for her to understand. She could only feel the edges of it. The power was staggering, and Vanessa saw light shining from between the hearts. The ground shook, and alternating waves of heat and cold washed over her. Vanessa was suddenly thrown back into a tree. It would have doubtless broken something except that Wonderland was more ghostly than solid, and she ended up passing right through it and skidding across the ground. There was a roar, and something thumped against the heart wall. A few seconds later, it hit again.

"Can it break out?" Vanessa asked after she had picked herself up.

"No," the Lady said. "The wall is only a representation. It's a barrier between worlds, and nothing so mundane as physical force can break through."

"But why is the Cat in there?" a voice from the wall said.

Some of the hearts peeled away in the shape of a rectangle, and the joker stepped out. His face was twisted in anger, and for a moment Vanessa thought he had razor-sharp teeth. He looked first to Will and then to Michael before his gaze fell on Vanessa and the Lady. He actually growled.

"Ah, I see. It makes sense now. Alice, I have heard of you."

"Oh really? What exactly have you heard?"

"That you bring chaos wherever you go. That you disrupt the natural order of the world."

"Order?" the Lady said. "In Wonderland?"

"You may have traveled here more than anyone else from your world, but you never truly understood this place." He looked back at the wall, which had closed behind him. "Would you care to tell me why you summoned a godling into my realm?"

"We were hoping you would hold it for us," the Lady replied.

"My realm is not a prison. It is a proving ground. It was never meant to hold a god."

The Lady suddenly looked unsure of herself. "Are you saying you can't do it?"

The joker sighed. "I can hold it, but only if it does not face its own fear."

"That seems too easy," Michael said.

"Oh?" the Lady asked. "How many times have you seen your friend Peter afraid?"

"That's different," Michael said. "That's just how Peter is."

"That's how every god is," the Lady said. "Believe me. I've met my fair share. When you have that kind of power, fear isn't the sort of thing you deal with on a day-to-day basis. It wouldn't surprise me if the Cat hasn't had a single moment of fear since it came into existence."

The joker nodded. "The brave are the ones who overcome their fear, not the ones who never feel it. It is very likely that I can hold the Cat for a long time. Years at least, if not centuries."

"So that's it, then," Will said. "We've won. The Cat is contained."

"We just can't go home anymore." Michael looked around, deflated. "I guess we can help rebuild this world. I can think of worse fates." He chuckled. "I was always pretty sure I would have one of those fates, actually, so this is better than expected. How exactly do we bring a land back from the ghostly realm?"

"I never thought you were one to surrender, Michael," Vanessa said.

"I'm tired, Vanessa. We just saved the world, or near enough to it, but we're also the ones who brought the Cat into the Looking Glass Land. None of this could have happened if not for us."

"They would have found someone else to manipulate," Vanessa said, "and then we wouldn't have been here to stop the Cat."

Michael nodded. "At least this way no one suffers but us."

"What's wrong with you?" Vanessa asked. "A few seconds ago, you were so sure everything would work out."

"It's the death of this place," the Lady said. "The twin worlds are much more related to emotions than other realms. It works both ways, too."

"Why hasn't it affected the rest of us?" Vanessa asked.

"Oh, I'm sure it has, but Michael has spent months obsessed with Hook, and Hook is here. That means he has the greatest vested interest in this place, so it makes sense that it would hit him first. I suspect that in a few days, he will find himself sitting in the middle of a field, lacking the will to get up again. We need to motivate him."

"That should be easy enough," Vanessa said. "Michael, Hook is still out there."

Michael looked up but then his shoulders sagged. "He's trapped here just like the rest of us. For better or for worse, we have won."

"You know he won't stay trapped. This is Hook. He doesn't just give up."

Michael nodded. He seemed stronger now, though only just. He looked to the horizon, and his eyes went wide. "I found him."

Vanessa blinked and looked behind her. Hook stood there amidst a crowd of ghosts. There were far fewer than had followed the pirate earlier, but they looked more solid, almost like Hook himself. The specters from before had been weak things. Only their numbers had made them fearsome. It was the same thing Hook had done in London, when he had thrown a legion against the headquarters of the Knights. This time, however, he had somehow managed to call up more powerful ghosts. These would have wills of their own, and if Hook were any indication, any one of them would be a match for either Michael or Vanessa. Hook had dozens of them, and they whispered to each other in a way that made Vanessa's skin crawl.

"Can you stop them?" she asked.

"Perhaps one or two, given time," said the Lady, "but I'd wager none of them are inclined to give me that."

"I must retreat," said the joker. "This battle is none of my concern, and I must remain neutral in the affairs of Wonderland if I am to retain my realm."

"They have to be coming for the Cat," Vanessa said. "That means they'll try to invade your realm. This concerns you as much as anyone."

The joker smiled. "No, it doesn't, not until they cross my threshold. Let them try that, if they dare. They won't be the first army I have captured."

Then the joker stepped back. The wall flowed around him as he disappeared into it.

The Lady shook her head. "He would have been useful."

"Why haven't they attacked yet?" Michael asked, having already drawn his sword.

Hook stepped forward, and the ghosts went silent.

"You know why I'm here," Hook said. "Open the way to the Cheshire Cat, and we'll let you remain in this world while we conquer yours."

Michael stood up straight. "You can't really expect us to accept that offer. This world is dying."

"Once I leave, I will have no interest in destroying this place. Who knows? You may even be able to save Wonderland. It's not as if you can return home."

Will's hand went to his sword, but Michael put a hand on him. He whispered something to Will, who then responded. Vanessa couldn't catch their exchange, but she heard Wendy's name. In the midst of this insane mission, Vanessa finally took a pause and thought about Wendy and Jane, as she imagined them anxiously waiting for Will to return home. She had to get them all out of Wonderland.

Vanessa turned back to Hook. "What are you afraid of?"

"Afraid? Me?" Hook laughed, and many of the ghosts with him did the same. "I fear nothing."

"Then why haven't you attacked yet? Why haven't you just taken what you want?"

"The joker was right," Michael said. "He can be trapped in the center, where he'd have to face his fear." He made clicking, clocklike sounds with his tongue.

Hook twitched but didn't otherwise respond.

"How would you like that? An eternity facing the crocodile?"

"I killed it. It can't hurt me anymore."

"Peter killed you, but that doesn't seem to have inconvenienced you."

Hook flew into the air. "How dare you?"

"Come on, Hook. With all those spirits with you, you're still afraid to take on three people?"

"What are you doing, Michael?" Vanessa pitched her voice low and hoped Hook couldn't hear.

"You know as well as I do that we can't beat him in a straight fight. If he's afraid of the center, then we have to use it."

"Do you have any idea how?"

"None whatsoever."

Vanessa groaned, but the Lady chuckled. "I would expect nothing else from a friend of Peter Pan." She raised her voice. "Did you hear that? You are so controlled by your fear that you are afraid to face even Michael as one trained by your ancient enemy. What a pathetic thing James Hook has become."

Hook cried in rage and flew to them. So sudden was his attack that it was several seconds before the rest of his spirits followed. That left Hook isolated, at least for a little while. That was apparently what Michael had been hoping for. He rushed forward, caught the pirate's attack on his own sword. He sidestepped, and Hook turned and attacked again with a flurry of blows. Michael met each one, but it left him no chance to counter. Instead, he kept on moving until his back was to the advancing ghosts. He managed a faint smile.

Hook's back was to Vanessa and her companions. She and Will exchanged looks before charging forward. Somehow, Hook sensed them coming and moved aside. He wasn't fast enough, though. Vanessa's sword bit into the ghost, spilling motes of blue light. Hook cried out and Michael pressed forward, attacking as fast as Vanessa had ever seen him move. Will attacked as well. He never hit, but his attacks managed to keep the ghost off balance. Vanessa was sure the other ghosts should have reached them by now. She spared an instant for a glance. A wall of blue energy had appeared between them and the spirits. They were trying to pass through it, but whatever magic formed it apparently served to prevent the passage of ghosts. The Lady was sweating, and Vanessa knew she wouldn't be able to hold this spell for long.

The three of them attacked Hook from every direction. There was no way any being, even a ghost as powerful as he, should have been able to defend against them, but the pirate was everywhere at once. Not only did he defend himself, he managed to attack as well. More than once, his blade sang against Vanessa's flesh, leaving her numb. She was slowing. Hook, however, hadn't taken any wounds beyond the first one.

"They're breaking through," the Lady said.

Vanessa glanced behind her, but before she could see anything, Hook's sword sliced into her shoulder. Her sword arm lost all feeling, and her blade clattered to the ground. She ducked under another of Hook's attacks. The pirate had now focused most of his attention on her. Michael tried to take advantage of that and break through Hook's defenses, but it was no use. Hook was skilled in a way that only someone who had spent centuries facing a god could be. Vanessa's arm tingled. In a few seconds, she would recover, but she couldn't count on a few seconds when facing an opponent as skilled as Hook. She reached for the Vorpal Sword with her left hand, hoping that the sword's magic would make up the difference.

Then she heard glass shattering. The Lady screamed, and the ghosts rushed forward. Vanessa threw herself to the ground before she'd had a chance to draw. Hook descended on Vanessa, but once he saw his army, he smiled. He motioned with his sword toward the wall. The ghosts spread out into four groups, each one standing at a corner. Hook rose up high and screeched. Vanessa had never heard a banshee screech before, but as the world went red, she was sure that was what this was. The Cat yowled in response from inside the joker's realm. Her vision cleared just in time to see each of the four groups attack their corner.

From within, the wall shook. The Lady threw her hands forward, but most of her strength had been expended in the shield wall holding the ghosts back. Whatever spell she had been attempting fizzled, and she slumped to the ground. The ghosts struck at the wall again. A heartbeat later, the Cat did the same.

"Stop them," the Lady said.

"I don't understand. I thought you said it wasn't really a wall."

"It's not, but ghosts don't exist in this world. The Cat has extradimensional properties of its own. They're not trying to break down the wall. They're trying to tear a hole between this world and the joker's realm."

Again, there was that peculiar double striking. They were closer together this time, and Vanessa could feel the vibration against her skin. She motioned to the group howling at the nearest corner. It consisted of at least a dozen spirits, but they didn't have much of a choice.

"That one. Attack."

The Vorpal Sword hissed as it came free of her sheath. She didn't even remember crossing the distance. She was just there, and the sword made that *snicker-snack* sound as it tore through the first ghost. Michael and Will were at her side, each one cutting down their own ghosts. The spirits didn't even try to defend themselves. They just attacked the corner again, almost at the exact moment that the Cat did from inside. Vanessa attacked all the faster, each stroke cutting down a spirit. There were only two left when they struck again, this time at the exact moment that the Cat made its attack on the inside of the wall.

Each section of the wall shattered in a shower of symbols so that the air was filled with floating hearts, spades, diamonds, and clubs. Beyond, where the wall had been, the air rippled. Lines forming impossible geometries shifted and changed so much that it hurt even to look at. Pain stabbed at Vanessa's head, and the Vorpal Sword fell to the ground. An amorphous blob flowed out of the distortion. It writhed, and violet fur sprouted out of its body as it shrank. A wide grin appeared followed by two bright yellow eyes.

"That was surprising," the Cat said. "I didn't think you'd actually be able to stop me." It looked over its shoulder. The distortion bubbled, and for a moment, Vanessa saw herself in a plain business suit. She just knew that there was no adventure in her life, nothing to make it worth living. She blinked and the image vanished, taking the idea along with it. The distortion, however, had grown bigger.

The Cat returned its gaze to Hook and bowed. "You have my thanks. If you had not convinced me to plan for this possibility, I might have never gotten out."

The Lady struggled to her feet. She staggered toward the distortion. "No, I won't allow it."

The Cat's body elongated as its front half walked until it was in front of the Lady, though the back half didn't move at all. "Alice, I do not believe that even you could stop something like this from consuming Wonderland."

She didn't bother to answer. Power welled up inside of her, and a net of blue light spread out from her body, surrounding the bottom of the distortion. It didn't go very high, no more than a few feet, but that seemed not to matter. The distortion tried to expand, and the net glowed brighter but didn't budge. The Lady was struggling. Her sweat streamed down her face, and her complexion had gone red. She clenched her teeth, and every breath was a struggle.

"Lady?" Vanessa said.

"Don't distract me. I have to contain this."

"Are you strong enough?"

"I have to be. If I don't, it could destroy both Wonderland and the Looking Glass Land. We'd be lucky if it stopped there."

"Oh, don't be so dramatic," the Cheshire Cat said. "Something like this will only affect the Looking Glass Land because you combined the twin worlds. It won't reach beyond the boundaries of this patchwork thing you've created. I wouldn't have unleashed it if it would have."

"You don't intend to stay in our world, do you?"

"Of course not. I've been to your world before, Alice. It's frightfully boring. And not even the good kind of frightful. No, I'll just use your world as a stopping point."

It yowled and shook its paw. The Cat looked at it and its eyes went wide. An ant had latched on to its leg. The ant was six inches long but was steadily growing. Other ants were sprouting as well. At the tree line, the bombardier beetle, cannon and all, had grown to the size of a small house. It stamped its rear legs. The cannon boomed, and the cannonball slammed into the Cheshire Cat. The ball was only slightly smaller than the Cat. By all rights, the creature should have been destroyed. Instead, the Cat's body bent inward. Its fur flowed around the cannonball and completely covered it. Then, the Cat's flesh bent around the metal until there was nothing showing of it.

"Did it just eat a cannonball?" Will asked.

The Cat just laughed. "You send bugs against me?"

"Not just bugs," the Lady said.

Card ghosts rose out of the ground, leaving frozen grass beneath them. They swarmed the Cheshire Cat. Hook's own spirits tried to intercept them, but though the pirate's ghosts were stronger, they were outnumbered many times over, and they couldn't hold back the tide of spirits. They slammed into the Cat, and its form wavered. The cards stabbed into it. Again, the cannon boomed. Hook moved to assist, but Michael got in his way. He smiled in the way that he always did when he was about to do something stupid.

"No, I don't think so," Michael said.

"Boy, you've never been able to stand against me, and you certainly can't in a realm that is more ghostly than physical."

Michael looked over his shoulder at the mass of ghost and insects assaulting the Cheshire Cat. He turned back to Hook and lifted his sword.

"That's the beauty of this. I don't have to kill you. I just have to slow you down until they can deal with the Cat."

Hook laughed. "Maybe if you had pixie dust, you'd be able to manage that. Grounded as you are . . ."

Hook rose into the air only to find Rosebud there to meet him. For a second, the old pirate stared at the tiny fairy. Then, he let out a laugh that shook the ground. "What is this?"

Rosebud flew in a circle and chattered something that was too fast for Vanessa to understand. Hook scowled and flicked her away, but she came back a second later. The Lady raised her hands and other glowing dots joined her, seemingly out of nowhere. Dozens of fairies, hundreds of them, filled the skies. Hook's eyes went wide, but he lifted his sword. It glowed with a blinding light. Every ghost around them, including the cards, glowed as well. The pale blue lights of wisps descended from the skies to meet the other fairies. A fairy darted down to Michael and sprinkled him with dust. Michael smiled and rose into the air. The fairy came and sprinkled Vanessa and Will, too. They had never flown before. Will rose off the ground almost immediately. He looked at Vanessa.

"Think a happy thought," he said.

"Like what?"

"I don't know," Will said. "Whatever makes you happy."

He flew off to join Michael. His aerial movements were more jerky and unsure than either Michael or Hook. There was no way he would last long in combat, but then Will knew that, too, and that didn't stop him.

"You have trained him well, Sir Vanessa," the Lady said, though it was obvious that every word was a struggle.

Still, as she spoke, Vanessa rose a few inches off the ground. She looked and smiled. The Knights of the Round. The Knights had been her whole life for years. That gave her meaning. That was her joy. She rose into the air. It took her a few seconds to figure out how to move around. By that point, Hook had already engaged Michael. Will tried to move in for an attack, but at best, he became a momentary distraction before he pulled away. Vanessa's flight was smoother, but not by much. She wouldn't be able to help any more than Will would, but there had to be something she could do.

The Vorpal Sword lay where it had fallen, several feet away. In spite of that, the weapon called to her. The Cat wailed, and she turned her attention to it. The Vorpal Sword could harm the Cat, and as much as Michael was obsessed with Hook, the Cheshire Cat was their real goal. She rose higher and then dove, snatching up the Vorpal Sword. The joy of combat rushed through her. She turned her body until she was parallel with the ground, then rushed right at her enemy.

The ghosts parted for her, opening the way to the Cat. It turned to her, its yellow eyes burrowing into her soul. The Vorpal Sword blocked whatever magic the Cat was throwing against her. There was a *snicker-snack* as it cut into the feline's flesh. The Cat was faster, though, and it flowed out of the way before the sword could sink more than a fraction of an inch in. She pulled up just in time to avoid crashing into a tree, but she wasn't fast enough to avoid its claws.

They burned like nothing she had ever felt. It was like acid flowed through her veins. The Vorpal Sword felt hot, and that heat spread into her body, burning away whatever the Cat had infected her with. Only then did she realize she was falling and quickly willed herself back into the air. The ghost of a ten of hearts stabbed a spear into the wound she had cut in the Cat's hide. Unlike the other attacks, this one went in. The Cat shuddered before turning to the ten and biting off its top half. Vanessa launched herself at it again, but this time it reacted faster, flowing out of the way as if it were made of water. Above her, a pale blue light fluttered, and her eyes went wide. That was too blue to be a wisp. It could only be Rosebud. Rosebud, whom the Cat had apparently feared. She resisted the urge to gasp as the answer came to her.

She flew at the Cat, feinting and pulling away at the last second. The Cat slashed at her, moving fast enough that if she had truly been trying to attack it, it would have disemboweled her. She slashed, trying to catch its paw, but it was like trying to cut a bolt of lightning out of the air. Rosebud crept closer. The Cat noticed Vanessa's attention was divided and started to turn. If it saw the fairy, it would probably flee, and there would go this opportunity. Vanessa cried out and threw herself at it. It turned its attention to her. Her blade sliced through empty air, though the Cat's head had been there a second ago. Just then, Rosebud got directly over it and sprinkled it with dust.

There were many types of fairies in the world, each with its own dust. Pixies, like the one that had sprinkled her, allowed a person to fly. Will-o'-the-wisps allowed them to affect spirits. Nixies allowed them to breathe water. There were other varieties as well, but as far as she knew, Rosebud, the ghost of a pixie, had dust that was completely unique. It did allow one to fly, but it only did so by separating the spirit from the body.

The Cheshire Cat roared. Its body seemed to boil over. The Cat was trying to resist it, but as far as Vanessa knew, Rosebud was the only ghost fairy in existence, and so the Cat had probably never learned how to deal with something like this. The body formed a long tube and shook violently until the Cheshire Cat's spirit came shooting out of one end. It was what Vanessa had been waiting for. She leaped at the disembodied spirit, her sword moving in a flash. The Cat widened its eyes before the sword cut into its head and split the creature in two. Whereas before, a destroyed spirit had collapsed into motes of light, this time, each half of the Cat let out a beam of brilliant blue energy. Everyone, even Michael and Hook, stopped what they were doing and turned to stare as the Cheshire Cat, a quasi-divine being who had been imprisoned in this realm for as long as the Knights had existed, cried out and was destroyed. The two halves fell to the ground and faded. The last thing she saw was the two halves of its mouth each giving a wide grin. The Vorpal Sword hummed in Vanessa's hand, and she knew that this time the Cat really was dead. The weapon had been crafted explicitly to battle this creature, and it was entirely possible no other weapon in all of creation could have destroyed the Cat.

Before anyone had a chance to celebrate, however, there was a loud roar. When she had seen others affected by Rosebud's dust, their bodies had fallen limp, but that had only been because most bodies couldn't operate without a spirit. Without the intelligence of the Cheshire Cat to guide the body, however, it was still the Jabberwock, one of the most fearsome creatures to ever walk the earth, or any other realm, for that matter.

The body became all teeth and eyes. A tentacle lashed out at Vanessa, but she sliced it out of the air with a *snicker-snack*. It roared from every mouth and backed up. The Vorpal Sword yearned to go after it, but its hunger had been sated, at least for a little while, when it destroyed the Cat's spirit. With an effort, she managed to put it away. If the Jabberwock wanted to retreat, she had no objections.

"No!" Hook said. "It can't be. Gods cannot be so easily destroyed."

Michael laughed as his sword darted forward. "You mean because you failed to destroy one, you think it can't be done."

Hook batted aside the attack, but only just. He was moving slower than before, as if the destruction of the Cheshire

Cat had done him real harm. Vanessa almost drew the Vorpal Sword and went after him, but she had a feeling that the destruction of a ghost, even one like Hook, would not be enough to quench the sword's hunger like the Cat had been. Instead, she drew her normal sword and flew up to join Michael.

Hook was on the defensive. He could still defend himself against the two of them, but he was panicking. Behind them, a bright blue light flared up. Vanessa spared just enough attention to see that the Lady was standing right in front of the distortion, her hands glowing brightly. Pieces of the shattered wall floated toward her and pushed the distortion back. One by one, the wall began to restore itself. They were winning. It was almost over.

Michael cut into Hook's shoulder just as Vanessa sliced into his leg. The pirate dove, bleeding blue light as he did. The two of them went after him, but he dove right into the ground. They both landed on the frost he'd left behind. Will crashed more than he landed, but he seemed unhurt.

The ants tore at the Jabberwock, but it wasn't noticeably hurt by the attacks. Vanessa and Michael exchanged glances before flying toward the monster. Vanessa hovered above it and tried to find where she had wounded it. As the creature was a completely different shape now, however, she had no idea where it was. Instead, she slashed at one of the eyes. Her sword pierced the skin, but when she withdrew, the organ reformed itself. It was like the Jabberwock was made of putty.

"Use the sword," Michael said.

"I'm not sure that's the best idea."

"I don't think we're going to kill this thing any other way."

"Do we really need to?" Vanessa asked. "What if we just let it get away?"

"Did you see how dangerous it is?"

"There are lots of dangerous things in the world. I think the price for taking this one down would be too high."

Michael cut at it again, but his attacks had no more effect than before. Most of the ants were down, and the ghosts had been destroyed. The Jabberwock was obviously trying to get away. They had apparently caused it a measure of pain, even if they had failed to seriously harm it. Finally, Michael nodded. They headed toward the Lady, but before they reached her, the White Queen came flying out of the air. She looked toward the Jabberwock and shook her head.

"No, you must not let that thing get away. Destroy it before it's too late."

"It's not a threat," Vanessa said, "and since when can you fly?"

She lunged for the sword at Vanessa's waist. Vanessa twisted out of the way, but she had forgotten the White Queen's peculiar abilities. The White Queen had known what she was going to do: she grabbed Vanessa's hand and slammed it against the hilt. The sword sang with joy and somehow forced her hand to close around it.

The sword rasped as it came free, and suddenly, all Vanessa could see was the Jabberwock as it shambled away. She flew toward it. Several of the creature's eyes turned toward her, focusing on her sword. It squealed and moved faster, but it wouldn't be fast enough. Her sword came down toward it just as Hook came out of the ground. He tried to catch her blade on his, but as before, the Vorpal Sword sheered through the ghostly weapon. It was enough to divert the attack, however, and her blade only cut a small piece of the Jabberwock. Black blood spilled out, filling the air with the smell of rot. The creature shrank and tried to flow into a rabbit hole. This time, it was

Hook who stopped it. He drove his sword into the ground at an angle so the remnant of the blade would be in the way of the hole. The Jabberwock squealed and withdrew. Vanessa realized what Hook planned to do. Hook threw himself at the Jabberwock, and its flesh closed around him.

"No!" Michael cried out.

Vanessa thrust her sword at the creature. It sank in, spilling more blood, but the thing quickly scurried back. Its form shifted and writhed. Ugly brown gave way to bright red. The bottom became black, and after a second, boots emerged. The red became a familiar greatcoat, and a head with a too-large nose and deep black hair appeared. Vanessa stared in shock as the Jabberwock took the form of James Hook. He looked down at his newly formed arms and smiled, in spite of the fact that even with a malleable body, he still had a steel hook.

"Well, well, well. This was the result I had hoped for, but I never imagined you would actually destroy the Cat to leave me with this empty vessel."

Michael threw himself at the pirate, but all of Hook's skill seemed to have returned, and he fended off the attacks effortlessly. Michael looked over his shoulder. "Rosebud."

"Now, none of that," Hook said.

Bat-like wings emerged from his back, flapping even as they grew. He rose into the air. Rosebud darted to him, but she hadn't even covered half the distance before Hook vanished in a red blur.

"No!"

Michael's voice was full of anger and pain. He zipped after Hook. Vanessa tried to go after him, but though she had learned a lot about flying in a short period, she was still no match for someone who had been taught to fly by Peter Pan himself. She landed next to the Lady, who was weaving her hands through the air, performing the last finishing touches on the wall. She let out a long breath and collapsed to the ground.

"Are you okay?"

"As well as can be expected. I've never tried to hold back the collapse of a world before." The Lady smiled. "That's one thing the Wizard never did."

"What about Michael?" Will asked.

The Lady blinked and got a faraway look in her eyes. "He's on his way back. Judging by the look on his face, he's not happy."

It was only a few seconds before a dot appeared on the horizon. It soon resolved itself into Michael. He landed, his face twisted with anger.

"Do you have any idea how stupid that was?" Vanessa asked. "You've never been able to stand against Hook alone."

"Hook has possessed the Jabberwock and has full control over its abilities," Michael said. "He outmaneuvered the Cheshire Cat to get it. Don't you realize how serious this is?"

"However powerful he may be, he's trapped in Wonderland," Vanessa said.

"No, he's not. He tore a hole. I saw Buckingham Palace through it. He's already back home."

"What?" the Lady asked. "How?"

"He flew all the way to the mountains. When he hit the wall at the border to Wonderland, I thought I would catch up to him, but he slashed with his hook, and the hole was there. He went through it, but it vanished before I could get there. He got away, again."

"What do you think would happen if you went through?" the Lady asked. "The Knights no longer exist."

Vanessa blinked. Her memory of Hook killing the White Queen was fuzzy, and there seemed to be something else there, too. She shook her head. "I'm not sure. I think there's another way. We might be able to save the White Queen."

"Vanessa, she was killed. We can't change the past."

"We can't." Vanessa pointed to the White Queen. "But she can. Why can she suddenly fly?"

"The laws of this land are so insane that no one can keep them straight," the Lady said. "Now that I combined the two worlds, they're even more crazy. Who knows?"

Vanessa motioned to the White Queen, and she walked over to them. "You got pixie dust, didn't you?"

"Yes, just now."

"Practice flying. Get as good as you can. Get to where you're fast and can fight in the air." She looked to the sky. "Rosebud, we need a pixie."

The ghostly fairy bobbed up and down. She darted into the sky and soon came back with a glowing green ball. That one sprinkled the White Queen, who suddenly floated to the ground. The images in Vanessa's memory changed. Hook didn't kill the White Queen. She caught his attack and flew away. Something shifted inside Vanessa, and she suddenly felt more solid. The Lady smiled.

"Very clever. You know temporal manipulation is forbidden, right?"

Vanessa shrugged. "Those rules were created by the Knights, and the Knights didn't exist when I broke them."

The Lady made a mock scowl. "That's a technicality and you know it."

"Nonetheless, I will stand by it."

The Lady chuckled. "Very well. I don't suppose you have an idea of how to get home."

"Can't you do it?"

"Unfortunately no, at least not quickly. It's my power that

melded these two worlds. Using my power to leave would break the nature of the spell I put on this place, and it would fall apart. They'd restore themselves eventually, but it wouldn't be for years."

"Can we use the joker's realm?"

"It was always a gateway from Wonderland to the Looking Glass Land. I might be able to redirect it, but that would undo the joining just as well as anything else."

"We could go through the ghostly realm," Michael said. "That's how Rosebud got here in the first place, and I assume she brought the fairies that way, too."

"Rosebud is a ghost," the Lady said. "She can pass through the ghostly realm, and fairies follow rules of their own. Neither one of those situations apply to us."

"What about the birds?" Will asked.

"What about them?" Vanessa asked.

"Do you think they can help?"

"Somehow, I don't think the cardinal will be able to help us."

He gave her a wry smile. "I wasn't thinking of the cardinal."

35

Being carried by a bird was a completely different experience from flying with the aid of fairy dust. Vanessa found that she didn't care for it. The talons gripped her shoulders so tight she thought they would dig into her flesh. The wind buffeted her face and the cold seeped into her, numbing most of her body. She cried out as they approached the mountains, half expecting the birds to crash into the same barrier Michael had seen. The air before her shimmered. Warmth then cold passed through her, and suddenly, Wonderland vanished. She was in the midst of a gray void. Fog swirled around her. She could just make out Michael on one side and Will on the other. The Lady flew in front of them.

"This isn't like crossing back from Neverland, is it?"

"Like you told me when this whole thing started," she said. "Neverland makes sense. Wonderland doesn't."

"I hope that means this won't take nearly as long. I don't know that I could make it that many days."

"It won't," the Lady cried out from in front of them. "Look up ahead."

Vanessa squinted, and after a second, she made out a bright yellow circle. It took her only a moment to recognize the face of Big Ben. The fog peeled away and the city of London stretched out before her. She had half worried that the bird would drop her when they came into the real world. A full-grown adult was well beyond what its species could normally carry, but it flew on, apparently employing some of Wonderland's ability to ignore its physical laws. It placed her down gently in front of the headquarters of the Knights. Each bird landed next to the person it had carried. Her bird stood nearly as tall as she did. Its black wings blended well with the night, and it had a bare head like that of a vulture, though its long beak was distinctive.

"A marabou stork," a gravelly voice said. "I didn't know they ranged this far north, though I take it they are not native."

As one, the birds squawked and took to the air. Vanessa turned to the voice, her hand going to the hilt of the Vorpal Sword. As soon as she touched it, however, her hand burned, and pain shot up her arm. She yelped and pulled back. A woman stepped out of the shadows. She wore a dark robe and had a long nose that ended in a wart. Her matted hair hung halfway down her chest, and her gaze made Vanessa shiver.

"Mora."

"The witch of Neverland?" the Lady asked. She raised her hands but there was a flash of red light. The Lady cried out and was thrown to the ground, unmoving. Vanessa rushed to her side, but Mora spoke before she arrived.

"Don't worry. She's not dead, but we couldn't have her disturbing our conversation." She looked at the downed form and laughed. "Even with much of her power not tied up in keeping Wonderland together, she could never be a match for me."

"We have nothing to talk about," Vanessa said, her hand moving toward the Vorpal Sword again.

"Indeed we do, unless you have ceased your hunt for James Hook."

Vanessa's hand stopped, but it was Michael who stepped forward and spoke. "You know where he is?"

"Yes, of course. He uses my power, after all. Perhaps, there is something you can do for me."

"A trade?" Vanessa asked. "You can't be serious."

The witch smiled. "Perhaps you will give me your name."

"I don't think so."

Vanessa eyed the headquarters. Mora might be more powerful than the Lady alone, but even she wouldn't be able to stand against the might of the full Court. Mora lifted a vial of blood and Vanessa froze. There was no way she could have been sure, but somehow, she knew the blood was her own, given to the witch as part of a deal the last time they had met. She didn't think Mora was using it just now, but that could change at a moment's notice.

"Why did you come here?" Michael asked, never taking his eyes from the vial of blood.

"James Hook has a new body."

"Yes, I know," Michael said. "We were there when it happened."

"That lessens my power over him, and that is *absolutely* unacceptable."

"Your power?"

"Yes. I taught him how to cross between worlds."

"He traded with you for that ability," Vanessa said. "I always wondered what he gave you."

Mora pulled a mummified hand out of her robes. Vanessa stared at it and the hairs on the back of her neck stood on end. "Is that a hand of glory? I didn't think there were any left."

"Not a hand of glory." Michael spoke in a voice barely above a whisper. "The hand of Hook. I thought the crocodile ate that."

"Ate but never swallowed," Mora said. "I gave Hook the ability to cross worlds, and in exchange, he promised me a pound of flesh. He was still attached to it when I wanted to claim it."

"That would be even more effective than blood," Vanessa said.

"While he was in his original body, certainly. I could bring him entirely under my power, if I so chose. It even had some influence when he was a ghost, but now that he has a new body, particularly one that powerful, it has moved him beyond my touch. That is where you come in."

"We're not going to trade with you for intel on where he is," Michael said firmly.

"I don't expect you to." Mora had a cunning look in her eyes.

"Then why did you offer me a deal?"

She gave an unnerving smile. "Because people make foolish mistakes sometimes. I didn't think you would, but I have been wrong before. This is the deal I offer you. Convince me you can actually take Hook down, and I will tell you everything you need to know."

"The Court would never agree to that."

"I am not asking the Court, Vanessa Finch. I am asking you, Michael Darling, and William Harden. Make a decision and contact me when you do."

"Contact you?" Vanessa asked. "How?"

"Tell a lizard. They will deliver the message."

The wind kicked up a cloud of dust, and when it vanished, Mora was gone, leaving a faint scent of brimstone behind her. Finally, the Lady regained consciousness and got on her feet. She looked from Will to Michael to Vanessa. "Well now. It seems I have missed something. Come, let's go inside and talk. I have the feeling this will affect the entire order."

Vanessa nodded and fell into step behind her, with her squires on her heels. Just before she stepped inside, she looked back to the spot Mora had vanished from. The witch had left blackened grass. Thunder rumbled above them and a few drops of rain hit her face. The Lady turned and met her gaze before her eyes wandered up.

"It will be a bad storm," she said, "in more ways than one."

Then, she turned and disappeared into the headquarters of the Knights of the Round. Lightning flashed overhead, and Vanessa and her companions rushed into the house after her.

36

It had been a long time since Vanessa had entered the headquarters with a member of the Court, and she had forgotten how easily the house's magic bent to the needs of the Knights' leaders. There was a single hall that ended at a gilded door. The air was still and held a faint, musty odor. The door swung open on silent hinges just before the Lady reached it. She paused in the doorway and motioned for them to follow.

They entered the council chamber and the Lady moved to sit in her place. She waved a hand at the ceiling. A single flame, about the size of a candle flame, appeared in the air above them and moved from one end of the room to the other.

"The others will be here soon. In the meantime, why don't you tell me what Mora wanted?"

"She's had dealings with Hook before," Vanessa said. "She doesn't like how powerful he's become and offered us a deal to bring him down, if we prove we can take him."

The Lady rubbed her chin. "I don't have to tell you that most people who make a deal with such dark forces find themselves stabbed in the back."

"I know," Vanessa said. "On the other hand, though, this is James Hook we're talking about."

The Lady was still considering that when a burst of flame

appeared at the King's position. When it faded, the Noble himself was there. He looked to the Lady, and though his face was covered, something in his stance told Vanessa that he was surprised.

"You're back," he said in a calm voice. "What happened to you?"

"Wait, if you will. I'd prefer not to repeat myself for each Noble in the Court."

The King nodded once and said nothing more. Over the next couple of minutes, three other bursts of flame brought the other Nobles. The Wizard was the last to arrive. Before he could speak, however, the Lady raised a hand.

"To answer the question you all have, Sir Vanessa and her companions employed ancient magic to summon all Looking Glass queens. As I still hold that title, I was summoned as well. It is a long story with details that I will relay later. The ultimate result of this, however, is that the ghost of James Hook has taken possession of the body of an Old One."

"An Old One?" the Wizard said. "Oh, come now. There hasn't been an Old One in this world for over a thousand years."

The Lady stared at him until he looked away. A chill seemed to rest on the council chamber.

"There is now," she said. "I witnessed it myself. The time for dissembling is over. We must turn all the resources of the Knights to stopping him."

"Lady, I'm wary of believing your alarming allegations, and a claim of this magnitude must be confirmed. If we do face an Old One's power, we may not have the strength to stand against him, at least not alone," the Knight Protector warned.

"Aren't we jumping ahead of ourselves?" the King asked. "This is what Michael Darling has been wanting from the beginning: free rein to pursue Hook. We cannot allow the obsession of one man to determine the course of the Knights, particularly when that man is only a squire."

"This would be not the first time one Knight's obsession led us to discover a threat that demands the entire organization's attention," the Queen said, "as you well know."

The King stiffened, and all the other members went still for a second. Vanessa was sure there was a story behind that, but she was just as sure none of them would reveal it to her. Then, the Wizard turned to Vanessa and her companions.

"This is not something that should be discussed in the open; you guys are excused."

"Pardon, but they were intimately involved in what happened," the Lady interjected. "They have a right to hear our decision."

"That is not your choice to make," the King said.

"There is no harm in it," said the Queen. "If we agree, all Knights will know of it soon enough. If we do not, it will hardly matter that they have heard."

"I agree," said the Knight Protector.

"We can work out the details later," the Lady said, "but the decision should be made now."

The King stared at her for several seconds before nodding once. "Who will stand in support of the Lady's proposal, to turn the efforts of the Knights of the Round to the opposition of James Hook's ghost, who now possesses the body of an Old One?"

The Lady stood right away, followed by the Wizard a heartbeat later. The Knight Protector gave Vanessa a level look, and it was almost a minute before she stood. Only three were needed to pass the proposal, but even so, the Queen stood a second later, followed shortly by the King.

"It is done," the King said. "We will inform all the Knights."

"I will escort Sir Vanessa and her squires out and return to discuss details."

Without waiting for anyone to answer, she walked toward the door. She paused.

"One more thing. Though it was not planned, I have observed Squire William's performance in the field, and on my authority as a Noble of this Court, I do hereby raise him to the rank of Knight."

Then she walked out. Will, wearing a wide grin, followed. Michael frowned but had the good sense not to say anything. He even waited for Vanessa to go first before exiting.

"That will cause talk," Vanessa said once they were outdoors. The storm had passed quickly, though its smell still lingered in the air. "When was the last time a Knight was raised by decree?"

The Lady pulled back her hood and smiled. "Not since I raised you."

"What about me?" Michael asked.

The Lady raised an eyebrow. "I have no intention of restoring you to full Knighthood, but you have earned some consideration. I will remove your probation. Get five full Knights to endorse you, and your rank will be restored."

"Why didn't you tell them about Mora's offer?" Vanessa asked.

"That a dark being has made an offer to one of the Knights is not so rare an occurrence that it deserves special notice," she said. "If you had accepted, that would be another matter. Now that the Court has made the declaration, however, that changes. I will leave it to you to decide whether or not to accept."

"You're making it my choice?"

The Lady nodded once. "We must do everything we can to stop Hook, and should they agree to work with her, it will not be the only questionable decision a Knight makes. Do as you will, but there is one thing that isn't up to you."

Vanessa felt the hairs on the back of her neck stand on end. "What's that?"

"You abandoned your magical training because you were eager to go out into the field. I supported your decision then but not anymore. If this mission was any indication, you are going to be in the thick of this, and you can no longer afford to ignore any resource. Starting tomorrow, I will begin your training again."

Vanessa took a deep breath and nodded. The Lady inclined her head first to her and then to Will. Michael clenched his teeth at being excluded, but Vanessa saw a faint smile on the Lady's face before she turned to reenter the house. Once she was gone, Michael turned to Vanessa.

"What do we do now?" he asked.

Vanessa pursed her lips, slightly surprised that he had asked her. Perhaps he had grown a little, or perhaps he had already guessed what she would do.

"We need to find a lizard."

ACKNOWLEDGMENTS

♠ ♣ ♦ ♥

Here we are at the end of book two where sometimes I wondered if I would ever get book one out there. Thanks go to Mireya Chiriboga who spent countless hours working on edits for this book, and of course, there is my agent, Jon Cobb. Alexi Vandenburg graciously allowed me a spot at his bookstore as they traveled from convention to convention. I've never so grateful and yet so exhausted because of the actions of any one person. Thank you for helping me make *God of Neverland* a success and thanks in advance for helping with this book.

Beta readers for this book were Andi Christopher and Jessica Guernsey. Thank you for all your help in making this book better. Of course, I must thank James A. Owen who provided the inspiration for one the major bad guys in this book. Not that he's evil or anything. Not completely. Anyway, let's change the subject.

As always, I must thank everyone involved in the Superstars Writing Seminar, hands-down the best writing event I've ever been to. Odds are, you will find me there every year. On that note, I must give my eternal thanks to a couple of mentors, founding members of that seminar who are no longer with us. Dave Wolverton did not live to see *God of Neverland* released, but he knew it was coming and had done me the honor of reading it. Eric Flint was another mentor who taught me a lot about the business of writing. I miss you both.

Gama Ray Martinez lives near Salt Lake City, Utah, with his wife and kids. He moved there solely because he likes mountains. He collects weapons in case he ever needs to supply a medieval battalion, and he greatly resents when work or other real-life things get in the way of writing. He secretly hopes to one day slay a dragon in single combat and doesn't believe in letting pesky little things like reality stand in the way of dreams. Find him at http://www.gamaraymartinez.com.